'23

HEX
YOU

SISTERS OF SALEM

HEX YOU

P. C. Cast / Kristin Cast

WEDNESDAY BOOKS
NEW YORK

First published in the United States by Wednesday Books,
an imprint of St. Martin's Publishing Group

HEX YOU. Copyright © 2023 by P. C. Cast and Kristin Cast. All rights reserved.
Printed in the United States of America. For information, address
St. Martin's Publishing Group, 120 Broadway, New York, N.Y. 10271.

www.wednesdaybooks.com

The Library of Congress Cataloging-in-Publication Data is available upon request.
ISBN 978-1-250-76569-7 (hardcover)
ISBN 978-1-250-76570-3 (ebook)

Our books may be purchased in bulk for promotional, educational, or business use.
Please contact your local bookseller or the Macmillan Corporate and
Premium Sales Department at 1-800-221-7945, extension 5442,
or by email at MacmillanSpecialMarkets@macmillan.com.

First Edition: 2023

10 9 8 7 6 5 4 3 2 1

To Diana—with a wink and a smile.

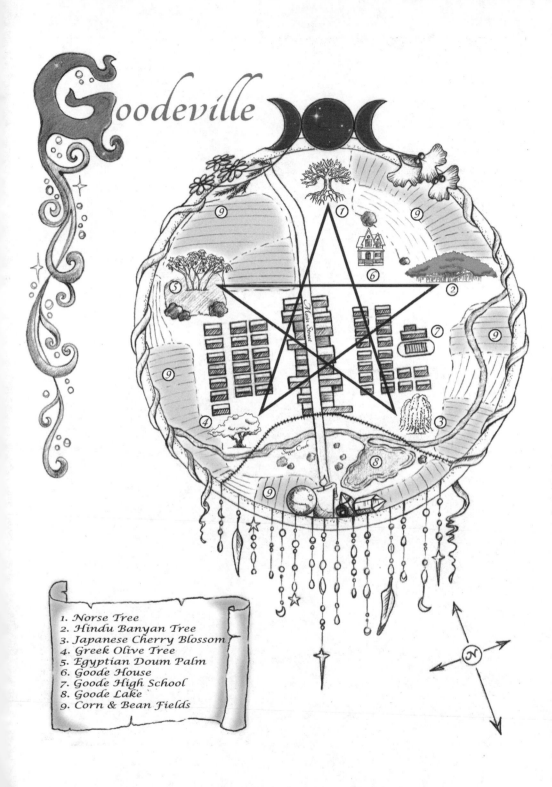

Goodeville

1. Norse Tree
2. Hindu Banyan Tree
3. Japanese Cherry Blossom
4. Greek Olive Tree
5. Egyptian Doum Palm
6. Goode House
7. Goode High School
8. Goode Lake
9. Corn & Bean Fields

PROLOGUE

TWO HOURS EARLIER

It would take a while before Jana Ashley felt at peace again. That's what happened when the devil came in. He flipped life upside down and made good, God-fearing Christians question themselves and their beliefs. But God would see her through, and He would be there to guide her.

Jana's glance roamed the sandy shore of Goode Lake behind her and the lone footprints that led to where she now stood.

"... *when you see only one set of footprints, it was then that I carried you,*" she whispered, fresh tears swirling her view of the water's calm blue surface as she clutched her daily devotional to her chest. Her lips moved again, this time in a silent prayer to the lord and savior she knew was always watching.

Another deity was watching, too. A supreme being not at all as forgiving and compassionate as Jana Ashley believed her god to be.

Amphitrite, goddess of the sea and wife of Poseidon—a philandering, egotistical, wet blanket of a god (although if anyone spoke about him out of turn, she would quickly fill their lungs with salt water)—stood in the shallow waters near the shore of Goode Lake, twirling her azure fingertips in the lengths of her skirts. They lapped like waves against her hands and shimmered in the orangey glow of the setting sun, tarpon scales in a crystal-clear sea. She had cloaked herself from this mortal, from *all* mortals. She was an observer, gathering enough evidence to wage war on the witch who had crossed her.

The fresh water around her feet bubbled and popped against her ankles, her anger heating it to a boil. With a deep inhale, she brushed her kelp-brown hair from her shoulders and cast her gaze to the edge of the water and the fluorescent-pink mound not too far in front of Mrs. Ashley. Amphitrite smiled.

Jana adjusted the small, checkered blanket tucked beneath her arm and mindlessly trailed her fingers over the large gold crucifix that rested against the collar of her shirt while she surveyed the curving shoreline ahead for a good place to spread out her throw and settle in for her daily dose of healing. Her brow pinched and her lips thinned as she squinted at the heap of clothes piled up ahead. She gripped her devotional and narrowed her brown eyes on the surface of the lake. If there were skinny-dippers out here, she would catch them. And if the owners of the castoff clothes were in the trees fornicating . . . Well, Jana wasn't quite sure what she would do then, but she knew exactly what the Lord God would have in store for them after their souls had departed this earth.

Seconds ticked by, and then minutes. No naked bodies surfaced.

Jana's cheeks reddened with both embarrassment and outrage as she realized that, unless Goodeville had suddenly been taken over by mermaids (and she would almost believe it with everything she'd seen over the past few days), no one could hold their breath for that long.

"Fornicators!" she spat, tightening her hold on her devotional as she picked up her pace and marched toward the discarded apparel.

City trails and playgrounds surrounded Goode Lake. Volunteers cleaned its beaches weekly. The church held summer camp activities on these shores. This was a good place, a clean place, a family place.

This wasn't Chicago, where oversexed heathens could get their jollies in the bushes!

"I'll call the police." She nodded to herself and tugged at her fanny pack as she closed in on the rumpled mound of fabric, any trace of embarrassment overtaken by the wave of self-righteous indignation that swelled beneath her ribs. "Yes, that's exactly what I'll do. And then let's see them explain their sinful actions to the—"

Jana stopped cold. Her copy of *Daily Wisdom for the Devoted Woman* slipped from her grip and hit the wet sand with a *thud*.

Stiff, white hands rested against the water-stained sand, poking out of a highlighter-pink windbreaker like formations of craggy, bleached coral. The unzipped flaps of polyester and baggy hood shuttered in the gentle breeze and hid the wearer's face.

Jana released a shaky exhale as her gaze trailed down the still torso and khaki Bermuda shorts to the bare calves, ghostly pale beneath the gently rippling water. The long ends of perfectly tied shoestrings stretched toward the surface as if reaching for air as small gray fish pecked at the naked flesh of the partially waterlogged body.

"H-hello?" The word scraped against Jana's dry tongue as the wind gusted and goose bumps flashed across her arms.

The only response was the quiet *whish whish* of the pink windbreaker.

"Are you o-okay?" Jana's throat tightened as she forced herself to inch forward, forced her trembling hand to reach out, her fingers to grasp the edge of the jacket. Her heart was a chunk of ice inside her chest as she pulled back the pink collar.

Blood as red and dry as brick crusted against a gash across the woman's neck and stained the shoulder of her lemon-yellow top.

Jana jerked backward and pressed the gingham blanket to her mouth, muffling the cry that crunched like gravel in her throat.

Her hands went numb and the blanket slid from her fingers as another gust blew back the jacket's hood, revealing a round nose and chin and open, cloudy eyes she knew all too well.

"Julie!" she shrieked and took another step back.

The blanket tangled around Jana's ankles, and she stumbled, as graceful as a newborn colt. The breath wheezed from her lungs when she smacked the ground. With a haggard breath, she sucked in a mouthful of sand. She lifted her chin and spit. Blond hair blew in front of her eyes, tangling with her own dark strands, and she brushed them back before realizing they weren't her own.

Her screams flooded her eyes with tears as she pawed at the shore, scampering backward, the heels of her shoes digging trenches in the sand.

Minutes went by, or maybe seconds, hours, years. Time had no meaning with death so near.

Finally, Jana's shrieks ceased, and her insides went numb. With shaking hands, she removed her phone from her fanny pack. It took three tries before she could dial 911 without error. When asked later, she wouldn't recall what she said to the operator or that she'd sent a text for help to her son, Jax Ashley. She would only remember the stillness of Julie Stoll's body, how pink her coat had looked against the deep red stain, and the gash across her neck that rippled and puckered like hardened candlewax.

Satan was loose in Goodeville, infecting its people, turning them all away from the Lord. This was proof. And this time everyone would see it.

Jana's fingers flew to her crucifix necklace. Her breath cracked around a noiseless sob as she clutched the gold cross so tightly the points bit into the flesh of her palm. *"Our father, who art in heaven, hallowed be thy name . . ."*

Still cloaked to human eyes, Amphitrite stepped onto shore next to Jana in a cloud of salt-scented air, the layers of her skirt undulating in time with the gently pulsing lake waters. A smile still played at her lips, the gentle curve of a dolphin's back, as she circled Jana Ashley.

"This is not the fault of Satan."

Sand flew as Jana jumped to her feet and whirled around. "Who's there?"

"It is I . . ." Amphitrite's grin fell as she lifted her algae-green gaze toward the heavens. *"My child."*

Jana blinked the tears from her lashes and scanned the banks of wildflowers and gently swaying grasses, expecting at any moment for the blades to burst into flame.

"God?" She opened her mouth to say more and closed it just as quickly. She had never been one to believe that the almighty would speak to her directly. At least, not with His words.

Amphitrite's sigh was a cloud of ocean spray. *"I have come in your time of need,* my child," she said, adding the last bit for good measure.

A single tear rolled down Jana's cheek. "Oh, Holy Savior, if I am truly blessed enough for it to really be you, please deliver me from this evil. Show me the way back to your light."

Amphitrite frowned down at the mousy woman. Mortals were so simple, almost not worth the energy to wring them out for the tiny drops of fun that dribbled free. But that *witch* had to be shown her place. And didn't they say that it took a village to raise a child? Well, Amphitrite would use one to burn Hunter Goode to the ground.

"Goodeville has been poisoned, tainted, infected by evil." Amphitrite studied Jana, the mortal's wide muddy-brown eyes twinkling with a reverence the sea goddess had gone so long without that she had almost forgotten its allure. *"Infected by witches."*

"I knew it," Jana whispered as she clutched her crucifix. "I've witnessed Hunter Goode, one of the devil's whores, practicing Satanism."

She had been right about that girl. Of course, Jana had known what she'd seen, but enough people had said that she had a few screws loose that she had started to agree with them. Then Kirk Whitfield had told her the Goode twins, Hunter in particular, were evil—that they worshipped Satan—and now God Himself had chosen her to be His instrument and send that harpy back to the fiery pits of hell.

Amphitrite cocked her head and let out another sigh of sea mist as a thick tentacle slithered out from under her skirts and swept up to catch her crown before it slid from her wet hair. The Goodes' magic was ancestral, in their blood, magic that came from this realm and this line of women, not Satan. But that was one of many things these non-magical bipeds would never understand.

"A means to an end," she grumbled low enough not to be heard by Jana before clearing her throat. *"Only someone like you—a true believer—can lead the charge and protect this town and the souls of those within it."*

Jana's chin quivered and her eyes filled with another round of tears. God had led her here, to Julie, to this example of what would happen to them all if she didn't follow His direction.

"Hunter Goode must be dealt with." Amphitrite's tentacle nestled her crown of starfish and seashells back against her hair and caressed her cheek before disappearing beneath the layers of her shimmering skirts. *"Her sister, too."*

Jana patted her crucifix. "I pray for them every night, especially Hunter with her pentagrams and devil worship. Although, I suppose you being the Lord and all are already aware of my prayers." Frowning, she brushed her dark hair from her face. "What more can I do? The town—" Sirens wailed in the distance as Jana slid her crucifix back and forth along its thin gold chain. "Oh, Holy Savior, they think I'm crazy. Barbara Ritter even offered me a Xanax when she saw me in the checkout line at the IGA."

Amphitrite's grin returned as the sirens grew nearer. The real fun was about to begin. *"Do you have faith?"*

"Of course," Jana offered before even drawing a breath.

"Then leave the town to me. I shall show them the light."

Goddess or not, had Jana Ashley been able to see Amphitrite's sinister smile or heard her laugh like knives on glass, she would have known without a doubt that true evil smelled of the sea and had eyes the color of envy.

Gravel sprayed into the tall grasses as two bronze-and-white sheriff's cruisers fishtailed into the small parking lot and skidded to a stop fifty yards from Jana, God, and the body of Julie Stoll. The ambulance wasn't far behind, the piercing howl of its siren masking the sounds of squealing brakes, muffler coughs, and crunching gravel from the cars whose drivers had spotted the emergency vehicles and quickly changed course to follow.

There was a blur of activity as the beach was cordoned off and the EMTs raced to the shore, the crash cart digging deep tracks in the sand. Deputy Carter tucked his cowboy hat under his arm as he questioned Jana, and she answered, slowly and carefully, all the while searching the breeze for the voice of God, her mouth tasting like salt.

The small parking lot was nearly full, and a crowd had gathered at the edge of the grass, literal ambulance chasers, for there wasn't much else to do in Goodeville than gawk at the fortune, or, in this case, *misfortune* of others. Their dramatically hushed whispers of *someone's dead, another murder,* and *what's this town coming to?* spilled out onto the shore and swirled around Amphitrite.

The great goddess of the sea let out a wave of laughter like clanging metal as she descended upon the townsfolk. The air grew sticky with a layer of salt-tinged mist that settled like morning dew on top the grass while Amphitrite poured her wicked lies into the ears of the people of Goodeville. Most of them drank it up, thirsty for anywhere to put their fear, parched for a place to lay blame, but there were some who were not so needy, some who stood firmly and did not let the rising tide sweep them off their feet.

By the time Jax Ashley reached Goode Lake, the parking lot was full, and he had to park in the grass. He elbowed his way through the crowd, mist collecting on his skin like sweat and salt burning his eyes.

"It was the Goode girls," one neighbor hissed as Jax pushed past on his way to his mother. "They're what caused all of this."

"Harlots!" said another. "The both of them."

"Worse than that!" came a shout from the back followed by murmured agreements. "They're *witches*."

Jax broke through the onlookers and charged toward his mother who sat with an EMT, her checkered blanket wrapped around her shoulders. He combed his hand through the salt-tinged moisture that beaded against his dark hair.

Burn them.

The words roared against his ears with a crash of ocean waves.

ONE

The plastic beads attached to the spokes of Hunter's bike wheels were a constant applause as she raced to the park and the Gatekeeper of the Egyptian Underworld that stood at its center. She ignored the screech of tires and honk of horns as she blew through the parking lot like a rocket. Her bike creaked and rattled when she hopped the curb and furiously pedaled through the grass to the doum palm. The sun had begun its descent beneath the horizon, and the lights of the tennis courts and baseball fields bit through the twilight and drew in townspeople like moths.

Hunter wasn't worried about onlookers. They could think what they wanted. They could capture her under cover of dark and tie her to a stake in the middle of Main Street for all she cared. As long as it was *after* she rescued her sister from the Egyptian Underworld.

Hunter had felt lonely, but she could never truly be alone while Mercy was alive. No matter what they went through, they were in this life together. They had been from the very start and no unearthly dimension would change that.

Hunter hopped off her bike and let it crash to the ground as she ran the rest of the way to the clump of doum palms that had protected the town from the ancient monsters of the Egyptian Underworld for generations. Xena was a blur of black, brown, and white fur as she raced toward Hunter and the tree. The cat mewed and circled Hunter's ankles as she caught up to her. The witch didn't need to hear the Maine coon's words to know what she said.

How many times and in how many ways had Mercy asked for Hunter's help? How many times had Hunter pushed her sister away?

Hunter pressed her hands against one of the palm's fragile shoots and called to the warrior she knew stood watch on the other side of the gate. "Khenti Amenti, Gate Guardian of the Realm of Osiris, answer my call."

The fabric between realms rippled and pulsed like a still lake around the rock of Hunter's call. She took a step back and clamped her hands into fists at her side. Khenti would give her answers even if she had to drag him into Goodeville to get them.

Xena arched her back and yowled as the gate came into focus. Hunter's fists unclenched and she stumbled backward as six warriors marched toward the gate. Their muscular bodies shimmered with each deliberate step forward and their sharp-tipped spears glinted in the Underworld's light. Hunter's heart clicked against her ribs as she focused from one snarling jackal mask to the next. Their painted fangs gleamed, and their red fur blazed like fire through the veil.

"Where is Mercy Anne Goode, the Green Witch from this realm?" Hunter screamed at the Gatekeepers. "What did you do to my sister?"

The jackal warriors stood at attention. Their masks had come to life and each of their pointed ears twitched.

Xena yowled and screeched a hiss as she stalked between Hunter and the warriors. They moved as one and each tightened their grip on their weapon, their snarling lips parted with a low growl of their own.

"Bring me Khenti Amenti!" Hunter shouted. "I demand to speak to the protector of this gate."

"We are the protectors now." They spoke with one voice, a low rumble that buzzed through Hunter's ears.

Hunter fisted her hands by her sides. "What did you do to my sister?"

"We do not answer to you, young witch."

The fabric that separated the realms rippled once more, washing the redheaded jackal warriors from view.

Xena howled as Hunter charged the vanishing creatures.

"Mercy!" she screamed and reached for the shimmering divide, but it was too late. The warriors were gone, and the realm's entrance was once more shielded by the doum.

Hunter wrapped her arms around the center shoot and pressed her forehead against the rough bark. "Mercy, if you can hear me, I'm sorry . . . for everything." Tears streamed down her nose and splattered the ground. "And I'm coming for you."

She wiped her eyes and stared through the palm to the warriors she knew lurked behind the gate. "I am a Cosmic Witch. Yes, I am young, but I have generations of power in my blood and the strength of the moon and the vastness of the universe wrapped inside my magic. I'll tear apart your world and this one to find my sister."

The pendant Tyr's magic had given back to her heated against her chest and a jolt of energy crackled beneath her skin. "I am Hunter Jayne Goode, and no one fucks with my twin, except me."

She let the message hang in the air between worlds for a moment before she bent down and scooped up the giant ball of hissing fluff. Hunter ignored the crowd, phones out and slack-jawed, that had gathered to witness the otherworldly event as she picked up her bike and set Xena in the basket next to her purse. She walked her bike to the parking lot as she spun her crescent ring around her finger and stared up at the brightening moon.

"We'll find Mercy," she whispered, hopping onto her bike and stroking Xena's hackles as she pedaled them to the Goode house to gather her arsenal. "And then we'll bring her home."

TWO

"Try not to worry. Khenti is a mighty warrior. He will defeat the In-tep demons. They are terrible creatures, but they cannot stand against my son," Meryt said.

Mercy watched Khenti's mom pace back and forth in front of the cave-like room's fireplace and decided her words would be more reassuring if Meryt didn't look so pale and worried. Although, to be fair, Khenti's mom was dead and spent most of her afterlife hiding inside from the demons outside in Duat, the Egyptian Land of the Dead, so maybe pale and worried was her norm. Mercy forced herself to smile. "Well, he did handle that In-tep that attacked us earlier pretty easily. You're right. He is an excellent warrior. I'm sure he's—"

Mercy's words were cut off by a gust of hot air that pushed Khenti, as well as a bunch of sand, inside her mother's Underworld sanctuary.

"Oh! Tee!" Meryt rushed to her son. "How badly are you injured?"

Mercy had stood from one of the many huge pillows Meryt used as chairs. She stared at Khenti, who was covered with blood and flecks of rancid flesh. She started toward him and then stopped—not sure what to do with so much blood. *He's gotta be hurt really bad!* "Do you have a first-aid kit or any medical supplies?" she blurted, and then realized the ridiculousness of the question. Meryt was *dead*. She couldn't get hurt. Why would she have a first-aid kit?

"Tee! Here, let me help you sit." Meryt moved to take her son's arm but he avoided her grasp.

"Muta, no, do not touch me. Let me wash this blood and gore from my body first." Khenti smiled. "And do not worry, either of you. This"—he used his scarlet-spattered weapon to gesture at his offal-covered body—"is not mine."

"Did you kill all of those zombie baboon things?" Mercy wrinkled her nose as the smell of the disgusting yuck on Khenti's body reached her.

"Yes. I discovered a whole pack of them not far from here and killed them all, but they will return." Khenti's smile faded. "I also killed an Ikenty, and I fear when it revives it will return with many more of its kind as well."

Meryt shivered. "Ikenty are terrible things. I have not seen one in quite a long time, but I have heard their yowls. When I do I remain here, where I am safe under Hathor's protection."

"What's an Ikenty?" Mercy asked.

"May I tell you as I wash? Ikenty do not have a rancid smell, but In-teps reek of the grave—and now I do as well."

"Yeah, that's a good idea. You are really stinky."

"Come, Tee, where the stream pools is an excellent bathing spot." Meryt went to a lovely tapestry that depicted her patron goddess, Hathor. She held it aside so that Khenti could enter the enormous room beyond without touching and soiling the fabric, then she and Mercy followed the warrior.

"I love this room so much." Mercy paused just inside the entrance to draw in a deep breath that was filled with the scents of flowers and fertile earth. *Room* was an understatement. The chamber seemed limitless—and because it was magic gifted to Meryt by Hathor, it might actually be. The huge place appeared to be a field filled with flowers and vegetables, mature wheat and trees bursting with fruit. The ceiling was domed, and even though Mercy logically knew they were inside a cave, above them a warm sun beamed life-giving rays onto the cacophony of plants. She let her fingers brush the tops of fragrant lavender as she followed Meryt and Khenti deep into the magic chamber to a wide stream that tumbled over smooth rocks. It wound around a grove of mango trees and then pooled in a perfect bathing place dotted with lotus that bloomed with ballerina-pink flowers.

Khenti didn't hesitate. He waded in, sandals, spear, and all, without taking off the short leather military loincloth-like clothes he wore. He sank down into the crystal water and dunked his hair several times, wrung the water from the dark length of it, and then began taking handfuls of sand and scrubbing himself. As he washed he explained, "An Ikenty is a demon with the body of a large bird of prey and the head of a black cat—with unusually long teeth and eyes that glow red."

"Sounds completely bizarre," said Mercy as she sat beside Khenti's mom on a simple wooden bench that overlooked the bathing area. Next to Meryt was a neatly folded piece of cloth that looked a lot like a bath towel.

"They are nasty creatures." Meryt shivered. "Their talons are particularly deadly because they purposely encrust them with rot, dirt, and feces."

"Isn't that overkill? I mean, everyone who is *usually* in Duat is already dead, right?" Mercy asked.

"Correct," Khenti said from the pool. "But Ikenty demons also guard the graves of mortals, where those poisoned talons make short work of grave thieves."

"Ugh. And you're sure the Ikenty and In-tep things are going to come back?" Mercy chewed her lip as her mind whirred.

"Absolutely. I tried to cover my tracks returning here, but it is only a matter of when, not if, they discover us." Khenti emerged from the pool, shook so thoroughly that Xena would have approved, and then joined them at the bench. "Thank you, Muta." He grinned at his mom when she handed him the towel, but his expression sobered quickly. "I am worried. As long as Mercy and I are here you are in danger. When the demons discover exactly where we are they will converge on this place. I will not be able to hold off a flood of them—and flood us they will." His dark eyes met Mercy's. "Has your sister made contact yet?"

Mercy purposefully refused to let her eyes wander down the warrior's mostly bare, glistening-wet, muscular body. *Get it together Mag! It doesn't matter how hot he is—I do not want us to die here!* "No. No, she hasn't, but she heard me. Hunter will figure out how to help us. We just need to be sure she has the time she needs."

Mercy glanced down at her chest and her stomach heaved. Hathor's mark, the henna image of the goddess's horns framing a large sun disc, continued to fade. There were currently no horns left at all, and the disc looked more like a crescent moon than the full, round sun. When the image completely disappeared it meant Mercy must leave the Egyptian Otherworld—or die there.

"Remember, time passes differently in Duat." Khenti's kind voice drew her gaze back to his. "Hathor's mark is fading, but I believe the goddess is watching. She has already blessed you. I cannot believe she will allow her mark to disappear before you find a way to return to your world."

"We," Mercy insisted. "You're coming with me. You're not dead yet, either."

Khenti's gaze went to his mother, who smiled sadly up at her son. "No. I cannot come with you, Tee. I *am* dead, my sweet son. I *do* belong here."

"You do *not* belong in Duat! This is not the afterlife you deserve.

It is a lonely eternity you were tricked into by Father. If Osiris knew he would not allow this travesty of justice."

"Then leave this place with your Green Witch, Tee. Find a way to get to Osiris. That is the only way I can escape this eternity," said Meryt.

"Okay, so we need time." Mercy's fingers drummed on the bench as she thought. Then she straightened and grinned at the verdant plants that thrived around her. "I think I can get us some time! Meryt, is there any chance you have some black candles?"

"I may. That would be up to Hathor," said Meryt.

"What does that mean?" asked Mercy.

"Hathor blesses me with things—fabric I fashion into clothes, wine and such things I cannot grow here—and candles. They appear in a wooden box. We shall simply check the box for black candles. The goddess often knows what I need before I think to prayerfully ask," Meryt said.

"What are you thinking, Mercy?" Khenti asked as he towel dried his long, dark hair.

"Remember the cloaking spell I cast so people couldn't see me talking to you at the park?"

Khenti's dark brows went up. "I do! Could you cast such a spell here?"

"Well, it'll take a much more powerful spell to cloak an area as big as the outside of your mom's cave, and there are no ley lines here for me to tap into, but I think I should be able to get enough power from the plants that fill this amazing room to set the cloaking. How long it'll last, I don't know."

"Long enough for us to sneak out of here so that the demons are no longer drawn to Mother's cave?" Khenti asked.

"I bloody well hope so," said Mercy.

"But how will your sister find you if you leave my cave?" Meryt said.

"We won't have to leave right away," explained Mercy. "I'll be able to feel when the spell is weakening. It's only then that we'll have to leave."

"The Mighty Cosmic Witch Hunter will find a way to reach you by then," said Khenti.

Mercy started to say she wished she had Khenti's confidence in Hunter, but then she realized she did have confidence in her sister! *I believe in Hunter. I always have. I just needed to remember that and stop being blinded by my own bullshit.* "You're right, Khenti. Hunter is a mighty witch. She'll do it. I know she will."

Meryt stood and nodded. "Of course Hunter is a mighty witch; her twin sister certainly is. Now, let us see if we are still in Hathor's favor."

Meryt led the way back through the growing room to what Mercy thought of as the living room of the cave. Meryt moved aside another beautiful tapestry—this one portrayed the fertile Nile, flanked by palms and flowers and a flock of hook-nosed ibises frozen in midflight. The room within was smaller than the living room, but the curtained bed in the center of it was spectacular, filled with linens the blue of the Egyptian sky. At the foot of the bed was a huge trunk decorated with Hathor's horns and disc and encrusted with semiprecious stones. Meryt lifted the lid, gasped happily, reached within, and then when she turned to face Khenti and Mercy her arms were with filled with fat black pillar candles.

Relief washed over Mercy. "We are definitely still in Hathor's favor."

"What else do you need?" Khenti asked.

"Just shadows and power," said Mercy. *And luck—a lot of luck—*she added silently.

"As you say, the growing room is filled with the energy of plants, and they have already recognized and accepted you," said Meryt. "Could you use the shadows beneath a tree?"

"If the tree's big enough. I'm gonna need a lot of shadows," said Mercy.

Meryt's smile beamed. "Oh! I do believe Hathor's sycamore fig will work. Come! Come!" With the litheness of a girl, Meryt rushed past them, nodding for them to follow. "Tee, bring one of the torches beside the hearth fire. Mercy can use it to light the candles."

They hurried back to the growing room. This time they had to walk farther. They crossed an arched wooden bridge and followed the stream in the opposite direction they'd taken to go to the pool. Mercy was amazed by the variety of plant life around them. She'd been to the Chicago Botanic Gardens several times, and had always loved the diversity of the flora there, but Hathor's creation for Meryt made that seem shabby in comparison. Mercy was so enthralled by a field of purple and blue and pink wildflowers that she didn't even notice the enormous tree until Meryt and Khenti stopped.

"Oh, wow! This is great!" Mercy stared up at the tree. It must have been at least one hundred feet tall with a huge, thick dome of wide, bright green leaves. Mingled among the leaves and rusty brown bark were clumps of figs that buzzed with wasps. Beneath the broad canopy the shadows were dark and plentiful.

"It is Hathor's tree—a sycamore fig—sacred to her. Its wood is often used for sarcophaguses, but the tree is worth far more than just its wood. Every part of the fig is valuable—her leaves make healing tea. Her sap makes the sweetest of sugars, and her fruit is almost as divine as Hathor herself," explained Meryt.

"She's perfect. Absolutely perfect!" Mercy approached the tree respectfully. She placed her hand on the skin of rough bark and closed her eyes. Immediately she felt the tree inhale and exhale, and she was greeted with curiosity and warmth.

"Hello, ancient one," Mercy said. "Your strength and beauty are truly magnificent. I am Green Witch Mercy, from a mortal realm far from here, and I need to borrow some of your shadows to keep Meryt safe. Is that okay with you?"

I serve Hathor and Meryt has the goddess's blessing—as do you, young one. I shall aid you.

"Thank you, Grandmother Sycamore. You'll be helping us a lot." In response the tree sent a burst of energy through Mercy that made her feel like she could run a marathon. She turned to Meryt and Khenti, who were standing just outside the canopy of the tree and motioned for them to join her.

"How may we help?" asked Khenti.

"First, let's place the black candles in a circle all around the tree, close to the trunk where the shadows are thickest." The three of them quickly made a tight circle of candles under the tree. "Okay, now we need to light all of them."

Khenti held up the lit torch he'd brought with them. "Do you need to do that, or may I?"

"You can do it. This spell is really an opposite spell, so it's not actually cast until the candles are blown out—and I'm going to have you and your mom help me with that part, too," Mercy said. Then she nodded in approval as Khenti lit all of the candles so that the darkness beneath the massive tree flickered with the soft illumination of firefly-like flames. When he rejoined her, Mercy continued. "We need to sit just outside the circle of candles, and we have to position ourselves so that we can be sure that we'll blow out all the candles at the same time. Do you understand?"

Meryt and Khenti nodded. The two of them followed Mercy's lead as she sat cross-legged before the tree. They positioned themselves around the circumference of the circle—equal distance apart. Then they looked expectantly at Mercy.

"First, we breathe together three times in and out to ground ourselves." Mercy breathed deeply and the mother and son joined her. "Next we set our intention, which is that these shadows expand and increase so much that they will cloak your cave from any demon searching for it. To do this you have to keep in mind that we are not afraid of shadows or the dark—that instead of fear we welcome their protection and concealment."

"I can do that, Green Witch," said Meryt.

"As can I," added Khenti.

"Awesome! I'm going to set my intention, tap into the power of the plants around us, and then speak the words of the spell. When I nod, blow out your candles with me and imagine the shadows multiplying like crazy. We should see something that tells us the spell is set and working. Ready?" Meryt and Khenti nodded. "Okay—set your intention and I'll begin casting the spell."

Mercy closed her eyes and concentrated. First, she focused on her intention. *The shadows under this amazing tree are going to multiply so much that they cloak this entire cave and keep Meryt safe.*

Still keeping her eyes closed, Mercy opened herself to the plant life around her. *Hello, beautiful, healthy growing things! This is Green Witch Mercy. Will you help me again by lending me some of your power?*

This time Mercy's mind wasn't filled with the enthusiastic voices of eager young plants. Instead she felt the already familiar presence of the mighty sycamore tree reach out to her and fill her.

You may borrow my power, Green Witch and friend of Hathor's blessed one. Take as you need. I have been greatly gifted by divine Hathor.

Thank you! Mercy was so overwhelmed by the magnanimous tree that her concentration was almost broken, but she grounded herself again and relaxed her shoulders, her face, and breathed deeply so that she remained intent upon her purpose—and then she began casting the cloaking spell.

"Come, shadows, cloak us from prying eyes
By your likeness we are disguised
In concealing darkness lent from Hathor's tree
Neither seen nor heard nor found shall Meryt be!"

As Mercy spoke the final words of the spell, she opened her eyes and nodded before leaning forward and, with Khenti and Meryt, blew out the circle of black candle flames. Then Mercy reached out to the sycamore and was immediately filled with a rush of power that reminded her of the Goode family's familiar ley lines, but this energy was denser. The sweet smell of figs surrounded her as Mercy channeled the tree's power through herself and into the shadows nestled under the tree.

For a moment nothing happened and then the thick trunk of the tree appeared to ripple—and Mercy realized it wasn't moving at all—it was the shadows that were moving, thickening, multiplying! With the sound of a forest of leaves rustling in a great wind, the shadows billowed up and up and up until they hit the magic ceiling—where they passed right through. Mercy closed her eyes again, tapped into the tree's power, and concentrated on settling the shadows over the cave like a blanket. *Thank you, ancient one.*

It is a pleasure to serve those beloved of my goddess.

Mercy opened her eyes and grinned. "It worked! I can feel it! I know it worked."

"Well done, Mercy! I knew you could do it!" Khenti rushed to her and lifted her from the ground into a hug.

And then his mom was there beside them, and Mercy allowed herself to relax into a much-needed mom embrace.

"What else must we do?" asked Meryt as she released Mercy and patted her cheek maternally.

"Nothing. Just leave the candles out here. The usual way to end the cloaking spell is to light the candles, but spells like this have a shelf life," said Mercy.

Meryt's brow furrowed. "Shelf life?"

"Oh, uh, sorry. That means that the spell will eventually just fizzle out when the power stops feeding it. So, you don't need to do anything to end it."

"Let us hope it lasts a long time," said Khenti as the three of them began to walk back through the growing chamber.

"Well, the sycamore is super powerful," said Mercy. "And that's a good thing. It should be able to hold the spell in place for a couple days—however long that is here." They'd come to the arched wooden bridge and Mercy paused in the middle of it. Khenti was beside her, with his mom next to him. Mother and son felt more relaxed, and Mercy was reminded of her mother with a sudden rush of longing. She blinked quickly as she stared down into the clear stream and fought back tears.

Then Khenti's hand slid within hers. "All will be well. You will see. All will be well. There is nothing witches as powerful as you and your sister cannot do."

Not trusting her voice not to break, Mercy only nodded and rested her elbows on the wooden rail of the bridge as she continued to will away her tears. Something caught her gaze as she blinked quickly—something gray and strange—and she realized the strange gray thing was her! Her hands were turning gray! Her gaze flew to her chest where Hathor's mark had completely disappeared. *We couldn't save our mom. We haven't healed the trees. We've basically been bickering babies instead of powerful witches. And now I'm going to die in this bloody awful place without even telling you how sorry I am!*

Hunter, I miss you and love you so, so much!

Unable to stop her tears any longer, Mercy watched them fall from her cheeks into the stream.

Then the water below her began to change. Instead of flowing musically over smooth stones and a sandy bottom, it shifted, swirled, and became a mini-whirlpool from the center of which lifted three words shouted in a voice as familiar to Mercy as her own.

"I found you!"

THREE

It took Hunter an hour to gather every moon-charged item she could possibly need in order to locate her sister and keep herself safe before she rode back to the doum with a cat-shaped Xena in tow. Within that hour, doubt hadn't been able to settle in. There had been too much to assemble, too much to plan. Now, as Hunter once again sat at the base of the palm, staring into her copper cauldron filled with crystal-clear moon water, and the battery-operated emergency light she'd taken from their tornado kit casting an eerie glow onto the gently swaying fronds, she wasn't sure she'd ever see Mercy again.

A small, white orb snagged Hunter's attention, and she squinted into the darkness that had closed in on her glowing, pale-yellow bubble. The starburst of light bobbed in time with the gentle *slap slap* of flip-flops and rustle of manicured grass. Xena twitched between Hunter and the approaching footsteps, back arched and lips peeled in a menacing, fang-wielding hiss.

"Achoo!"

The sharp curve in Xena's spine softened, and Hunter released a stored breath.

Emily clicked off her phone's flashlight as she and Jax entered Hunter's illuminated sphere. "We've been looking for you for hours," she said with a sniffle before swiping the back of her hand across her nose.

Jax combed his fingers through his dark hair, the ends curled like he'd been caught in a rainstorm. "It's been, like, thirty minutes."

The thin strap of Emily's maxi dress slid off her brown shoulder as she shrugged. "Either way, you should really turn your phone on."

Hunter dug her phone out of the bottom of the floral-patterned tote she'd used to haul her supplies. She pressed the power button, but the screen remained black. The day had been filled with too much for her to worry about whether or not her phone was charged.

For a second time, Jax mussed his tangled hair, his dark eyes wide and searching. "We have a problem."

Xena let out a low, mournful *meow* and climbed into Hunter's lap.

Not another one. Hunter's face heated, and her breath hitched. *I can't . . . I can't . . .*

"I can't get her back," she choked as tears rolled down her cheeks. "Mercy's gone, and I can't get her back."

Jax and Emily rushed over, crouching on either side of her. A hand was on her back, smoothing circles against her spine.

"Mag is gone?" The hand stopped as Emily chewed her lower lip. "She wasn't at school and didn't text me back, but I thought . . ." She wrapped her arms over her chest. "Well, she told me she and Xena got into it and that she had to stay home all weekend."

Xena let out a pitiful mew.

"Mercy's in trouble. She used our connection to contact me. She's trapped in the Egyptian Underworld. She needs me." Hunter's voice caught as she lifted the end of her shirt and swiped at the tears streaming down her cheeks. "She needs me, and I have no idea what to do."

"Looks like you have some sort of idea." Jax nodded toward the copper cauldron, the poppet and ball of twine, and the rainbow of crystals Hunter had removed from their pouches and placed in a circle around the basin. "You have a plan. You always do. You just have to trust yourself, H."

Confirming Jax's statement, Xena pressed her front paws against Hunter's shoulder and leveled her amber gaze at Hunter, erupting into a long series of chittering meows before nuzzling her fluffy head against Hunter's cheek.

"Jax and Xena are right," Emily began, her eyes watering as she held back a sneeze. "You can do this. You said yourself that Mercy used your connection to contact you. That bond goes both ways. It's, like, the law of twins." She scooted closer, their knees touching, and took Hunter's hand in hers. "Not only are you family, you're connected through magic."

"And you're a badass witch," Jax said, leaning against Hunter and wrapping his calloused fingers around hers. "Believe in yourself."

Hunter gripped their hands tight and took a deep breath, drawing strength from her friends and the reminder of the special bond she shared with Mercy. She was Hunter Goode, twin sister to Mercy Goode, fueled by the cosmos, the god of the sky, and the ancestral magic that flowed within her veins.

Her pendant heated against her chest, and she envisioned the core of the opalescent jewel swirling a deep purplish-pink with the power of her magic and the grace of Tyr. Her god was there. Tyr believed in her . . . along with her friends and the familiar that had been with her for as long as she could remember. She owed it to them—more importantly, she owed it to herself—to believe in and trust her power.

"I've got it!" She released Jax's and Emily's hands and reached for the two blue crystals to the left of her cauldron. "Celestite." She lifted the lighter of the two, its prismatic shards glinting like icicles in the low light. "It activates psychic abilities and elevates spirit in order to see and understand messages at a spiritual level."

Hunter's fingertips heated as she pressed the crystal to her lips. "Help me to see my sister."

The pendant thrummed against her chest in time with the rapid beat of her heart as she dropped the crystal into the cauldron of moon water. Sparks shot from the jagged points of the delicate blue and crackled against the surface of the water like fissures in broken glass.

Emily sucked in a breath and pressed her fingers to her lips as the rough outlines of the phases of the moon etched into the cauldron's side lit up as white as the foaming crests of ocean waves. "There are some things I will never get used to."

A smile ticked against the corner of Hunter's mouth as she refocused on the task at hand and scooped up the second crystal. "Blue kyanite encourages communication and breaks down fears and blockages." The bladed crystalline structures looked like jagged azure glass. "Help me to overcome my insecurities and speak directly to my twin," she whispered, smoothing her fingers over her pendant, warm against her skin, as she released the crystal into the basin. Another shot of sparks exploded against the water's surface in a shower of glitter. Once again, bright white light beamed from the etchings, illuminating Jax's and Emily's wide-eyed wonder as they stared at the magic unfolding under the doum palm.

The water stilled and the cauldron dimmed, and Hunter, Jax, and Emily waited.

Jax leaned forward, squinting down at the liquid. "Did it work?"

Palm fronds creaked overhead as warm air blew around them, tepid gusts that signaled the fast-approaching heat of summer, but the water remained still, a pane of glass.

Hunter picked at her jagged thumb nail. The magic still called to her, a tugging on her heart that would surely make it explode within her chest if she didn't follow. "The spell's not finished yet."

She pressed her palms against either side of the cauldron and let her heart guide her.

"To the power of the ley lines that stretch from this realm to those beyond, I beseech you."

The earth shuddered beneath them, a great giant awaking from slumber.

"Help me find what I have lost—the other half that makes me whole."

The ground hummed, tickling her spine and raising the hairs on the nape of her neck.

"We're connected by blood, by love, by magic. No matter how far apart, I always feel her with me."

Green light rose from her arms like mist. The same green as the power at the cherry tree. The same green as her sister.

"To the power of the ley lines that stretch from this realm to those beyond, I beseech you," Hunter repeated.

Green light, the lush emerald of living things, radiated from the moon phases etched into the copper cauldron. It rained from the points of the crescents and dripped from the round slopes of the full moons, pooling against the grass.

"Help me find what I have lost—the other half that makes me whole."

Verdant light blazed against the ground beneath them, illuminating the line of magic that ran from the doum palm and connected it, in a pentagram, to the four other ancient guardian trees that stood at the gates of the Underworlds.

"To the power of the ley lines that stretch from this realm to those beyond, I beseech you."

The green track raced back to Hunter. A scream tore from her throat as power reached up from the earth and buried its teeth into her flesh.

"I beseech you!"

A flash of lightning ripped through her chest. Jax and Emily shielded their eyes as green flames engulfed the palm fronds, an umbrella of otherworldly fire.

Hunter submerged her hands in the basin of crystal-charged water and threw up a handful of liquid. "Find my sister!"

The droplets burst apart, and magical bluish-green rain extinguished the flames and fell into the cauldron as if being called home.

As the water stilled, shapes appeared on its surface, fuzzy at first as if seen through sleepy eyes, then clearer and clearer. Mercy stood next to a bare-chested Khenti, her dark hair hanging around her shoulders as she leaned over a wooden railing to blink down at Hunter. Her tear-filled eyes were the bright green of butterfly wings pressed into her chalky-white face. Hunter choked back a sob as she took in her twin's graying arms. If she didn't act fast, Mercy would be gone for good.

"I found you." Hunter leaned forward, bumping into the cauldron and nearly sloshing the magical portal all over the grass.

"Hunter?" Mercy's eyes filled with tears. "Is that really you?"

Emotion choked Hunter's voice, and she could only nod.

"I miss you." Mercy sniffled, tears falling down her cheeks.

I miss you, too, Hunter mouthed, and she meant it.

Emily released a shaky breath. "Oh, thank god, or goddess, or whoever. That was intense."

Jax nodded and dragged his palm down his cheek. "Too intense."

Mercy's thick eyebrows lifted. "Em! Jax! I've been so worried I wouldn't see you again!"

"Come home already." Emily tucked a mahogany curl behind her ear as she peered down at Mercy. "You look terrible."

Mercy wiped at her eyes. "I wish I could, but Khenti and I are stuck in the hell part of the Egyptian Underworld. I've tried to get out. *We've* tried. The demons are closing in, the mark of Hathor that protected me is gone, and I don't have enough power to get us out."

"What if you use this portal thing?" Eyeing Hunter, Jax motioned toward the cauldron. "Or that doll? Can't you just, I don't know, combine the magic forces and pull them out?"

Hunter rubbed her knuckles against her aching chest. She'd asked for a way to locate and communicate with her sister, not pull her from a different realm. "Transporting people to and from different worlds is god-level energy. Plus, the doll isn't any doll. It's a poppet." She ran her fingers along the silky fabric she'd cut from an old blue nightshirt. "It's made for someone specific."

Someone, she knew, who would eventually come back.

He shrugged. "But the portal is worth a try."

Jax was right. And Hunter wouldn't be able to live with herself if Mercy never made it home because she'd refused to attempt the easiest solution.

Mercy tucked her hair behind her ears and smoothed down her dress. "Ready?"

Hunter nodded. "On three."

The twins counted in unison, "One, two, three!"

Hunter's fingers slammed into the water, and she bit back a shout. "It's like glass."

"Or concrete," Mercy whimpered, shaking out her hand.

Jax's cheeks pinkened. "Guess we can strike that one from the list."

Hunter sucked in a breath as pain shot through the protective pentagram she'd carved into her stomach. She clapped her hands over the scar that rested in bumpy cords beneath her shirt.

Jax stiffened and his gaze swung out over the darkness that surrounded them. "Do you hear that? Waves crashing. I've heard it before . . ."

"*Before?* What do you mean—" Hunter's question was halted by a shriek of laughter that splintered against her ears.

"Hunter, what was that?" Mercy shouted, her watery voice nearly swept up in the thrum of crashing waves. "What's happening?"

Emily held out her hand, her trembling finger pointing to the glowing figure fast approaching.

"She's here." Hunter grabbed the poppet and twine and shot to her feet, flanked by Jax and Emily. "Amphitrite's here, and I'm ready."

The sea goddess's azure skin was alight with a bioluminescent glow that smoothed her features into the liquid softness of a jellyfish. *"They're coming for you, Witch. Don't only take my word for it. The mortal can tell you."* Amphitrite's hair lapped against her shoulders as she nodded toward Jax. *"He was there."*

Hunter stepped in front of her best friend. Last time she'd seen Amphitrite, she'd used blood magic and the power of the ley lines to temporarily expel the goddess of the sea so she could finish healing the cherry tree and the gate to the Japanese Underworld without the oppression of lies and threats. But Hunter had known Amphitrite would return, and the goddess always knew how to get down to business.

Jax didn't falter, didn't call a personal time-out to deal with the fact that a glowing sea goddess had washed up in the middle of Goodeville. Instead, he and Emily exchanged a glance as if to say *wherever Hunter and Mercy go, we go* and then stepped closer to Hunter. "The town, they—" He swallowed. "Well, a bunch of people think you and Mag are evil witches who have cursed Goodeville."

The air grew humid, tinged with the briny scent of the sea. *"I can help you,"* Amphitrite purred.

Hunter snorted. Amphitrite didn't give without taking. "I can help myself."

The sea goddess narrowed her eyes and craned her long neck as she twirled her hands in the flowing lengths of the skirts that hid the writhing tentacles of a sea monster.

Hunter wailed, her knees buckling, as pain seared her scar. Tears flooded her eyes, and her jagged nails dug into the clover-dotted field. "I banished you," she howled. "You can't get in my head or touch my body."

Amphitrite shrugged her thin, glowing shoulders. *"Can't blame a goddess for trying."*

Jax and Emily were at Hunter's side, hooking their arms under hers and helping her to her feet.

"So nice that you have such good friends." Amphitrite's grin revealed a

set of pearlescent teeth as pointed as a shark's. *"It would be a shame to see anything happen to them."*

Hunter clutched the poppet and twine in one hand while she brushed the grass from her legs with the other. "Jealous much?"

Amphitrite's grin remained fixed, her teeth sharp, the tips of a trident. *"Oh, dear Witch, I don't get jealous. I get revenge."*

Hunter cocked her head and lifted a brow. "And I thought we didn't have anything in common."

She held out the poppet and released the spool of twine, pinching one frayed end between her thumb and forefinger.

"Mighty Tyr, God of the Cosmos! Acknowledge this poppet of the goddess Amphitrite." Power crackled like lightning and the heavens churned as Hunter's god answered her plea, and she squinted against the brilliant blue light that beamed through each stitch of blue silk.

"Naïve!" Amphitrite spat. *"You think your simple incantations will work against me?"* She stalked forward, and Hunter, Jax, and Emily held their ground with a yowling Xena ready to attack. *"I am a goddess! An immortal! Ruler of the—"*

"Enough!" Hunter shouted over the roar of ocean waves that battered her ears.

"We don't want you here!" Emily's energy rooted her to the ground, a glimpse of who she could be if ever gifted with magic.

"Go back to whatever seashell you climbed out of!" Jax joined in, all traces of fear and unease erased.

Amphitrite's torso rippled and grew as a great swell of water surged along her outstretched arms and shot from her fingertips.

"With this knot, I bind your body from doing harm in this realm!" Hunter boomed, wrapping the twine around the glowing poppet's middle and tying its arms to its sides.

A sharp hiss, and the devastating waves burst into steam.

"Witch! I will—" Amphitrite's howls were cut off as Hunter tied knot after knot along the poppet.

The once-great goddess of the sea wriggled and thrashed but couldn't break free from the magical restraints that prevented her from giving life to her evil.

"Blessed Tyr, bind this goddess's body from doing harm to anyone in this mortal realm!" Hunter thrust the poppet into the air, and lightning bisected the sky, slamming into the twine-covered doll.

A scream like a train scraping its tracks and Amphitrite popped—a stuck balloon splashing onto the grass.

Emily groaned, stepping back as the wave of salt water lapped against their shoes.

"Goddess guts." Jax frowned, tapping the toe of his shoe against the shallow waves as Xena let out a series of disgruntled meows and lifted one dripping paw and then the other.

But Hunter wasn't bothered by the surge of cool liquid surrounding her boots. Instead, her attention was fixed on the poppet, each knot the same glimmering sapphire as the depths of the sea.

"Amphitrite?" she whispered, brushing her thumb over the cold, wet twine.

Hunter sucked in a breath, her eyes wide.

"Mercy!" she shouted and took off toward the cauldron, Jax, Xena, and Emily in her wake. "I can get you out!" Hunter panted as soon as she made it to the enchanted moon water.

Mercy stared up at Hunter, her brows nearly lifting to her hairline. "What the bloody hell was that? What happened?"

"I'll explain everything *after* you're safe." Hunter swallowed the lump growing in her throat. She had so much to reveal, so much to apologize for, and she was terrified her truth, not the Egyptian Underworld, would be the thing that would take her sister away for good.

Mercy tented her hands on her hips. "What's your plan?"

Hunter winced as Jax jabbed her bicep with his pointy elbow. "Our H just slayed an octopus woman."

Emily's curls bounced with another series of emphatic nods. "Turned her into a puddle."

Mercy dropped her head back and groaned. "Oh my goddess, you all are on drugs."

Ignoring her sister, Hunter clutched her pendant and whispered a silent prayer to Tyr as she stared at the shimmering poppet. She closed her eyes and reached, up, up, up, to the treetops, to the clouds, to the stars. She was fire and light, collapsing and forming, a star in the making. She wrapped the scattered bits of herself around the moon, the stars, and the vastness in between. Magic washed through her, a steady pulse that would lift her physical body off its feet if her heart wasn't tethered to earth.

Beside her, Jax and Emily gasped.

Hunter's eyelids fluttered open. Blue flames crept along her hands from the poppet, and the goddess energy trapped in its knots and licked up her arms.

In the cauldron, Mercy sucked in a breath and pressed her fingers to her lips.

Hunter reached her flaming limbs into the basin and through the magical portal that had denied her access before she'd harnessed the energy of a goddess.

"I am Hunter Goode, and I command the power of the cosmos."

She gripped two outstretched hands and pulled Mercy and Khenti from the Underworld.

FOUR

I t was quite horrible, kitten. Horrible I tell you!" In human form
Xena was curled up in the corner of the couch swathed in
Abigail's plush bathrobe with a chenille throw wrapped around
her shoulders. Her hair was drying in a crazy halo around her
head, but she still looked drenched. "I should have been faster.
I should have pounced on her and raked my delightfully sharp
claws down her watery"—the cat person paused there to shiver in
disgust—"body."

"I'm glad you didn't." Hunter was sitting on the arm of the big
recliner that was always Jax's favorite and the seat he'd claimed when
they'd all piled out of his car and the Camry and hurried into the
Goode family home. "Amphitrite would've just found a way to hurt
you to get at me."

"And you really were sp-sp—*ACHOO!*—spectacular. Totally
very scary." Wiping her nose and smiling apologetically, Emily scooted
farther away from Xena to the opposite side of the couch.

"Goddess bless you, kitten. Did you not take your medical pill that
keeps you from being allergic to my incredibly powerful dander?"

"I forgot." Emily sniffed again.

"Here ya go, Em." Mercy emerged from the kitchen and handed Emily two pink pills. "Benadryl," she told her friend with a grin. Following her, Khenti carried a tray filled with mugs of steaming hot cocoa, which Mercy passed out to everyone before she and Khenti sat beside each other on the couch between Xena and Emily.

"This is gonna put me to sleep in, like, thirty minutes—which is actually good because Mom just texted me and reminded me it's a school night so I gotta get going in a sec, but . . ." Emily's gaze—along with everyone's except for Mercy's—went to Khenti.

"What is this called again?" Khenti asked her after he took a second big swallow of the cocoa.

"Hot chocolate or cocoa," said Mercy. "Here, you have some marshmallow on your, um . . ." She took a napkin off the tray and dotted the white goo off Khenti's upper lip.

He grinned at her. "Thank you. This is my new favorite drink."

"Wait until you try pizza," said Xena. "It's especially delicious with extra tuna."

As Khenti's smooth, umber brow furrowed in confusion, Mercy said, "Now that we're settled and not in the middle of the park it's time for formal introductions. Hunter, you've already met Khenti."

"Nice to see you again, Khenti," said Hunter with a little wave, the tips of her fingers caked with dirt from digging a hole near the banyan for the sea goddess's poppet.

"Mighty Cosmic Witch Hunter—thank you for coming to our rescue." Khenti gave her a little seated bow.

"Us Gatekeepers have to stick together," said Hunter.

Khenti's shoulders slumped. "I am Gatekeeper no more."

"Why? What happened?" asked Hunter, picking dirt from under her nails.

"It's a kinda long story. First, introductions." Mercy gestured at Xena. "This is—"

"I know this lovely creature," interrupted Khenti. "In human form or feline, your fur is as I recall it, quite magnificent, even if it is wet."

"Thank you, Khenti kitten. I do appreciate a demi-god who acknowledges furred excellence," Xena said, then went back to lapping her cocoa.

"Demi-god?" Emily chimed. "I've never met a demi-god before! And by the way, you two being pulled from that water thing was one of the most awesome things I've ever seen."

"Khenti, this is my best friend, Emily," said Mercy.

"It is nice to meet you, Emily," said Khenti.

"Hey, I haven't met a demi-god, either, though I used to really love those Percy Jackson books when I was a kid," said Jax.

"And that is Hunter's best friend, Jax," added Mercy.

"It is a pleasure to meet you, too, Jax. Though you still have not met a demi-god. My father took my position of Gate Guardian away from me and disowned me. I'm afraid I am only a mortal human now."

"Is that why you're not dying or turning gray or whatever here?" asked Emily.

"No, I have no ill effects from being in your realm because I'm a living being. Were I, say, an In-tep demon from my realm I would eventually sicken and die if I didn't take another's form," explained Khenti.

"Gross." Mercy shuddered. "Those things are disgusting."

Xena looked up from lapping her cocoa and licked marshmallow from her lips before she said, "I am quite pleased you aren't a dead demon, Khenti kitten, and I do hate to correct you when you have only just arrived, but what you said about your father taking away your status as a demi-god is impossible."

"I do not mean to contradict you, but it is more than possible. Mercy witnessed it," said Khenti.

"Khenti's right. His dad's bloody awful. A major bully. For basically no reason except that Khenti stood up to him, he took away his position as Gatekeeper, disowned him, and banished us to Duat. That's why we were stuck in Egyptian hell," said Mercy.

"Oh, I did not mean his father couldn't disown him or take his magical position from him." Xena licked her hand and smoothed back her hair as she continued. "I simply meant that he could not reverse what is Khenti's through the right of his blood. Gatekeeper no more, but he is certainly still a demi-god."

Everyone turned to stare at Khenti again who said, "How do you know this?"

"Oh, I know almost everything important," said Xena before she returned to licking her hand and grooming her hair. Between licks she added, "You can prove it easily. You are a warrior, which means you should have a magical weapon under your command, correct?"

Khenti nodded slowly. "My khopesh." His gaze found Mercy's. "It came to me in Duat when I called. I assumed it was because I was still in our Underworld—which has a magic of its own."

"Well, call it to you now, Khenti kitten. Then you shall see that your father cannot take away what was gifted to you through your blood. It is a simple fact. Let us pretend for a moment that our beloved Abigail had become angry at Mercy and Hunter. She could have stripped them of their duties as Gate Guardians, but she could not have taken their magic from them. That is a gift given through blood and ancestors—and it cannot be revoked." Xena licked her hand again and reached out to rub a smudge from Mercy's cheek. "Though our Abigail would never have done something so awful."

Mercy leaned away from her and into Khenti. "Xena, I love you lots and missed you super bad, but you gotta quit putting your spit on me."

Xena made a pouty face and sighed. "You let me lick you when I am a cat."

"You're not a cat now!"

"I'm always a cat!"

Mercy rolled her eyes and turned to Khenti. "You should try calling your weapon."

"I—I am almost afraid to," Khenti said softly.

"Why?" Hunter asked.

Khenti moved his broad shoulders restlessly. "Because if I am still a demi-god without being a Gatekeeper it will be as if I am only half whole."

Hunter leaned forward. "Have you been a Gatekeeper since you were born?"

Khenti shook his head. "No, Cosmic Witch, children are not Gatekeepers. Like you and your magical sister, I had to mature into my power before I was named Gatekeeper."

"Well, then, if you're still a demi-god you'll have your power and be free to decide what to do with it now that you're not tied to a gate," said Hunter.

Khenti cocked his head to the side and asked, "Could you simply walk away from being a Gatekeeper?"

"Yes," Hunter said without hesitation. "As long as I was still a witch I'd still be me."

Khenti nodded. "I shall consider what you have said." He lifted his hand, and commanded, "To me, khopesh!"

There was a flash of light and a sound like a tearing cloth, and a weapon that looked like a cross between a sickle and a sword appeared in Khenti's hand, gleaming the black of moonless nights and dark, bottomless waters.

"I am still a demi-god." Khenti said the words softly as he gripped the weapon with both hands and bowed his head.

Mercy put her arm around his broad shoulders. "I'm so glad, Khenti!"

He met her gaze. "I must go back. I must save my mother."

"You mean go back through the Egyptian Gate?" Hunter asked.

Khenti nodded. "My father tricked my mother, and because of

that she is trapped in Duat, our Underworld's version of hell. It was unjustly, unfairly done, and I must discover a way to undo it."

"Um, no one is getting through that gate," said Hunter.

Xena shuddered. "Not as long as those jackal-headed creatures guard it."

Khenti looked from Hunter to Xena. "You tried to go through?"

"Of course," said Hunter. "I figured that would be the easiest way to get Mercy back, so Xena and I went to the gate. I tried to call you first, and when the jackal guys showed up instead I asked about Mercy."

"The jackal warriors were very unpleasant. They would not help us at all," said Xena primly.

Khenti blew out a long breath. "Well, I'm going to have to find a way to get past them. I have to save my mom."

"But what can you do except get banished to Duat again?" Mercy shook her head. "No. She doesn't want you to die to be with her. She made that clear. Even if you could get past those guards wouldn't your dad just re-banish you?"

"It is a risk I am willing to take," Khenti said stubbornly.

"Well, it's not a risk your mom wants you to take! You'd die, Khenti, and your mom definitely doesn't want that. Neither do I!" Mercy brushed her hair back and then picked at her lip. "I wish Osiris didn't let your dad be such a douchebag. It's really not right."

"Douchebag?" Khenti asked.

"I've got this," Emily spoke up. "A douchebag is a guy who is basically useless and usually mean and arrogant, too. We also call them toxic males or mediocre, angry white men."

"Excellent definition, kitten," said Xena.

"Thanks!" Emily grinned at the cat person.

"Oh, I understand," Khenti said. "But Osiris probably has no idea my father is a, um, douchebag. He is too busy running the Underworld. He trusts that Upuant is doing his bidding justly."

Mercy sat up straighter and turned to Khenti. "Wait, what if

Osiris did find out what your dad did to your mom—and you—and me, for that matter?"

Khenti's brows lifted. "He would more than likely be angry. Perhaps *very* angry."

"Enough that he'd free your mom and reinstate you?" Mercy grinned.

Khenti retuned her smile. "I cannot speak for the God of the Underworld, but Osiris is just and reasonable. I do not know if he would reinstate me, but I absolutely believe he would remove my mother from Duat."

"Then we need to figure out a way for you to get back to your realm without being torn apart by those jackal guards," said Mercy.

Hunter snorted. "Get in line. We have to figure out how to fix the gates first. Well, three of them."

"Three?" Mercy stared at her sister. "You healed one?"

Hunter picked at her thumbnail. "Yeah. The Japanese Gate is healed."

"H! Really! That's amazing!" Mercy's jubilation was short-lived as Hunter didn't reflect her joy. "Why aren't you all happy-schmappy? And why aren't the rest of the gates healed now, too?"

"Long story," said Hunter. "I'm not sure if I can recreate the spell that closed the Japanese Gate. It has to do with Amphitrite."

"Oh! That wretched goddess! Must we speak her name?" Xena manically licked her hand and groomed her hair.

"How about I do some more research?" Hunter evaded her twin's gaze. "After school tomorrow I'll go to the cherry tree, be sure it is completely healed, and then we'll go from there."

Emily yawned. "Oh, sorry! I'm not bored or anything, but the Benadryls are going to kick my ass. I really have to go home. Can we put all this on pause until tomorrow?"

"Yeah, I've gotta get back home to my mom," said Jax. Then he smacked himself on his forehead. "Sheesh! All this"—his gesture took in Mercy and Khenti—"made me totally forget. You guys—there's been another murder."

"What?!" The word burst from Hunter. "More missing eyeballs? That can't be possible."

"No, no, nothing like that. It was Mrs. Stoll. She was killed out at Goode Lake. I don't know how. She might have drowned. Or, well, something worse might have happened to her."

"What do you mean?" asked Mercy.

Jax shrugged. "My mom found her and when I got to Goode Lake she was still pretty upset. I don't know exactly how Mrs. Stoll died. I did hear people say that she was drained of blood."

"Oh, bloody buggering hell!" Mercy said. "Something else has gotten through one of the other gates!"

"It kinda looks like that," said Jax.

"You mean a demon from one of the other realms?" Khenti asked.

Mercy blew out a long breath and said, "Yes. Unfortunately."

"Then I must remain here in your realm with you until we track this new monster," said Khenti.

"That's really nice, Khenti, but you don't have to do that," said Mercy.

"Of course I do. It is part of being a Gatekeeper. And as none of you are demi-gods you will need me," he said.

"What does that mean?" Emily asked.

"Demons or monsters from other realms can only be vanquished by a demi-god or a god," said Khenti.

Jax shook his head. "No, Hunter killed Polyphemus and she's just a kick-ass witch, not a demi-god."

Hunter cleared her throat and they turned to look at her. "Well, I had help, which is also how Amphitrite got all into our business. Khenti is right. I couldn't have gotten rid of Polyphemus by myself."

"Will you remain with us long enough to dispatch any demon that has escaped into our realm, Khenti kitten?" Xena asked.

Khenti's smile was fierce. "I would consider it an honor."

Mercy took his hand and squeezed it, smiling her thanks to him.

"That's awesome," said Jax. "But there's more about the new body situation that you should all know." He took a deep breath and then in a burst of words said, "Hunter, Mercy, I gotta tell you that there were a lot of people out at the lake after Mrs. Stoll's body was discovered, and they were saying a bunch of crap about you two—like the fact that you're witches and that you could be hexing people, which is why there have been so many deaths recently."

"That's ridiculous!" Emily said.

"Why would the witches who protect this realm hex it?" asked Khenti.

"We wouldn't," said Hunter. "But there will always be people who blame witches for things they don't understand. It's why only people we trust know about the gates and the fact that we have real magic. It's better that way." She didn't look at Jax, but everyone else did.

"Your mom was spreading a bunch of the rumors, right?" Mercy asked gently.

Jax nodded. "Yeah. I'm sorry." He cleared his throat and continued. "Also, I didn't think much of it then, but now it makes a lot more sense. When I was out at the lake getting Mom I swear I smelled the ocean—a lot. Like, with salt and everything. It was definitely *not* a normal Goode Lake smell."

"Fucking Amphitrite!" Hunter said quickly.

Jax nodded. "Yeah. It was the same smell as when she showed up at the park."

"She was probably whispering about us to the people at the lake," said Hunter. "At least she's gone now."

"I wonder how much damage she did before you got rid of her?" Em asked around a yawn.

"I'm sure we'll find out at school tomorrow," said Hunter.

"I guess that means there's no taking Khenti to school as an out-of-town visitor," added Mercy.

"I don't think that would be a good idea," agreed Jax.

"And, Mag, you can't miss another day of school." Hunter met her twin's turquoise gaze. "We can't give any of them an excuse to say we're up to something."

"Yeah, okay, I get that." Mercy turned to Khenti. "Sorry, you'll be on your own tomorrow until I get home from school."

"Oh, Khenti kitten and I shall be just fine," said Xena. "Are you, perchance, a hunter as well as a warrior?"

Before Khenti could respond, Mercy said, "No! No bird hunting inside the city limits!"

Xena frowned and tossed back her mane of half-dried hair. "Kitten, we most certainly won't be hunting in town. Not when the fields are filled with delectable birds ripe for the plucking." The cat person elbowed Mercy. "Did you get that? Ripe for the *plucking*?"

Mercy and Hunter rolled their eyes in unison.

"Just keep a low profile," said Mercy.

Xena blinked her yellow eyes innocently. "Don't I always?"

FIVE

"Thanks, Jax!" Mercy called and waved from the porch as she clutched the sweats Jax had let them borrow from the gym stash he had in his car. She turned and grinned at Khenti as she handed him the clothes. "Here you go. Jax is taller than you and the sweatshirt might be, um, kinda tight around your shoulders and chest, but these should do until we can get you some real clothes."

Khenti looked down at his military uniform—that was basically a linen diaper, a leather skirt, and a jeweled neck collar. "These are not *real* clothes?"

Mercy pointed at the gorgeous dress Hathor had gifted her with. "Well, they're real—and I love mine—but what I meant is that we'd stand out here if we wore them in public. It'd be like me showing up in my jeans and a fringed shirt in your Underworld."

"I think your dress is quite lovely," Xena called from the couch.

"Love the belt," added Hunter. She smiled at her sister and Mercy returned the smile, but neither twin maintained eye contact for long.

Mercy wondered when it would stop being awkward between

them. Initially when Hunter had pulled them from Duat, she'd fallen into her sister's arms and the twins had clung to each other and sobbed. Then they'd all had to run for their cars and get away from the park, which, thankfully, had been mostly empty. Of course now they knew Goode Park had been so empty because most of the town had been at Goode Lake watching a body being hauled away and talking about them.

Hunter's yawn broke through Mercy's thoughts. "You look tired," she told her twin, noticing for the first time the dark circles under her sister's eyes and how pale she was.

"All this magic . . . I'm worn out. I need sleep." She stood and Tyr's necklace caught the living room lights as it flashed fiery opal.

Mercy moved to her sister. "H! Tyr's necklace! You got it back. Does—does that mean you and Tyr are together again?"

Hunter's gaze shot to hers and her hand cupped the rune. "Yeah. My god and I are okay again."

"I'm so glad!" Mercy pulled her sister into a warm hug. At first Hunter's body was stiff, but within just a few seconds she relaxed and her arms went around Mercy. She hugged her back quickly and then stepped out of her embrace.

"See you in the morning, Mag. Night, Khenti." She only paused long enough to kiss Xena's cheek before Hunter disappeared upstairs.

Mercy sighed and sat down beside Khenti on the couch again. "I shouldn't have asked about Tyr."

"Don't worry, kitten," Xena said. "The important thing is that my girls are home and well. You will soon be back to finishing each other's sentences."

Mercy chewed her lip, but didn't say anything.

"You have only just returned." At her side, Khenti spoke softly. "Give yourselves time." He slipped his hand into hers and squeezed it.

"Yeah. You're both right. Hunter and I just need to get used to each other again." Mentally, Mercy shook herself, squeezed his hand in response, and smiled at Khenti. "But it is getting late. How about

I show you around a little before explaining about bathrooms and such."

"Sounds lovely, kitten." Xena stood and stretched, arching her spine like a proper feline. "You should show Khenti your greenhouse. It is your special place. Whilst you do that I shall be sure no one left catnip toys on the spare bed."

"No one?" Mercy lifted a brow at the cat person.

"One never knows when a stray feline might enter the house. You know we often keep windows open and those feral beasts do love a cozy spot in the afternoon for a catnip toy and a lovely nap . . ." Xena's voice trailed away as she went up the stairs.

"You're not allergic to cats, are you? I promise you no feral cats have broken into our house. Xena is talking about Xena; she likes to nap in the spare bedroom," Mercy said.

Khenti's full lips curled up. "I appreciate felines. They do not make me sneeze like your friend Emily. And I think Xena is magnificent. She would be worshipped as a goddess in our Underworld."

"Don't let her hear you say—" Mercy began, but Xena's voice came from the second-floor landing.

"Then I must visit your Underworld, Khenti kitten!"

"Come on, I'll show you around before Xena corners you and starts asking you exactly *how* she'd be worshipped." Khenti's hand in hers, Mercy led him to the back door.

From upstairs Xena's words drifted after them. "I would prefer to be worshipped with plenty of tuna—and an occasional fat sparrow . . ."

Just a few steps outside the back door Khenti paused and drew in a deep breath. "Your world smells like green, growing things. I like it very much."

"Thanks! You're here at a good time. In the winter it's cold and we get a bunch of snow, and the summer is hot and humid—really a mess. But right now, in the middle of spring when everything is fertile and healthy and stretched up toward the sun, it's perfect."

"What is this greenhouse of which Xena spoke?"

"Here, it's this way." Mercy gestured for him to follow her. She didn't take his hand again, but they walked close enough beside each other that their arms occasionally touched. Mercy liked how comfortable she felt with him, and she loved that he actually listened to her and cared about what she had to say—and he was definitely off-the-charts hot, but when she thought about more—as in a relationship—she felt uneasy. She'd misjudged Kirk. She didn't believe she was misjudging Khenti, but she hadn't believed Kirk was an ass and had been totally wrong about that. Mercy liked Khenti—a lot, but she had to go slow. She had to be able to trust her judgment. She stopped in front of her mother's last present to her. "This is my greenhouse. It's my sanctuary. Come on in." She opened the door and flipped on the light switch, but even before they were fully inside, the scent of flowers and tomato plants, ferns and fertile soil, filled her senses and worked on her nerves like a balm.

"This is wondrous!" Khenti walked slowly down the middle row of the glass house. "It reminds me a little of my mother's growing chamber."

"Yeah, only I'd have to multiply this several times to catch up with your mom's chamber."

Khenti stopped before a table filled with healthy tomato seedlings. "What are these interesting plants?"

"Tomatoes. They'll be ready to plant in the garden outside at the end of this month."

"Tomatoes?"

"You know, red, round fruit that are really more like a vegetable. They make great spaghetti sauce, but my fav is to slice them thick for tomato sandwiches on toasted bread with lots of mayo." When he just shook his head, Mercy pulled her phone from her pocket and quickly googled tomatoes to show him a picture.

"We do not have that plant in my world," said Khenti.

"OMGoddess! Seriously? I'm gonna tomato you up while you're here!"

Khenti grinned. "Whatever that means I shall look forward to it because it makes you happy." He touched her cheek gently. "I like it when you're happy."

Mercy covered his hand with hers. "Me, too. It's good to be home." Then, as she thought about the awkwardness with Hunter, her smile faded and her hand dropped from his cheek. "Weird, but good."

"It will get better. And your sister's powers are impressive."

Mercy nodded. "They are. And she said she closed a gate, which is great news. Well, unless she has to have Amphitrite's help to do it again, which is not great news."

"Let us not worry about that until tomorrow. Tonight let us take joy in the fact that we are no longer in hell."

"You're absolutely right. We're not in hell. We're not going to die. And you're here in *my world* now—my filled-with-yummy-tomatoes world!" Mercy brushed her hand gently over the baby tomato plants so that their distinctive scent filled the air around them.

"And we're alone." Khenti turned from the tomato sprouts to face her.

"We are," Mercy said.

"Thank you for saving us." Khenti met and held her gaze.

"Hunter saved us." She was unable to look away from his dark, expressive eyes.

"But only because you used your powers to reach from one world to another and call to her. You are amazing, Green Witch Mercy." Slowly, gently, Khenti cupped her face and pressed his lips to hers.

The kiss was a sweet question that Mercy allowed herself to answer with a *yes* as she deepened the kiss and wrapped her arms around his broad shoulders. Khenti held her as they explored the kiss, until they both were breathing hard. When Mercy pulled back just a little Khenti relaxed his embrace so that she could easily step out of his arms.

"I need to take this part of our relationship slow," said Mercy.

"That is understandable. As I have never had a girlfriend, I, too, would like to take it slow—though I very much enjoyed our kiss."

"Wait, you've never had a girlfriend?" Looking at Khenti—strong, super hot, and an authentically nice guy—Mercy was shocked by his words.

Not appearing shy or ashamed of his inexperience, Khenti shrugged nonchalantly. "As you are already aware, it often ends badly when mortals and gods, or demi-gods, are lovers. Mortal parents warned their daughters about me; none were willing to cross their parents— not that I blamed them. And when I became Gate Guardian I was too busy focusing on the impossible task of making my father proud to have time for much else. So, it is good to be here with you— getting to know you—learning to care for you. I understand and appreciate taking it slow."

"You are a fantastic change from the guys in my realm," said Mercy.

"Jax seems nice," Khenti said.

"Yeah, he's very nice. But he's also like a brother to me."

"Ah, I understand. And I am not like a brother to you." Khenti's eyes glittered in the greenhouse lights.

"Not at all." Mercy wanted to kiss him again, but she didn't. She wouldn't. Not right away. Slow meant slow—and the fiasco with Kirk still had her confidence shaken.

Khenti continued to hold her gaze as he took her hand gently in his and lifted it to his lips. He kissed it and smiled. "I am glad you do not feel as if I am your brother. Very glad." He did not release her hand. Instead, he threaded his fingers with hers and remained so close to her that Mercy could feel the heat of his skin.

Her stomach flip-flopped and she had to clear her throat before she spoke. "W-would you like to see my mother's grave?"

"Yes, very much."

Hand in hand, Khenti and Mercy walked slowly through the Goode family cemetery. When they came to Abigail's grave Mercy touched her fingers to her lips, and then pressed them to the grave marker—a large stone owl that was Athena's symbol.

"I love you and miss you so much, Abigail," she whispered.

Surprising her, Khenti also pressed his fingers to his lips and then to the owl and murmured, "Rest peacefully, Abigail Goode, and know your daughter is safe and cherished."

Mercy blinked quickly to keep her tears from falling and squeezed Khenti's hand.

Behind and above them, the sound of a window opening was jarring in the silent night. Then Xena's voice echoed around them. "Kittens! The room is ready! It is late! I shall take my bath with my cannabis treats now and bid you good night! Come to bed now, kittens!"

"Xena!" Mercy yell-whispered up at the open window and the mane of untamable hair silhouetted there. "Shh! You'll wake the dead!"

"Oh, silly kitten! The dead do not need to sleep!" Xena shouted. "Now come to bed!"

"We better go inside. She won't leave us alone until we do," said Mercy.

"She would make an excellent goddess," Khenti said as they made their way from the cemetery to the back door.

"Yeah, but do not tell—"

"Of course I would be an excellent goddess!" Xena shouted from the window before slamming it shut.

Just inside the house, Mercy said, "Don't let her bully you tomorrow. Remember, if Amphitrite has people gossiping about us it's best we keep a super low profile—and Xena is what we call *extra* in this world."

"No low profile?"

"She doesn't understand the meaning of the word—literally," said Mercy.

"So, no hunting in town?" Khenti asked.

"No! Actually, not hunting at all would be best! I'll encourage her to hunt in her cat form, and I'll show you how to binge Netflix. That'll keep you both busy while Hunter and I are at school."

"That is for the best. My khopesh would make a mess of a bird," Khenti said as he grabbed Jax's borrowed clothes and they headed upstairs.

"I like messy birds!" Xena's voice came from down the hallway and Abigail's open bedroom door.

Mercy opened her mouth just as Hunter stuck her head out of her bedroom door and at the same time the twins shouted, "GO TO BED, CAT!" Then together they laughed as Xena slammed the door closed.

"Night, Mag." Hunter grinned at her.

"Night, H. Thanks for bringing me home," Mercy said.

"Always."

"I love you, Hunter."

Hunter paused as she was closing her door. "I love you, too, Mag."

Feeling a lot lighter, Mercy showed Khenti to his room—and began a long explanation about toilets and showers and electric light switches . . .

SIX

Being a goddess went beyond the physical. No matter what tricks Hunter Goode had up her sleeve or which bastard of a god she had by her side, she would never win. Getting rid of a goddess wasn't that easy. And getting rid of Amphitrite would be even more difficult.

The great goddess of the sea was without a body, in this realm at least, but a form was the least important aspect of her being. After all, she had cloaked herself from most mortals, hiding in the dew on the grass or the sweat on their skin. Yes, some of her powers would be missed. Filling spongey lungs with the salty waters of the ocean or hurling a hydrant of seawater with the flick of her wrist had been fun, but this type of war suited her better. This type of war separated mere witches from the goddesses they would always strive to be.

Amphitrite drifted over Goodeville—nothing more than salt and humidity, an exhale of breath. At least, in form. In actuality, she was a burbling ocean trench, spilling lava, spewing toxins, the beginning of something far more deadly.

Over the centuries, her targets may have changed, but her mission remained the same: revenge. In this year, in this realm, Hunter Goode was the perfect mark.

For now, Amphitrite would watch and wait. She was good at this part: planning, calculating, being still before a strike. Sailors had called it *the calm before the storm,* but it had never been a storm. It had always been a goddess.

Included in her long list of strengths was cunning—an additional reason having a body meant nothing at all. Amphitrite had already put another piece in play in the witch's short game of life, and it was one the insolent mortal would never see coming.

Make that two things . . .

Had she lips, she would have smirked.

Amphitrite drifted above the creek that encircled the town of Goodeville and through the boughs of swaying junipers until she came to a large building with a mighty stadium. It was there she found him, the spawn of the Christian, god-fearing woman Amphitrite had already made her own.

He jogged from one end of a large lawn of well-tended grass to the other, passing peers who exercised and joked with the ease of naïve mortals.

So moldable. So weak.

Amphitrite floated to Jax as he ran laps around the field, hate wafting from her in gusts of salt-tinged air.

"Tell me your troubles, boy, and I'll tell you who's to blame."

Jax brushed the sweat from his forehead and licked the salt from his lips.

"Boy!" Amphitrite's shout was a hiss of steam that Jax batted away like a gnat.

Anger flared within the goddess. The mortal had ignored her. More than that, he hadn't heard her words at all. Was it her? Had that witch stolen her power after all?

Impossible!

She hovered above Jax, an invisible storm cloud churning with fury, as his pace slowed. He pulled his phone from his pocket and stared at the illuminated screen, his steady jog veering from the gravel path and onto the grass.

No, the problem wasn't with her. It was him. His head was too full of compassion for the witch.

Distracted, Jax crashed into another mortal. The ball he'd been about to throw fell to the grass with a *thud*.

"Hey, man! What the hell?"

Amphitrite swelled with genius. Within Goodeville, Hunter had more enemies than friends.

Jax brushed his hand through his sweat-streaked hair. "Sorry, dude. Kylie . . ." He held up his phone as evidence. "You know how it is."

"*Lies!*" Amphitrite swarmed the boy. "*It's that witch. That Hunter. She made him do it. Made him hit you.*"

The boy's chest swelled, and his chin lifted. "You did it on purpose."

"I was distracted." Jax's brow furrowed, and he tucked his phone back into his pocket. "Why would I run into you on purpose?"

"*She's made him hate you. All of you.*" Ocean waves crashed as Amphitrite whispered.

The boy pulled on the collar of his shirt, suddenly drenched with sweat and stinking of the sea. "You think I have shit for brains?"

"*Hunter Goode is a witch. A spawn of Satan. This is her doing.*"

Jax took a step back. "Dillon, chill—"

"This is because of that witch." His shoulders seemed to harden as he inched closer to Jax. "Kirk was right all along."

"*She wants you all gone. To bring forth the devil and take this town as their own.*" Mist collected around Amphitrite's formless being and twinkled in the afternoon sun like a star.

"She's made you her bitch." Dillon spat the words like a threat.

"Seriously, man, it was an accident. I don't know why you're freaking out."

Jax turned to leave, and Dillon struck out, nearly shoving Jax off his feet. "Hey, asshole!" Dillon fisted his hands. "Tell your little witch girlfriend that she can't hide behind you forever."

Jax took a deep breath and clenched his hands into fists before relaxing them. "Whatever, Dillon," he mumbled, and jogged back to the track.

"Hunter Goode is a witch."

Dillon stood on the field, body stiff as a corpse, a puddle forming around his feet as the great goddess of the sea flooded the mortal with wrath.

"And that witch needs to burn."

SEVEN

Hunter sat in the red laminate booth at Shake It, debating whether to order curly or regular fries. She chewed the inside of her cheek as she envisioned the complexities of dunking a corkscrew-shaped fry into her shake without getting her fingers sticky. She wrinkled her nose.

Alex Feretto, Hunter's locker mate since freshman year and the newest Shake It employee, set two chocolate shakes on the table before tucking her blond hair behind her ears. "Straight fries make for the best dunking," she said, her cat eyes creasing in the corners with a grin. "And I don't know how much you want to mix Old Bay with chocolate."

"You totally solved my problem." Hunter returned Alex's friendly grin with one of her own, although she was positive that it didn't reach her eyes. "Straight, unseasoned fries it is."

With a nod, Alex scribbled the order on her notepad. "Always happy to help out a fellow Mustang," she chimed, tucking her pencil into her black server apron before heading to the POS.

If only Hunter possessed half of Alex's kindness toward her fellow students.

Hunter pushed the menu in front of the silver napkin holder and sagged against the puffy booth. She dug her phone out of her back pocket and scrolled through her texts with Jax.

Skipping practice. Need to talk. Meet at Shake It after school.

Hunter checked the time. Maybe he'd decided to go to practice after all.

A bead of water slid down the old-school milkshake glass and joined the ring pooling around its base.

If she continued to hold in all her lies, she would spare her friends. Sure, the guilt would eat her alive. Hell, it might give her an ulcer or two, but at least she'd still have friends. That wasn't too unhealthy, right?

She stifled a groan as the door chimed and Jax strolled in.

He waved to Alex and a couple his mother's age lunching at the counter before seeing Hunter and rushing over, his cheeks plump with the crooked-toothed grin that had already begun to lose its catawampus-ness thanks to his Invisalign.

Hunter set her elbows on the table and cupped her chin in her palms. Guilt burned in her throat, and the syrupy scent of the melting milkshakes made her stomach lurch. She had to tell Jax all the unfortunate decisions she'd made. It was the right thing to do.

He slid into the booth, grabbing a wad of napkins to wipe the sweat from his face. "Ran here," he explained. "Got sweat all in my mouth on the field, but figured I should keep it going and do something active since I'm missing practice."

A wobbly smile twisted Hunter's lips.

"You look green. You didn't get a dairy shake again, did you?" He shook his head. Droplets of sweat fell from his hair and dotted his T-shirt–clad shoulders. "Isn't that why you're vegan and not vegetarian? The whole mucous, pooping, cow milk thing?"

Hunter's cheeks flamed with the memory of a twelve-year-old Jax in the woods next to Goode Lake frantically clawing at the dirt to make sure she had a proper hole in which to release all the demons warring in her stomach after they'd shared a whole bag of string cheese.

"I have to tell you something. *Things,* actually. I—" Hunter's confession was cut short when Alex returned to set a plate of hot fries on the table between the friends.

Hunter watched Alex's white sneakers as she and Jax discussed their latest biology assignment, finally looking up when Alex departed, her shoes squeaking against the black-and-white-checkered tiles.

"So," Jax began around a mouthful of fries. "Since I called this meeting, I feel like it's only fair that I go first."

Hunter nodded. Unease trudged up her back with weighted boots, rounding her shoulders.

"This is harder than it was in my head." He took a drink of his shake and flattened his palms against the table. "Amphitrite would have killed Em and me if you hadn't been such an intense fire-breathing dragon."

Hunter dragged her pendant along its thin rope cord and frowned.

Jax held up his hands. "I mean that in the most badass way possible."

She smiled and cautiously popped a hot fry into her mouth.

"You've clearly been dealing with some heavy things, but . . ."

She swallowed and felt the mushy fry slide down her esophagus in slow motion. Here it was. The *you're a terrible human, and I don't want to be friends with you* speech. And she deserved it.

Jax leaned forward, his chin nearly touching the tip of his paper straw. "The spell with Kylie . . ." He paused and offered a quick smile to Alex as she passed with another table's milkshakes. "Not okay. I feel . . ." He grimaced. "*Wrong.* What we did was wrong."

As if planned, his phone buzzed, and a picture of Kylie glowed up at them from the screen, her eyes closed and round face tipped toward the sky.

He stared at it unblinking until her photo vanished and a missed call notification was added to the tally on the screen. "She's obsessed," he said, his glass leaving a slug trail on the table as he pushed it back and forth between his hands. "It's not normal. Yesterday she started crying because I said I didn't like Whoppers. Somehow that meant that, because she *does* like Whoppers, I must hate her."

Hunter blinked. "You love burgers."

"Malt balls not burgers!" he shouted, blushing as the couple at the counter turned to look at them. Clearing his throat, he whispered, "But that's not the point. The point is—whose identity is wrapped up in malt balls?"

Hunter hiked her slumped shoulders. "Who even eats malt balls?"

With a sigh, Jax leaned back and crossed his arms over his chest. "I'm serious, H. That spell didn't let out feelings she already had. It turned her into a stalker who thinks trips to the bathroom require a partner. The Kylie I liked had her own thoughts and loved her independence."

Again, his phone vibrated, and Kylie's influencer-worthy pose stared up at them. He winced and flipped his phone facedown on the table.

"Maybe something's actually wrong." Hunter grabbed his phone and answered it, the perverse desire for a car accident to have taken place making her feel like an even shittier human. "Jax's phone!" She grimaced at how high pitched and fake her attempt at cheer sounded.

"Where's Jax?"

"He's—" Jax flailed his arms and shook his head as if being attacked by spiders. "In the bathroom."

"The locker room bathroom?" A shrill firework of giggles erupted in the background followed by the squeak of door hinges and hushed silence. "I haven't seen him on the field. I want to make sure he's okay."

"At Shake It. We're having a good ol' fashioned best friend roundup." Hunter dropped her face into her hand and groaned inwardly at the ridiculous word vomit her guilt kept spewing past her tongue.

"Oh . . ."

Hunter swore she heard Kylie sniffle. "The stuff with his mom." She bit her bottom lip as another surge of regret tightened her throat. "He just needed to talk."

"It's fine, H. I get it." In the background someone sharply called Kylie's name. "I have to go. Tell him I'll talk to him after cheer practice."

Hunter hung up and slid the phone back to Jax.

"Well?" Jax asked, blinking at her expectantly. "Wild, right?"

Hunter pressed her napkin against the puddle of water at the base of her milkshake glass. "She just sounded worried."

"She's not worried. She's obsessed," he said for the second time before letting out an exhausted exhale. "You'll see."

Thoughts racing, Hunter jabbed at the frozen core of her milkshake with the mushy end of her paper straw.

Tell him now. Say that you didn't know what would happen. That he's right, everything's not okay. Say it. Say it! Say—

"What my mom saw on the beach. What she still claims you did in our garage apartment. The things people are saying about you and Mag . . ." Jax's dark eyes met hers, and she froze, her breath trapped in her chest. "I know you're not some horrible evil witch, but—"

There it was again. That *but* that could take away the only person in the whole world who saw her for who she truly was.

"There's something going on. If you don't want to tell me, that's fine, but I won't sit here and pretend like everything's peaches and that we didn't hurt Kylie."

"*We* didn't hurt Kylie. *I* did." The words exploded from her on a breathy exhale. "I didn't really know what that spell would do, but I needed the magical energy it created." The backs of her bare thighs sounded like Velcro against the sticky booth as she shifted. "Amphitrite gave me a spellbook, and I believed her when she told me that, if I fed it enough spellwork energy, it would give me what I needed to fix the gates."

Jax scratched his chest, his forehead creasing with the beginnings of an idea. "If you used the book to do the spell, it has to have a way to undo it. Do you have it with you? We can—"

"I don't want to use the book!" It was Hunter's turn to blush as customers swung around to gawk at the outburst. "It's tied to *her*. I don't even know if it's still alive now that she's gone."

"Alive?" Jax grimaced. "That's what you meant when you said you needed magic from the Kylie spell. To give it to the book?"

Hunter opened her mouth to respond with a quick *yes* but caught herself before she let another half-truth masquerade as the whole truth. "It likes blood way more than it does spell energy."

Jax stopped mid-drink, shivered, and pushed his milkshake to the edge of the table.

Her stomach churned and gurgled, warning her to hold on to her lies, but she had to keep plowing forward. She had to tell Jax everything. They both deserved the truth, and she wouldn't be free until she did.

"You know Chuck, the *repent your sins* guy who hung out downtown?"

Jax's lips moved with a *yes* Hunter couldn't hear over the roar of her heartbeat.

"He had a knife . . ." Her mouth went dry, and tears stabbed the backs of her eyes. She blinked them away, the deep scarlet of Chuck's blood flashing in the empty space of each fall of her eyelids. "He tried to give it to me. He had killed someone. Amphitrite was there. He heard her. I know he did."

Jax's thick brows furrowed, and his mouth opened and closed with an unspoken question.

Slow down, she scolded herself before taking a deep breath. This time, she didn't stop the warm gush of tears from washing down her cheeks. "Amphitrite led me to the alleyway between Suzette's

Creperie and Main Street Meats. I thought I'd have to jump into a bloody meat dumpster with the book, but she had something else planned." Hunter dropped her gaze to the pile of fries, unable to look at her best friend. "Chuck was there. He'd just murdered a man. The voice of God had told him to, but I know it was Amphitrite poisoning his thoughts." She lifted the soggy napkin from the table and pressed it against her hot cheeks. "He brought me the knife he'd used, held it against my hands. He wanted me to take it—"

Her voice caught on a sob, and she clutched her pendant to remind herself of her strength and Tyr's support. Even after everything she'd done, the god of the sky had come back to her. She hadn't been terrible. She'd been lost.

"Amphitrite was right behind me. I thought she would help me. I thought she would help both of us." Crystals of salt shimmered like stars against the crispy fries as tears once again welled in Hunter's eyes. "She pushed me, and the knife"—she bit down on the inside of her cheeks to keep from wailing—"there was blood everywhere," she said, hiccupping back another sob.

Jax covered her hand with his. "I'm sorry you've been alone with this."

"He's dead." Hunter's watery gaze flew to Jax. "And it's my fault."

He squeezed her hand. "He's dead, and it's Amphitrite's fault."

That might be true, but nothing would make it better. It had calloused a part of her heart, and Hunter would spend the rest of her life filling the world with good in an attempt to erase the bad of that night.

She cleared her throat and wiped her nose on her sleeve. "There's more," she whispered, staring down at his hand over hers. "I used magic to break Kirk's fingers. He assaulted me, and I fought back. I don't know if I feel bad." She chewed her lower lip. "Sometimes I do, and then I remember his hand on my throat and that look in his eyes, and I want to break his fingers all over again."

Jax smoothed his thumb across the back of her hand. "Hate to say it, but that's what he gets." He hiked a shoulder, his eyebrow arching. "I don't feel bad, either."

A smile scratched her lips, brittle and sharp. She didn't deserve such a good friend. She wanted Jax to be angry, disgusted, make her pay for what she'd done. The act of telling wasn't the release she thought it would be. Confessing didn't wash her clean. She needed to do that on her own, forgive herself. But how?

Hunter stared at her milkshake, suddenly wishing she was five years older and they were at a bar. "Your mom is telling the truth. I was doing blood magic, banishing Amphitrite from the garage apartment and from my body, when she walked in. I used another spell to clean up the mess and didn't correct anyone when they said she was lying." Her voice was flat, unflinching. The wash of tears and visions of Chuck, his warm blood on her hands and the way he'd slumped against the pavement like a wet paper bag, had drained the compassion from her tone.

It wasn't fair, not to Jax. A part of her knew that. A part of her wanted his anger so she could focus on his needs and not her own.

Jax pulled his hand from hers and leaned back against the booth, his throat tightening with a thick swallow. "People are saying she's crazy. My dad called six psychologists, and the whole time you knew she was right." He ran his hands through his hair. "Jesus, Hunter!" He stared at Hunter as if trying to find a way to understand why she'd let so many people think his mother was crazy for so long. Why she hadn't even told *him* the truth. Whatever he was searching for in Hunter's face, it clearly wasn't there, because he snatched his phone off the table and got to his feet. "I can't even look at you right now."

Her chin quivered and another slow leak of tears slid down her cheeks. *I'm sorry!* she mouthed, but only the gentle cracks of a whimper escaped her lips.

Feet from the exit, the door to Shake It flew open in front of him, the bells above it seeming to clang instead of chime.

The scent of fresh grapefruit hit Hunter, bringing goose bumps to her arms. "Hunter Goode, you traitorous bitch!"

The diners turned to face Hunter as Kylie stormed past Jax, her hair swirling around her shoulders in a whirlwind of glossy red as the closing door forced in a gust of warm air. "I turn my back for five seconds and you try to go after my man?"

Hunter wiped her cheeks as anxiety flew from her lips in a burst of laughter.

"Why are you laughing?" Kylie screeched, her hazel eyes brimming with tears. "We're supposed to be friends."

Hunter swallowed. Jax was right. There was something very wrong with Kylie York.

"We *are* friends."

"Friends don't take another friend's boyfriend!" Kylie hissed, her clenched fists brushing the hem of her Mustang-red practice shorts.

Jax's forehead creased with worry as he gingerly placed his hand on Kylie's shoulder. "You know Hunter and I are just friends."

Kylie whirled around, and their audience shifted uncomfortably as she channeled her rage at her innocent boyfriend. "Oh, like I'd ever believe you. You skipped practice to meet her. *Behind my back.*"

He snatched his hand from her shoulder, his expression hardening, as unreadable as stone. "I skipped practice because I didn't want to deal with team bullshit. My mom has been an even bigger wreck since finding Julie Stoll's body, and Hunter—" His hands were fists now, too.

"Hunter what?" Kylie demanded with a stomp of her red-and-white sneaker.

He walked backward toward the exit, chest puffed, chin lifted. "You two work it out."

Another chime of the bells, and he was gone.

"Jax!" Hunter and Kylie shouted in unison.

Kylie spun back around to face Hunter, her cheeks nearly as red as the strawberry lengths of her hair.

"You don't get to say his name!" she shouted, and swiped Jax's discarded shake from the table. "He's mine, not yours!" With a flick of her wrist, soupy chocolate flew from the glass.

It coated Hunter's face and slid in thick globs down her chin, splattering against her T-shirt.

Gasps and murmurs flew around them while Hunter groped the table for the napkins.

Hunter flinched as Kylie slammed the empty glass onto the table. "People—*these* people—"

Hunter wiped her eyes and stared at Kylie's outstretched arm, her long finger pointing at the patrons of Shake It.

"They're all saying that you're the reason bad things keep happening. I haven't believed them, but I see now that they're right." In a burst of grapefruit, she whirled around and stormed out of Shake It.

Hunter buried her sticky face in her sticky hands. She didn't care that people now whispered about her, about Jax, witches, and murder or that Alex had accidentally flung mop water all over her bare legs and patches of skin revealed by her strappy sandals. Hunter just wanted to melt onto the floor like Jax's milkshake and get absorbed by the dirty cotton ropes of the mop head. She should leave Goodeville, disappear into the crowds of tourists boarding the commuter trains to head back to their real lives after a weekend in the quaint town, and start a real life of her own.

EIGHT

After Nure-Onna had embraced and drained the mortal woman at the lake, she was languid and filled with the sweet warmth of mortal blood for the first time in centuries. Lazily, she'd swam to a deserted area across the lake and slithered onto the rocky bank, where she'd stretched her serpentine body to bask in the fading sunlight. Flushed with borrowed mortal heat, the enormous viper had dozed amid the sun-warmed rocks until she had been interrupted by the garish sounds of mortal hysteria at the discovery of the body of the discarded woman.

Nure-Onna had raised herself to her full height. Her small, heavy-lidded eyes had flashed red as she stared across the lake at the mortal pandemonium. She'd imagined diving deep and swimming to the shore where they had already covered the woman's corpse. She would've loved to have surged from the depths of the lake to attack the mortals. First, she would've slashed them with her poisonous fangs and then, as their bodies succumbed to her toxin, she would have drained them all dry. As she'd readied herself to dive and then strike, the creature had swept back her long, dark hair and noticed that her arm had changed color from porcelain to slate. More surprised than disturbed, she had studied her serpent body. Her beautiful scales, usually the turquoise and jade that reflected the waters that surround Kyushu, the island of her birth, had also shifted to different shades of sickly grays. It was then she had realized that even though she had been so recently filled with fresh mortal blood, she was feeling increasingly weak and dizzy.

Ah, I understand. I may visit but not overstay in this realm of living mortals. Nure-Onna dove deep into the lake to easily avoid prying eyes as she retraced her watery journey from the lake to the creek that washed past the weeping cherry tree, which held the entrance to the World of Darkness.

Reluctantly Nure-Onna had slithered from the stream and followed her trail of slime to the newly opened hole in the rotting tree. She had reentered the tunnel and returned to her realm, but Nure-Onna would be back . . . lesson learned. Next time, she would be wiser.

NINE

Hunter ditched her bike in the front yard and ran up the porch steps, bursting into the house in a cloud of syrupy-sweet coconut milk. She raced up the stairs, thankful Mercy, Khenti, and Xena had already left, and she wouldn't have to explain her appearance or what she was about to do. Her talk with Jax had made it clear that simply confessing wasn't enough. She needed to fully rid herself of Amphitrite and focus on getting her life back on track.

She reached her room and shucked off her T-shirt, still soggy with chocolate shake, and tossed it into her overflowing hamper before pulling a face wipe from the pack on her bedside table and scrubbing the sticky mess from her skin.

Even though Amphitrite was gone, Hunter wasn't completely free. She wouldn't be until every piece of the sea goddess was erased from this realm.

Her fingers traced the bubblegum-pink bumpy scar against her pale stomach. "I guess some things will always be here." She chewed the inside of her cheek. "It's a reminder. Never let power turn you into someone you're not."

Hunter threw open her closet door and pulled another tee from the hanger before yanking her luggage from deep within the closet's shadowed corners. She didn't stop, didn't think, only acted. She unzipped the duffle and reached into the cavernous black interior. The spellbook was no longer puppy-ear soft, alive, and pulsing beneath her fingers. Its cover, once reddish pink with blood, was now dull and lifeless, the watery brown of a coffee stain. She opened the cover as rough as sandpaper and thumbed through the pages. They crunched beneath her fingers like fall leaves.

The book was dead.

Hunter ripped out the only page she still needed and shoved the *WANT* spell into her back pocket before tucking the book under her arm and dashing back down the stairs. She jogged toward the back door, pausing in the kitchen to gather the lighter fluid and long lighter from the grilling accoutrements section of their pantry.

The afternoon air was still and thick. The kind of weather that makes the earth feel as if it's stopped spinning. Hunter swiped the sweat from her brow as she ran to the old Goode graveyard nestled behind the Goode house. The place where her mother and grandmother were buried along with all the ancestresses before them.

The wrought-iron gate opened with a *creak,* and Hunter didn't bother to close it as she ran through the maze of headstones, her sandals slapping against her soles with each rushed footstep.

She came to a stop at the iron firepit in the center of the cemetery.

"You were never mine," she said to the spellbook as she tossed it into the pit and doused it with lighter fluid. "Go back to hell." She touched the lighter to the book's crisp cover and pulled the trigger. The only power Hunter needed was her own.

Flames engulfed the spellbook, and its curling, black pages sent a flutter of satisfaction up her spine.

As she turned her back to the blaze and headed toward her next duty at the cherry tree, her hand shot into the air, her middle finger extended to the memory of the vanquished goddess.

TEN

Goodeville was awash in hate for the foolish young witch who had banished the sea goddess's body from this realm. If the pliability of most of the townspeople's opinions of Hunter Goode been a meal, Amphitrite would have been more than satiated.

Her laughter cracked through the air like shattering glass as she glided like a wispy cloud above Main Street.

The witch doesn't know what she has done or who I have awakened.

The goddess swirled over the high school and finally dipped down beneath the boughs of the fetid cherry tree.

She was next—the creature Amphitrite's wisdom and cunning had thought to call forth before her run-in with that pubescent mortal.

Amphitrite admired the streams of ichor that ran like silvery veins from the dark hole in the base of the guardian tree. The creature was already awake, active. No doubt, she had begun to feed.

Had she a true form, Amphitrite would wrap her azure fingers around the ripples of otherworldly energy that seeped from the hole like smoke and pull, yanking the bloodthirsty beast from her hiding place.

A spark of anger crackled within Amphitrite, and waves of heat shimmered from her fog-like form. She stretched and flexed, gathering power from the droplets of water resting in the clouds. She didn't need a body. She only needed her magic.

> *"Creature from the Underworld*
> *Come forth, come forth, come forth.*
> *Through water, you are bound to me.*
> *Come forth, come forth, come forth.*
> *By ocean, rain, and river*
> *We are tied to this realm.*
> *Come forth, come forth, come forth.*
> *By sea, ice, and sweat*
> *We share purpose.*
> *Come forth, come forth, come forth.*
> *By lake, snow, and breath*
> *We seek revenge.*
> *Come forth!"*

Slime spurted from the large fist-sized hole that served as a conduit, connecting the Japanese Underworld and Goodeville.

"Come forth!"

A forked tongue lashed out, licking the air, testing the surroundings.

"Come forth!"

The Nure-Onna slithered from her cave, her thick body swelling to its true form as she emerged.

Amphitrite's smile slid across her lips like the tentacle of a jellyfish. She had a body. She saw it reflected in the Nure-Onna's glossy black eyes. To this realm, to these mortals, she was sea and salt, wrath and waves, but to the Nure-Onna, to those who held true power, she was as real as the earth itself.

"Hello, my pet." Amphitrite's laughter cracked like gunfire. *"Shall we begin?"*

ELEVEN

Hunter's nails were jagged nubs that she couldn't keep from chewing while she once again waited for Jax. She hadn't thought it was possible, but she dreaded this talk even more than the one before. She'd confessed to everything at Shake It, and he'd walked out on her. She was surprised he'd still agreed to meet her at the cherry tree.

"At least I got rid of the book."

She kicked a clump of dirt along the grass, her heart, butt, and stomach all clenching as Jax's car pulled down the easement to park a few yards from the tree. She waved, a frantic, startled-goose type of movement that made her white cheeks flame.

Jax unfolded his tall frame from his vehicle and strode toward her, his dark eyes firmly fixed on the stiff grass.

"Hi!" Another flap of her arms.

He continued walking, staring down, brushing past her as if she were a ghost. She was invisible. They were no longer friends.

She followed him to the cherry tree. With each step, she deflated. Another inch and her knuckles would drag on the ground.

He stilled, finally lifting his gaze to stare at the tree, but Hunter could only look at him. Her best friend. Her brother. Her person.

Hunter's anguish spun up her throat and erupted in a gasping sob. "P-please d-don't hate me." Her sadness bent her at the middle, folding her like a paper doll.

He wrapped his arm around her heaving shoulders and pulled her against him. "I don't hate you."

She couldn't stop another choking wail from cracking in her throat. He didn't hate her, but that didn't mean he was still her friend.

Jax pulled her into a bear hug and rested his chin on her head. "But I am mad at you."

"You don't want to be my friend anymore," she cried, completely aware of the growing wet spot turning his heather-gray tee deep charcoal.

His chest vibrated against her with a laugh. "We'll always be friends, H. No matter how much of an asshole you are."

"I've been a h-huge asshole," she hiccupped.

"You have been." His chest rose and fell with a sigh. "But that doesn't mean I'll stop being there."

She pressed her cheek against him, his heart thumping a gentle, reassuring beat. "I love you, Jax Ashley."

"I love you, Hunter Goode."

She stepped back, blinking the last few tears from her eyes. "Friends?" She held out her hand.

"For life." Jax clapped his palm against hers before shaking it.

She didn't deserve him.

"So," he began, his forehead creasing as they turned to face the withering cherry tree. "How exactly do we check that everything's"—he gestured toward the tree—"fixed?"

Hunter picked at her thumbnail, her gaze roaming the drooping branches, leaves sliding from them like sauce from limp noodles, before returning to the best friend who'd set aside his anger to be there for her. She *did* deserve that—the chance to make everything better.

She deserved him. Yes, she'd done bad things, but she wasn't a bad person. Not too long ago, she'd been here, close to this very spot, performing a spell to save her town, save the world. She deserved a universe of Jaxes. Everybody did.

"The tree will just be *better.*"

They parted the boughs, and crispy, brown leaves rained down on them. The sour scent of wet garbage hit her, and she choked on a cough. The gate should be fixed. The cherry tree, its guardian in this realm, should be healing, but it wasn't better. It wasn't even close.

How had she gotten it so wrong?

Jax wrinkled his nose and brushed a curling leaf from his shoulder. "It stinks."

Hunter stared up through the large gaps in the once thick and verdant foliage as she rounded the ancient cherry's wide trunk. Her sandals squelched against moist earth and cold liquid seeped between her toes. She glanced down, lifting her foot. A thick string of mucous trembled in the breeze. Hopping on one leg, she shook her foot. The shoestrings of goo slapped the air but didn't fall. She kicked out, still balancing on one foot. Another squelch, and her grounded foot flew out from under her. Her arms windmilled and smacked into Jax. She grabbed onto his shirt and crashed onto the ground, yanking him down with her.

Air fled her lungs as the full weight of her wide receiver best friend slammed down on top of her. He rolled off her, and she let out a squeak of pain before sitting up and blinking bursts of light from her vision.

"You okay?" he asked, picking shriveled leaves from her hair.

Wiggling her slimy toes, Hunter pointed, her finger an arrow aimed at the trail of ichor that lapped against the base of the tree and flooded the grass in a thick mucosal path that led to the edge of Sugar Creek.

"Well, that's new." Jax got to his feet and bent down, taking her hand in his.

She let him pull her up, unable to keep her eyes from the pearlescent trail. She'd closed the gate. She'd done a spell. She'd used mortal blood. She'd—

Hunter's breath stilled within her chest. *"Amphitrite."*

Jax's thick brows lifted. "Think she did this before you poofed her out of here?" His fingers flashed out, mimicking an explosion.

"I think . . ." Hunter chewed her lower lip as thoughts rang between her ears.

. . . she used me.

I listened to power instead of myself.

I was naïve.

It was all for nothing.

"Amphitrite wanted revenge," she said, landing on the truth without giving further voice to her shame. "She was here when I performed the spell that I thought would close the gate and heal the tree, and I used her spellbook to do it. If there was a way to not only keep the gate open but call a being from the Underworld into this realm, she would have made sure that's the spell I had." She tightened her hands into fists. "I was so focused on one-upping Mercy and being the first to close the gates that I didn't stop to look at what was happening right in front of me."

Jax shoved his hands into his pockets and squinted at the oozing trail. "Your priorities have been super fucked."

"I'm sorry." Hunter leaned her head against Jax's shoulder. "I'll fix it."

"I know you will."

Hunter's chest swelled. She didn't have to extrapolate, didn't have to explain the whats or whos or whys. He trusted her. Jax was mad at her, and he loved her, and he believed in her, and he regretted parts of their friendship. Their relationship wasn't black-and-white. *Life* wasn't black-and-white but shades of gray.

He pushed her, a playful grin plumping his cheeks.

And she was getting comfortable with gray.

"Hey." She returned his smile with one of her own. "You might need me. You never know what made that mess." She motioned to the thick layer of slime that hadn't even begun to crust under the harsh burn of the sun.

"Next time," he began as he followed Hunter to the backside of the tree, "remind me to bring some salt."

Slick goo slid between her mucous-covered toes as she cautiously wound around the base of the tree to the side that faced Sugar Creek. She stopped, her toes clenching against her sticky wet sandals. A hole no bigger than a softball stared up at her from where the trunk met the earth. Thick globs dripped from its black maw, as squishy and putrid as rotted fruit, splatting against the gelatinous film that oozed around the base of the tree.

"This is where it came out," Hunter said, her gaze never leaving the black circle pressed into the tree like a Looney Tunes tunnel entrance.

Jax plucked a stick from the splintering tree debris surrounding them and squatted next to the trail. "Do you think whatever it is has poisoned the water?" He stabbed the slime. The stick sank a few inches, the mucous squelching, enveloping the thin branch.

Hunter's ponytail slipped off her shoulder as she shook her head. "The creek runs into Goode Lake, and they're always testing the lake water. We would have heard if there was something wrong with it."

Jax pulled the stick from the trail, studying the threads of slime that quivered in the wind. "Whatever's coming out can't be that big."

Hunter tilted her head, grimacing at the otherworldly ooze. "Polyphemus literally stuffed his body inside Sheriff Dearborn's skin." She squatted down next to Jax and peered into the slick black hole—a conduit between this realm and the Japanese Underworld spilling out from the cracks in the crumbling gate. "We can't use this to judge the creature's size."

Jax tightened his hold on the stick and stretched out his arm. "You'll come save me if I get sucked into the Upside Down?'"

Hunter clapped her hand on his thick shoulder. "It'll have to pull us both in."

With a sharp inhale, he plunged the stick into the dark.

Every muscle in Hunter's body tensed, and she forced her eyes to stay open, unblinking, fixed on the portal to the Underworld. Her chest ached as she held her breath, determined not to move, to hear and see and be ready for anything.

They waited.

Jax flicked his wrist, wiggling the stick back and forth, baiting whatever creature lurked inside.

Still they waited.

Hunter's heartbeat roared and her lungs burned.

Jax pulled out the stick. Another string of goo, but no chomped-off tip, no evidence that anything was home.

"I definitely thought that would go down differently," he said, dropping the stick and brushing his hands on his shorts as he stood.

Hunter peered into the darkness, steeling herself for the horror movie moment when the creature emerged just as the main characters thought it was safe.

A glob of mucous splatted against the steadily rising puddle that dripped from the entrance.

Hunter frowned. She didn't want to get attacked, but she did want to know what had gained entry into her town.

"I'm doing a spell." She pushed herself to her feet and ignored her sticky toes as she straddled the slime trail.

"Now?" Jax shoved his hands back into his pockets.

"Yes, now." Hunter clutched her pendant and squatted over the ichor. "Something escaped from the Japanese Underworld and killed Julie Stoll. It'll kill again. Just like Polyphemus. We need to figure out what it is before it hurts someone I care about."

Jax nodded as if settling an argument with himself. "This is the kind of magic I can get behind." He knelt back down beside her and gripped her shoulders.

"Ready?" She was asking herself, but Jax's confident *yes!* chased away any doubts that sheltered in the shadowed corners of her mind.

She plunged her hands into the moist pocket between this realm and beyond. The air was hot and damp and rolled across her hands and out of the hole in fetid gusts. Jax coughed, a sudden burst of air that exploded against her back. "It smells like the zoo."

And it did. Like the rainforest exhibit. The smell of too many pent-up animals and too many sweaty humans packed into a building filled with fusty, stagnant air. Every time she'd gone to the zoo, she'd run through that exhibit, away from the stench, but she wouldn't run now.

Instead, Hunter pictured the ley line beneath her, stretching from the ancient cherry tree and flowing in a cosmic blue current through Goodeville. Her pendant hummed against her chest as she reached up, up, up, through the clouds and into the cosmos.

Reveal yourself. Her mind was clear, blank, primed for a picture, a clue, of what had come through.

The power beneath her feet sputtered. A spitting shower replaced the hurricane of energy she knew the ley lines possessed.

Behind her, Jax cleared his throat and patted her on the shoulder. "Ready whenever you are."

She glanced down at her arms, her wrists and hands thrust into the mouth of the Underworld. Maybe she hadn't made her request clear enough.

She closed her eyes and returned to the vastness of the universe.

"Reveal yourself!"

This time, the ley line barely flinched, a resting worm, soft and quiet, beneath her feet.

She pulled her hands out and stood, nearly knocking Jax to the ground for the second time that afternoon.

"Did you see it?" he asked, flattening his hand against the ground to steady himself before he fell. "Is it gross?"

Hunter used the bottom of her tee to wipe her moist palms. "It didn't work."

Jax tilted his head, opening his mouth and closing it before finally saying, "But you're a witch."

Hunter stared down at the shriveled leaves, willing the ley line to awaken and lend her its power. But it was hidden, sleeping, hibernating.

"I need to rest." She shoved her hands into her pockets and surveyed Sugar Creek a final time before turning to her bike and Jax's car. "That's what the ley line is doing. I should do the same."

"Makes sense," Jax said, his strides shortened to keep pace with her. "A lot has gone on. As soon as you're recharged, you'll be back to throwing witchy powers all over the place."

Hunter forced out a weak chuckle as she spun her crescent moon ring around her finger. She wanted to agree with him, wanted to fully believe that a nap and a warm mug of tea would fix her problems and put her back in touch with the magic of Goodeville, but the weight on her chest and the churning in her belly told her it would never be that simple.

TWELVE

S o, you're sure Hunter is good with you and Khenti and me checking out the banyan tree without her?" Emily asked as she pulled into the driveway of Mercy's house.

"Yeah." Mercy tapped out a quick text as she reassured Emily. "I'm just talking to H now. She's at the cherry tree waiting for Jax. They're checking to be sure the gate really is closed. She already knows the Greek Gate is still messed up, and we all know the Egyptian Gate is hanging on by a thread and jackal-headed assholes, so we need to check the Hindu Gate to see how it's doing. The Norse Gate is perfect, though."

"Your mom's sacrifice made sure of that," said Emily.

Mercy nodded as a wave of grief crashed over her. When she could control her voice again, she said, "We'll all meet back here for dinner and to report what we found and figure out next steps." She turned to grab a big shopping bag out of Emily's backseat. "I'm glad Burton's Department Store had a decent selection of jeans and tees—and, of course, Mustang hoodies. Going all the way to Champaign would've been a pain in the ass. Hope all this fits Khenti." She started to get out of the car, but Emily's voice stopped her.

"Mag, can we talk for a sec?"

Mercy turned to her friend. "Sure, but if we don't get inside soon you know that Xena will be out here—and she comes with cat spit ready to smooth on your hair."

Emily shuddered. "Don't remind me. But I did take my allergy pill this morning, so at least I won't explode into snot and hives if she does put cat spit on me. Again." Then her expression sobered and she cleared her throat. "Did you notice anything weird at school today?"

Mercy snorted. "Yeah. I noticed the stares aimed in my direction, especially by the cheerleading Stepfords," she said as she rolled her eyes.

"You were friends with them just, like, a week or so ago." Emily met and held Mercy's gaze. "And they're not all Stepfords. Kylie's a cheerleader. I like her. Hunter and Jax like her. She's actually really nice." Emily drew a deep breath and continued. "And they weren't just staring at you. People watched all of us—you, Hunter, *and* me."

"Yeah, people are assholes."

"See, that's part of what I want to talk to you about. Mag, you know I love you, right?"

"Well, yeah. You're my best friend. And I love you, too. Em, are you okay?" Mercy turned in her seat so that she could look directly at Emily.

"I'm okay. But I don't think you are."

"Well, I've been through hell recently. Literally."

"Yeah, and you're back, you're safe, and you and Hunter are talking again. But, Mag, I don't think you're *really* back," Emily said slowly.

"What does that mean?"

"I don't want to piss you off, but I gotta say this." Emily's fawn-colored cheeks flushed. "When your mom died, you, like, withdrew into yourself—and pretty much just thought about yourself." She held her hand up to stop Mercy when she started to speak. "Let me finish, 'kay?"

"'Kay," Mercy said softly, afraid of what Em was going to finish with.

"You almost got stuck and dead in Egyptian hell because instead of facing your problems here you took off—you ran away—and you *lied* to me and to Xena. Did you think about how that would make us feel?"

Mercy moved her shoulders. "I thought I'd be back before either of you knew about it."

"Girl, and I say this with love, you only thought about *you*. And the problem is you've been doing a lot of that lately. I know you're not really shallow—and you're not really selfish—but Mag, you were so out of control and only worried about yourself that *you almost lost your sister and almost got yourself dead*. Did you even think about what losing you would do to Hunter *or* to me—especially so soon after losing a mom and a dad?"

Emily reached over and took her hand. "I just want you to think about that—and also about how judgy you've gotten since the Kirk thing."

"Em! The *Kirk thing* was major! He was horrible. He's *still* horrible. You saw how he glared at me—I mean *us* today. He attacked H. He attacked me. He's the worst!"

Emily nodded, still holding her hand. "Yeah, he is—and that's something Hunter and I had been trying to tell you since you started dating him."

Mercy opened her mouth to shout at Emily that what had happened between her and Kirk was bad enough—she bloody well didn't need her best friend rubbing it in her face! But then she really looked at Emily. Her eyes were filled with tears and her cheeks were blazing.

Emily's super upset. Oh, bloody hell. Emily's right. I didn't even think about what it would do to her or H if I didn't come back. I didn't think about anyone but myself.

"Shit. I've been a selfish bitch."

Emily's lips tilted up. "Selfish—yes. A bitch—only sometimes. And have you really made up with Hunter, or are you just living under the same roof again?"

"Well, coming back from Egyptian hell was pretty traumatic for me and there hasn't actually been much time for me to—" Mercy stopped herself. "I'm making it all about me again." She sighed heavily.

"Yeah, but at least you realized it this time. Mag, you're a good person; you've just gotten lost lately. Come back, okay?" Emily squeezed Mercy's hand before letting it go.

"Okay," Mercy said. "Em, thanks. I know that wasn't easy to say to me."

"If we weren't besties I'd just let you turn into a mean, crusty old cat woman."

"She's my familiar! That does not make me an old cat woman," Mercy said. "Or crusty!"

"Only because you're not old and crusty. Yet." Emily grinned.

"Kittens!"

Mercy and Emily turned to look at the front porch. Xena, in Abigail's bathrobe, was standing in the middle of the open doorway squinting at them.

"Kittens, are you ever going to come inside?" she shouted.

"Is she squinting?" Emily asked.

"Well, yeah. I mean, I wouldn't say this where she could hear, but that cat is old. She probably needs glasses." Smiling impishly she added, "And since you're on a roll with telling your friends hard truths—how 'bout you break it to Xena that she needs spectacles?"

Emily snorted a laugh as they got out of the car and headed up the sidewalk. "Oh, girl, *hell no*. Hell, *no no no!*"

"Do you have everything? You didn't forget your dried juniper stick, did you?" Xena followed Mercy, Emily, and Khenti as they went out onto the porch.

"Xena, relax." To soften her words, Mercy hugged the cat person and didn't flinch when Xena licked her cheek affectionately.

"The whole point of going to the banyan tree is to check in with it, then to cleanse and try to strengthen it while H is making sure her spell worked on the Japanese tree. So of course I brought my juniper stick. It's right here in my basket." She patted the spellwork basket she carried.

"Why 'of course'?" asked Khenti, who, except for his long, dark hair, looked like any other teenage guy who went to Goode High School in his new jeans, tee, Mustang hoodie, and Converse All Stars.

"Oh, I know!" Emily bounced on her toes, making her dark curls dance around her shoulders. "Because juniper smoke is excellent for fighting malefic magic, negative energy, and illnesses in general."

"You are quite right, kitten!" Xena clapped, then hugged Emily, who stepped out of her embrace quickly enough to avoid a cheek lick.

"Have you been studying witchy stuff?" Mercy asked.

"Absolutely." Then Em's expression fell. "Wait, that's okay, isn't it?"

"Of course!" Mercy said quickly. "It actually helps if you under-stand the basics. Well done, you."

"Oh, good! But the phases of the moon still kinda confuse me," said Emily.

"There are two that are most important, kitten," said Xena. "The full moon is for completing projects. The new moon is for begin-ning projects. Everything else is like feathers on a bird—pretty, but not as important as what's beneath them."

The three teenagers stared at Xena.

"What?" The cat person smoothed her hair. "Is my fur out of place?"

"No, you look great, Xena," Mercy said quickly. "We were just thinking about the fact that you love to *eat* what's beneath those feathers."

Xena laughed. "Of course I do, kitten! Though I do take time to appreciate a well-dressed meal."

"Gross," Emily whispered.

"Okay, well, we gotta go," said Mercy as she herded Khenti and

Emily out the door. "And, speaking of dinner, we'll swing by the pizza place on the way home and get dinner if that sounds okay to you."

"Oh, yes, kitten! Please be sure they—"

"I know—you want extra tuna on your pizza and not much else," Mercy said.

"I do like the cheese, too," said Xena.

"Right, but not many vegetables."

Xena shuddered. "No. Please. They are too crunchy. Not like sparrow bones. Sparrow bones have exactly the right amount of crunch."

"All righty then. We gotta get to the tree. Love you and see you soon!" Mercy blew Xena a kiss as the three of them hurried from the porch to Emily's vintage T-bird, climbed in, and took off.

"That cat," said Emily.

"Right?" said Mercy.

"She is a unique creature. Today she introduced me to albacore tuna and something called *The Bachelorette* on Hulu," said Khenti from the backseat.

"Oh, Freya! That cat is way too into trash TV. Wait, did she pour cream over your tuna?" Mercy spun around to look at Khenti.

"She gave me the option of adding cream or not. When she gave me the choice it made me think that perhaps she did so because that isn't the way humans in this realm usually eat albacore tuna, so I told her I'd try mine without the first time," said Khenti.

"Smart," said Emily as she turned onto an old one-lane gravel road that snaked around the northeast side of Goodeville and through the fields that surrounded the banyan tree that held the Hindu Gate.

"Khenti, seriously, don't eat anything Xena recommends," said Mercy. "I shoulda told you that before I left for school. I'll show you how to use the microwave tonight, and also how to order delivery." She shuddered. "*No one* eats cream on tuna except cats."

"So disgusting," Emily murmured.

"Yup," agreed Mercy. "Em, see that dirt road up there on the left? That's the one you need to take."

"Okay, got it. I forgot how close to the school it is. Hey, remember our freshman year when we used to sneak out to this tree and cut class to drink your mom's wine coolers?" Em said.

"How could I forget? Abigail grounded me for a month when she caught us. But *worth it!*" They both grinned.

"Wine coolers?" Khenti asked from the backseat.

"Think wine that's watered down and too sweet," said Mercy.

"Sounds terrible," Khenti said as they bumped up the dirt road.

"Totally!" Mercy said and Emily laughed. "Em, see the tire tracks I left the other day? Right over there?" Em nodded. "Just follow them and you can park not far from the tree."

Emily did so, and soon they exited the car and approached the old banyan.

"This tree is spectacular," said Khenti. "I have never seen one quite like it. Are there many of them in your realm?"

"Yeah, but not in this part of our world. The only reason this banyan lives here is because my ancestress summoned it to guard the gate. Illinois winters should kill it," Mercy explained as they approached the impressive tree.

"But magic keeps it alive?" Khenti asked.

Mercy sighed, and then coughed as the scent of sulfur and decay hit her. "Yeah, well, magic is *supposed* to keep it alive, but it's definitely not doing well."

"Yuck, the smell is way worse than at the palms." Emily held her nose as she gagged and backed several steps away from the tree. "Hey, do you need me in there with you?"

"No, it's okay," said Mercy as she took a fat stick of dried and bound juniper from her spellwork basket and a long rectangular box of wooden matches. "You and Khenti can wait by the car. I can already tell that the tree is sick. I'll cleanse it with smoke and then pull some energy from the ley lines to bolster it—then I'll be back at the car."

"'Kay, I'm definitely waiting in the car," said Emily.

"I shall accompany you," said Khenti, moving to Mercy's side.

"You don't have to. Really. I can handle this just fine by myself," said Mercy.

"I have no doubt about your magical prowess," explained Khenti. "But I am curious about these other gates. The only one I have seen is my own—and, of course, the Norse tree."

"Xena took you there today?" Mercy asked as she and Khenti entered the shadows under the thick canopy.

"Yes, I asked her to. I know how much it means to you. I also thought it would be a safe place for Xena to hunt her delectable sparrows—though I was confused when she killed the first one. They are so tiny!"

"Bloody hell, Khenti! She didn't make you eat it, did she?"

"Oh, no! She said she'd rather not share, and I said I wasn't hungry." Khenti grinned.

"That cat . . ." Mercy muttered. "Okay, seriously. Like I said, from now on don't eat anything Xena offers you, 'kay?"

"Okay. What can I do to help you with this gate, Green Witch?"

"You can catch me if I pass out or hold my hair back if I start to puke after I greet the tree," said Mercy.

"If you fall I will catch you—of that you need never worry. I am here for you."

And Khenti was. He was there, just a few feet behind her, lending her strength and support as she approached the main trunk of the banyan. Because of its cluster of trunks the banyan could be mistaken for several trees growing in a tight group like the doum palm, but it was only one very old, very large tree with several joined trunks and vines dangling from what was usually a thick, verdant canopy of dark emerald leaves. Today Mercy noted the dead leaves crunching under her feet and how so many of the vines had fallen to the ground—as if they couldn't bear to touch the sick tree.

Mercy shifted her juniper stick and the matches to her left hand and pressed her right palm against the tree. "Hello, banyan. How are you doing?" Instantly sickness poured from the tree into her palm and through her body to take up residence in her stomach. "Oh, bloody hell!" She turned to the side, bent, and puked up the salad she'd had for lunch.

"Just breathe. I'm here. All is well." Khenti held back her hair and put his arm around her waist to support her.

When she was done retching, Mercy stood and with a shaky hand wiped her mouth. "Eesh, I hate to puke. I shouldn't have left my basket in the car. I always have a bottle of water in there for—"

"Here! Here!" Emily's voice was nasal as she held her nose and ran to them, a water bottle held in front of her like a shield.

"Thanks, Em." Mercy washed out her mouth and then took several long swallows of water as Emily raced back to her car—still holding her nose. "Okay, before I pull energy up through the ley lines I'm going to fill this whole area with juniper smoke."

"Do you want to go back to the car for a moment to regain your strength?" Khenti gently brushed a dank length of hair from her face.

Mercy met Khenti's worried gaze. "No, I'll be okay. It's totally normal for me to get sick when I communicate with plants that aren't well. Now I know this tree will make my stomach feel awful, so I'll be prepared for that when I touch it again." Mercy glanced up at the banyan. "And this tree is super sick."

Khenti nodded slowly. "Yes. I can feel it. Not like you—it does not make me ill. But there is a thickness, a darkness in the air here that is not right."

Mercy turned to him. "You're right. Even though I'm not touching the tree right now I feel the wrongness of it—and I mean more than just the crumbling gate and the stink of it. I wonder if whatever killed Mrs. Stoll could've come from the Hindu Underworld?"

"Can you ask the tree?" Khenti said.

"That's a really good idea. I can communicate with the tree, even though it might not speak to me in words. Hey, would you cleanse the area all around the trunk and under the canopy with juniper smoke while I try?" Mercy asked.

"Of course! I would be happy to help."

Mercy gave him the thick stick of dried juniper that she'd bound together with purple thread. Then she struck a long match against the box, lit the stick, and demonstrated to Khenti how to waft it around. Fragrant blue-gray smoke billowed from the juniper stick, cresting like waves up into the branches of the sick tree.

"Does it always smoke this much?" Khenti asked.

"How much it smokes depends on how much negative energy there is to cleanse. Apparently, there's *a lot* of bad stuff hanging around here."

"Shall I speak the words of a spell as I cleanse the tree?" Khenti asked, wafting the smoking stick around.

"No, the smoke itself is the spell. It changes the energy around it, but it helps to focus on intent as you're cleansing the tree," said Mercy.

"So, I think about the tree being cleansed of negative energy, correct?"

"Yep, absolutely correct." As smoke filled the area around them, Mercy returned to the central tree trunk. She centered herself and then pressed both palms against the tree. She asked it nothing at first. Instead she reached down, down, down and tapped into the pulsing lime-colored river of power beneath her feet. Concentrating, she drew power from the ley line—and it answered readily, filling her body with warmth and strength that soothed her protesting stomach. Then, imagining she was a hose attached to the green power by her feet, with the nozzle being her hands, she guided the surging ley line through her and up into the ailing tree.

The power responded. It came willingly. But as before, it was like her hose was kinked and it only dribbled into the tree. Mercy kept her eyes closed and even pressed her forehead to the rough bark as she concentrated, willing more healing power into the tree. She felt the sweat trickle down her back and between her breasts, and still she held on until her knees turned to mush and she had to stagger back before she passed out.

"Mercy!" Khenti hurried through the thick smoke to take her arm and make sure she remained upright.

"I'm okay. I'm okay." Mercy was breathing hard as she clung to Khenti's strong arm, but as soon as she'd stopped trying to force power into the tree she felt fine—better than fine. The power she'd been attempting to fill the tree with was now filling her! "Keep cleansing the banyan. I just gave it as much ley line juice as I could force into it. Now I'm gonna ask it about whether anything has come through."

"Are you sure you should—" Khenti cut off his own question and bowed his head slightly to her. "Luck to you, Green Witch."

"Thanks, Khenti. Going in for a third time." Mercy tossed back her sweat-slick hair and strode to the tree. She didn't hesitate. She pressed her palms against the bark. She could easily feel the difference even just a little of the ley line power made. The tree wasn't as cold or sick. Mercy sighed in relief, even though she realized she'd just bandaged the problem instead of fixing it. She concentrated on the banyan—on its breath and the life she felt under her hands. "Mighty banyan, guardian of the Hindu Gate, has anything—a creature or spirit or *anything* passed through you recently?"

Mercy's answer came within seconds. From her palms she could feel a definite negative and a closed sensation, like a door slammed shut. She sighed in relief. Khenti returned to her side and she smiled up at him, hands still resting against the tree.

"Nothing has escaped from the Hindu Underworld. I'm sure of it. The tree is sick, but its gate is still closed."

Khenti nodded. "I am glad to hear it."

"Me, too! At least that narrows our focus to the Greek Underworld and the Japanese Underworld." Mercy paused. "Well, maybe not the Japanese Underworld. If Hunter really did heal the cherry tree then we know that whatever killed Mrs. Stoll had to have come from the Greek Underworld." Mercy bowed her head and touched it against the tree. "We're going to fix you—Hunter and me—I promise. Just hang on. Be strong. We'll be back. Soon. Until then, blessed be."

Mercy patted the tree's bark affectionately before she stepped away from it. In a movement that was natural and comforting rather than possessive, Khenti put his arm around Mercy and she rested her head on his shoulder. They stood like that for a little while without speaking. Mercy knew she should move away—head to the car, go get dinner, and take it back to the house for everyone—but it felt so good just to stand there, encircled by Khenti's warm arm, that she didn't move.

"The tree seems better," Khenti said softly as his fingers drew slow circles over the skin of her shoulder, causing her to shiver. "Are you chilled? Do you feel ill again?"

Mercy lifted her head and looked up at him. "No, I'm not cold and I feel just fine. The tree is better, but that's only temporary."

"I wish it was permanent," Khenti said.

Words blurted from Mercy's mouth before she could stop them. "I wish a lot of things were permanent."

His brown eyes held hers and his fingers returned to drawing circles over her skin. "I will remain in your realm to help you vanquish whatever demon has been loosed here, but Mercy, I must return to save my mother from—"

Mercy quickly pressed her finger against his lips. "I know, and I really appreciate you staying to help us. I'm sorry. I—I shouldn't have said that." She started to turn away, but Khenti put both of his hands on her shoulders and turned her so that she had to face him.

"I must help my mother, but I will not abandon you. I am here for you, and will remain here until the demon that plagues your town is vanquished."

Mercy wanted to lose herself in his eyes, but she forced herself to shake her head. "It's not really fair. You should go back and get your mom out of hell."

His smile was gentle. "And I will *after* I aid the witches who pulled me out of hell."

Her lips tilted up. "Even if one of those witches pretty much got you stuck in hell?"

Khenti shook his head. "My banishment was not your fault. My father is responsible for that, and much more. When I return I will make him pay for his crimes."

"But not right away?" Mercy asked.

"Not right away," he said, touching her cheek. "Remember, my mother is safe again. Now that we are no longer with her, Hathor can hide her and care for her as she did before we arrived in Duat."

"I'm so glad she's safe. And thank you for being here for me—for us. Thank you for being willing to stay and kill whatever monster is here." She stepped into his embrace again. This time she wrapped her arms around him and rested her cheek against his chest. She could hear the strong beat of his heart, which seemed in sync with her own pulse.

Holding her close, Khenti asked, "What do we do now, my Mighty Green Witch?"

Mercy snuggled closer to him and sighed. "Well, we get dinner and then hope like hell Hunter will tell us the Japanese tree is fixed and whole, and that she can cast the spell that healed it on this tree—like, right away."

"And we have to discover what killer escaped and track it down," added Khenti.

"Again."

Khenti's arms tightened around her. "We will do it. All of us— you, Hunter, Emily, Jax, Xena, and me." He smiled. "That is almost an army."

She grinned against his chest. "An army of six?"

"It isn't the size of the army that is important. It is the weapons and their disposal and how much courage they have that is important, and we have a magnificent Green Witch, a powerful Cosmic Witch, a spectacular feline familiar, and two loyal friends. *All* are courageous."

"And a demi-god who is a monster killer," added Mercy as she finally stepped back to smile up at him.

"And a demi-god who is definitely a monster killer." Khenti bent and kissed her.

In her pocket, Mercy's phone bleeped with a text message. She pulled it out and read: *KITTEN I AM QUITE FAMISHED!!!!!!!!!* 🐱♡.

"Is it a problem?" Khenti asked.

"Well, yes and no. Xena is hungry, so we'd better get that pizza and get home. Plus, Hunter and Jax should be there soon, too."

"Excellent." Khenti draped his arm around her shoulder again as they headed back to Emily's car. "I believe I am what Xena would call *hangry*."

"Did you just say *hangry*?" Mercy looked up at him, laughter in her eyes.

"Did I use the word correctly?"

"You definitely did," said Mercy.

"Xena is quite an education," said Khenti.

"Well, Xena's quite *something*, that's for sure." They laughed together at Emily's car, but as Mercy moved the seat forward so Khenti could climb in, she felt a prickle along the back of her neck and down her spine. She turned and stared at the tree, expecting to see someone watching her.

No one was there.

She glanced at the cornfield that separated the tree from the campus of the high school. No one was there, either. Or she was unable to see anyone within the thick shadows of the tall corn.

"What is it?" Emily asked as she peered up at Mercy.

"Nothing," she said automatically and then silently added, *or at least nothing I want to face out here without my magical sister at my side,* and got hastily into the car.

THIRTEEN

That fucking coach had actually kicked him out of football practice. Kirk didn't think about where he was going when he left practice—his need to get away before he punched that has-been in his face was too urgent. As he stomped through the cornfield that framed the stadium he replayed what had just happened over and over in his mind.

He'd showed up at practice—like always. Sure, his hand was still in a cast, but he was the team captain. It was his job to be there for the Mustangs, even if he couldn't throw a ball.

So, Kirk was there—in his workout jersey—ignoring the pounding in his hand as he jogged warm-up laps with his team when Coach Jamison finally joined them.

Yeah, okay, he'd noticed the guys acted weird around him, like some broken fingers had changed who he was, which was complete bullshit. He'd also noticed that Coach had been staring a hole in his practice jersey as he jogged around the track. Then he'd blown his whistle and told Derek Burke to start leading them through their warm-up drills. *Derek* fucking *Burke.* Kirk was just going to complain

99

to Coach and remind him that it was the team captain's job to lead drills when the old man called him over to the sidelines.

"Mr. Whitfield, I applaud your tenacity," Coach had said. "But you can't be out here."

"Hey, Coach, don't worry. My hand is hardly bothering me at all. I might even get this cast off early," Kirk lied. Actually, his hand hurt like hell, even though he was eating hydrocodone like M&Ms.

"Whitfield, it's not about your hand. It's about your behavior and your attitude. Have you gone to even one anger management class?"

"I'm going to. I just haven't had time yet," Kirk lied again. No way was he going to some lame counseling class crap. That was for losers.

"Listen to me, Whitfield. Get yourself to those classes. Learn the tools it takes to manage your anger now, before it destroys more than your high school football career," lectured the coach.

"Coach, this is about a lot more than my high school career. Football is my ticket to college!"

"Football *was* your ticket to college. I will not have a young man on my team who strikes a woman. You've been suspended indefinitely. Now you're also banned from practices. I wish you well—I truly do, son—but you have a lot of growing up to do before you'll be an asset to anyone's team. Be sure you turn in your uniforms ASAP—that includes your practice jersey. Now I've gotta get back to the team. Good-bye and good luck, Mr. Whitfield."

And then that old fucking man turned his back on Kirk.

Kirk had started walking. He felt the stares of his teammates—*his friends*—on his back as he escaped into the concealment of the cornfield and just kept walking. What the hell had that old man been talking about? He was an asset to *any* team. He was a natural leader. His one-hundred-meter-dash time was the fastest in the school, and he wasn't scared to hit and hit hard. He could tackle linebackers who outweighed him by fifty pounds. Kirk's anger simmered until he heard voices.

Voices? Out here? Kirk had come to the edge of the cornfield, but he remained inside the shadows of the growing plants as the voices drew him.

He recognized her voice before he saw her. It was Mercy! And she was with someone. Kirk could hear a deep voice in conversation with her, though he couldn't make out their words. Was it that pussy, Ashley? He hadn't been at practice because of some lame excuse about his mom needing him. Kirk perked up and even actually smiled. What if Jax and Mercy were sneaking around together because they were a *thing*? He'd bet that would freak Hunter out—and Kirk Whitfield was just the guy to let the whole school know about it.

Eagerly, Kirk snuck closer to the voices. Then he smelled the smoke. He could even see weird bluish-gray stuff billowing up over the corn. What the hell was she doing? Then Kirk froze. She was probably brewing some witch crap. Now was his chance to video it! Then people would believe him! That asshole coach might even let him back on the team once he proved those twin bitches were also twin witches—*real* witches. He automatically reached for the phone in his pocket and had to stifle a groan of frustration. He was wearing his practice jersey. It didn't have pockets, so he didn't have his damn phone with him.

That's okay. Figure out what she's doing. The more info you have, the more stuff you'll be able to use against the twins.

Kirk crept through the field following their voices until he could see them through the thick, green stalks. It definitely was Mercy—and she definitely was doing some witch shit. She had her hands pressed against the bark of that weird group of trees in the easement between fields.

Wait, that's one of those special trees they'd told him about. She for sure was up to some magic shit! Kirk wished he'd actually listened to what Hunter and Mercy had said about the witch tree crap, but all the details didn't really matter. The fact that they were witches was what mattered.

Mercy was with some dude, but it wasn't Ashley. It was a guy Kirk had never seen before—some brown guy with long, girly hair—who wore a Mustang hoodie and held what looked like dried parts of a tree wrapped together by thread, which was smoking like crazy. *What the fuck are they doing?*

Kirk watched Mercy stagger from the tree, sweating and breathing hard, and then the long-haired dude rushed to her and was all touchy-feely. He held her hair while she puked and acted like he was her fucking mommy. When she was done barfing Mercy went back to the tree while the dude continued to mess around with the dried smoking stuff. Then Mercy did whatever to the tree and the dude came back to her with more touchy-feely crap.

Fuck. He kissed her!

Wait, it's only been days since we broke up. Had that bitch been cheating on me?

Kirk stared as the dude put his hands all over Mercy as they went back to Parrott's T-bird.

At first Kirk couldn't believe it. No damn way could Mercy have been cheating on him. But as he stared at the T-bird his mind was filled with what had to be the truth. *She'd been cheating the whole time they were together. No wonder she gave him a bj so easily. She'd probably been passing them out to the dude with the girly hair, too. So, not only was she a witch, but she was also a cheating slut.*

For a moment Kirk thought he saw something from the corner of his eye and he whirled around, ready to kick someone's ass, but no one was there. He dragged his tongue, suddenly sticky with salt, against his teeth and tugged on his earlobe. Was it just him, or could he actually hear the ocean?

Make them pay. The thought floated to him on a gust of mist.

He nodded, his mind boiling over with anger that built and built and built as he cut back through the cornfield, avoided the stadium, and headed to his Jeep.

"I will. I'll figure out how to show everyone who they really are, and I'll make those twins pay."

FOURTEEN

Over the next days Nure-Onna tested her ability to remain in the mortal realm. She had to—and not just because she craved fresh blood and the clean, sweet water of this world. Nure-Onna had become the servant of a goddess—and her new mistress had tasked her with targeting allies of the mortal who had offended her.

Nure-Onna did not truly care about the mortals in this realm; she cared only about herself and her lost child. But the goddess had made promises to her. She had also threatened, but it was not surprising that a deity of such power would also have mercurial moods. Nure-Onna would navigate this new relationship carefully, do as the goddess commanded, and then finally, *finally* reap her reward.

She slithered from the moist, sludgy tunnel that bridged realms and swam freely up and down the little creek until her skin began to gray. Then she checked the sun's position in the sky. Half a day. That was how long she could remain in the mortal realm before her body began to sicken. A short time compared to centuries in the World of

Darkness, but it was enough to allow her to hunt and to fulfill the goddess's command.

The next time Nure-Onna swam along the creek she knew how long she had to hunt and drink. She moved with deadly purpose, camouflaged by the mud her serpent body swirled up from the creek bed as the goddess had directed until the enticing sounds of laughing girls beckoned. Nure-Onna glided up the gentle creek bank and found herself at the edge of a field that acted as a conduit to the girls' voices. Nure-Onna slithered silently between the rows of tall, green-leafed crops and followed the trail of voices until she peered from the edge of the field to a large, grassy area where several—*many*—girls were laughing and frolicking together. She coiled her viper body beneath her, so that from the shadows within the field she could sit and study the hapless mortals and see if she recognized any of them as one of the allies of Amphitrite's enemy. Hidden in the tall, green ocean of algae-like corn, Nure-Onna settled in to wait.

She had learned patience from the World of Darkness. She had also learned stillness. Like all serpents—she was an expert in stealth. So, though she salivated with hunger, Nure-Onna took pleasure in knowing that she would be the vehicle through which one of the innocents before her would today begin her own Underworld journey.

The girls had divided into two groups. One was more distant than the other. The more distant group was attempting athletic stunts—rather unsuccessfully. The second group was smaller and closer to Nure-Onna. They moved together in a dance-like routine. After a short time they seemed to get bored with the exercise and the girls lounged in the spongy grass, gossiping amongst themselves.

Nure-Onna felt a moment of nostalgia for her distant mortal life where she had been a servant to a powerful Shogun. Long ago she, too, had gossiped with other girls, combed each other's hair, and sworn forever friendships.

But Nure-Onna had been beautiful, and to a servant beauty was truly a curse.

Then Nure-Onna was pulled from reflecting on her miserable past by one of the girls who suddenly drew her interest. The young woman had fire-colored hair and skin that was, unfortunately, freckled. She had to be one of the mortals the goddess had described, for there were no other girls there with flame-colored hair.

The serpent's body shivered with excitement. The red-haired girl was intriguing. She had a distinctly citrus scent, like yuzu, only stronger and sweeter. Nure-Onna remembered yuzu and wondered if the child's blood would taste as tart and refreshing.

She hoped so.

Nure-Onna had to get closer. Slowly, silently, she glided from the field to a clump of bushes much nearer the group of gossiping girls. She did not coil her body, but remained on the smooth, powerful scales of her underbelly. She rested her chin against the fertile ground and squinted through the brush, breathing deeply as her yuzu-scented target paced back and forth restlessly before her little group while she tapped on a rectangular device held tightly in her hand. *Come closer, child,* Nure-Onna silently beseeched, *closer!* When she spoke, the yuzu girl's voice was as refreshing as the juice of a newly squeezed fruit.

"Guys, seriously, none of you heard anything about why Jax isn't at practice?"

A dark-skinned girl whose hair cascaded in thick braids down her back shrugged. "Nope. All anyone's talking about is how brain-dead imbecilic Kirk is to show up at practice like he's still on the team."

A second girl, this one with long, golden hair pulled back in a single tail added, "Well, that's not *all* we're talking about. There's also a lot of twin witch gossip going around."

Nure-Onna's tongue flicked out, tasting the scent of the girls' words. They were speaking of the witch and her sister! The one who had offended the goddess! She had followed the correct path. The yuzu-scented girl was her target!

The dark-skinned girl sighed. "Yea, well, I didn't mention that 'cause I think it's kinda shitty to talk about the twins so much. I mean, come on! Their mom just died. If my mom died I would—" She shivered. "I can't even think about how awful it would be."

Fascinated, Nure-Onna continued to listen to their conversation.

Golden hair put her fist on her slender waist and leveled her gaze at the yuzu girl. "Kylie, Jax is hot and all."

"And tall!" interrupted a girl with wavy hair that was light brown and reminded Nure-Onna of ribbed sea sand. "Don't forget how tall he is, Tiffany!"

"Well, yeah, tall is good," continued golden hair Tiffany. "And he's, like, pretty sweet. But is he hot enough *and* sweet enough to put up with his bff Hunter Goode? She's a piece of work. And so's her sister."

Yuzu Kylie frowned. "I like Hunter. She's actually a lot of fun. She has a really awesome sense of humor. And I think Mercy is nice, too, even though I don't know her as well. But you guys do—or you did. You hung out with Mercy when she was hooking up with Kirk. I even remember that you, Tiffany, used to talk about what great fashion sense Mercy had. So, I gotta agree with Heather." Yuzu Kylie nodded at the dark-skinned girl. "Talking crap about the twins just seems really mean, you know? Especially since you guys used to kinda be friends—plus, seriously, *their mom died.*"

Golden hair Tiffany wrinkled her brow and shrugged. "Yeah, I hear you, Kyles. Maybe we have been too mean to the twins. My mom and I fight sometimes, but I don't know what I'd do if something happened to her."

Dark-skinned Heather spoke up again. "Hey, have you texted Jax?"

Yuzu Kylie sighed, sending sweet-scented breath to tease Nure-Onna. *If she would just move a little closer!* "Yes, of course. I've been texting him since I realized he wasn't at practice."

She gestured to a larger field that adjoined theirs. A fence that was partially flanked by tall evergreens and stadium seating surrounded it. On the field boys were running and throwing balls. Nure-Onna barely glanced at the distant group of mortals. The only male the goddess had commanded she hunt was the one called Jax, and yuzu Kylie had just said he was not among the others. They did not smell like yuzu. Even from such a distance they smelled of sweat and hormones, which repulsed the serpent.

Golden hair Tiffany spoke again. "Kyles, call him."

"Yeah, that's totally what I'm gonna do." She tapped at the rectangle in her hand and then brought the device to her ear as she frowned and sighed again. "He's not answering."

"Try again," said golden hair Tiffany. "He might be someplace where it's hard to hear his phone or whatever."

"Yeah, you're right, Tiff." Yuzu Kylie looked down at the rectangle again and lifted her hand to tap on it.

"Miss York, you know my rule about phones at practice. Put it away—now!"

Yuzu Kylie flushed as red as her shorts and hastily put the phone in her pocket. Nure-Onna bared her fangs silently at the intruding adult, who continued to give the girls orders.

"Look, I know school is almost over for the year, but we have two more pep rallies—not to mention tryouts for next year's squad in six weeks. So you girls need to look sharp. I want you to practice the dance for the routine you're doing to the Taylor Swift medley, and I mean full-out. Perform like you're in the gym with everyone watching. Then I want to see some tumbling passes." The adult looked around the grassy area. "I thought the mats were already out here, but I see I'm mistaken. Okay, well, while you're practicing the dance I'll grab one of them and drag it over here so I can spot you."

"Yes, ma'am!" the girls shouted together.

"Good. Now I'll go get that mat while you get that dance practiced."

As soon as the adult left, the dark-skinned girl touched yuzu Kylie's arm. "Go over there by the field and call him. We can start the dance without you."

"Thanks, Heather." Yuzu Kylie hurried to the edge of the field.

Nure-Onna gnashed her fangs. Had she practiced her usual patience she would now be within striking distance. She could coil around yuzu Kylie, inhale her delicious citrus scent—and then drink all of her blood. Why had she moved? She knew better! Slowly, silently, the enormous serpent slithered backward. If she could just reach that edge of the field yuzu Kylie would be hers!

"Where's Jax?" Yuzu Kylie's voice had gone flat and lost its sweetness.

The group of girls yuzu Kylie had walked away from laughed as one of them did what Nure-Onna considered a rather awkward dance move and music blared from yet another small rectangular box. Yuzu Kylie frowned, covered one ear, and stepped even closer to the field.

"The locker room bathroom?" asked yuzu Kylie, clearly angry.

Nure-Onna had finally made it to the field. As she glided silently toward the sweet scent of yuzu, Kylie's voice got harder, more clipped, more filled with anger.

"It's fine, H. I get it. I have to go. Tell him I'll call him after cheer practice."

Yuzu Kylie tapped the rectangle again just as the adult woman tossed a thick mat down near her and said, "That's it, Miss York. I'll take that phone."

Yuzu Kylie whirled around and stared at the adult, her freckled face pink with anger. "Actually, Coach Livingston, I have a family emergency and I need to go. My mom will write you a note or whatever." And she stormed past the gaping adult.

Nure-Onna had been seconds from striking and feeding, and as yuzu Kylie strode from the field she was filled with gnawing anger that was almost as dark and urgent as her desire to possess the blood of the sweet young girl. She considered attacking the adult—of making her pay for the loss of her delectable yuzu fruit—but Nure-Onna was not a fool. The other girls would see her strike the adult. They were mere children—they had no katana with which to strike her head from her shoulders. They could not harm her. They could not even subdue her. But they could warn others—and by *others* Nure-Onna meant her yuzu Kylie. That would make the goddess angry. An angry goddess would not reward her servant, and she *must* be rewarded—she *must* have her child returned to her from the depths of the lake into which they had both disappeared, mother and son, so very long ago.

A wave of longing washed through Nure-Onna, making her scaled body tremble with need.

She would kill yuzu Kylie—for the goddess and for her own insatiable need to be reunited with her precious child. Nure-Onna only had to be just a little patient—and she was exceptionally good at exercising patience.

FIFTEEN

Emily parked the T-bird on Main Street directly in front of Foxfire Woodstove Pizzeria.

"My parking karma is golden," Em said.

"I don't know how you do it," said Mercy as she folded down the front seat so Khenti could climb out of the car. "And Main Street's hopping tonight." She looked up and down the unusually busy street that bisected the heart of the town and grimaced as she wiped salty sweat from her face. "Ugh, it's barely spring and *already* so humid it's like I could squeeze water from the air. Everyone should be inside in the air-conditioning."

"Maybe the stores are running some kind of special," said Em as they made their way to the pizzeria.

"Is it Mustang Days already?" Mercy frowned as she watched a man she thought might be the potbellied guy in charge of the IGA's deli park his vintage Camaro just a couple spots down from them, slam its door, and practically charge out into traffic to yell *"You need to learn how to fucking drive"* at Mrs. Ritter—who looked super shocked as she sped around him.

"He is very angry." Khenti watched the deli manager get back into his car and fishtail away, tires smoking.

"Yeah, that's super strange," said Mercy. "He was yelling at Mrs. Ritter. Did you see her face? She was totally not expecting that."

"Adults are weird. Road rage is a real thing with them," said Em.

"Yeah, I guess so. They're—" Mercy began, but as they reached the door of the pizzeria she stopped. "Wait, guys, did you hear that?"

"Hear what?" Em asked, pausing behind her.

"I swear I heard waves. Or water. And do you smell—" Squealing tires interrupted her and pulled their attention back to the street in time to see a man get out of a car stopped at Goodeville's only light. He sprinted to the car behind him just as another man was getting out of his car. The two men were red-faced and shouting, though she couldn't make out their words. Then the first man pushed the second, who fell against his car and then as he straightened he came up swinging punches at the other guy.

"OMG, are there actually two grown men *fighting* in the middle of Main Street?" Emily shook her head in shock as they stared.

"Is this normal behavior for your people?" Khenti asked.

"No. I really don't think so," said Mercy.

A sheriff's car pulled up, lights flashing but sirens off. Deputy Carter jumped out of the car and rushed to separate the two men, who were now rolling around in the street.

Across from the pizzeria the bell on the door to Kingpin Lanes chimed manically as two matronly women burst from the bowling alley.

"I know you threw that water on me!" the first woman shouted as she shook water from her damp hair.

"Oh, Judith, don't be ridiculous. You're just going through The Change and sweating like a whore in church. Stop blaming me and get you some hormones, old woman."

"Is that the Freeman sisters?" Emily asked as their attention shifted from the street fight to the bowling alley.

"Yeah," Mercy said. "Patricia and, um, I can't remember her sister's name. Wow. They're a big part of the booster club. I've never seen them so much as say one mean word to each other before."

"Don't you dare tell me what to do *or* call me old!" Patricia's hand snaked out and she slapped her sister across the face before spinning around and stomping away.

"I won't be going to the city with you for Sunday dinner this weekend!" her sister shouted after her.

"You're uninvited anyway!" yelled Patricia without turning around.

"Something is wrong," Khenti said. Then he wiped moisture from his forehead.

"It didn't feel this humid earlier. Maybe there's a storm rolling in," said Mercy as she lifted her hair from her neck. "Ugh. Where's a breeze when you need it? Let's get our pizza and go home."

Mr. Mitchell looked up from the bar at the sound of the door opening. "Oh, hey there, Hunter and Emily."

"I'm Mercy," she corrected automatically. "I wanna place a to-go order." She, Emily, and Khenti slid onto barstools and Mercy quickly ordered Xena's disgusting pizza and two large veggie pies with four salads—as well as root beer floats for the three of them while they waited.

"What is a root beer float?" Khenti whispered to her.

"Well, it's usually a yummy dessert, but with what's going on outside I thought we deserved a treat," said Mercy as Mr. Mitchell put the floats in front of them. "Thanks, Mr. Mitchell. Hey, um, have you noticed any weirdness in town this evening?"

Mr. Mitchell sighed and placed his hands on his hips and jerked his chin in the direction of the street. "Well, I don't know about out there. I've been too busy taking care of business in here. I've had to kick three people out of the pizzeria this afternoon for rudeness—and that's a first in my two decades of owning this place."

"I like it," Khenti said.

"I don't." Mercy frowned as she stared out the picture window at the second Freeman sister, who was backing out of her parking space and narrowly avoided hitting a car. She actually rolled down her window and, red-faced, shouted at *and flipped off* the driver of the car she'd almost hit.

"I meant the root beer float."

"Oh, sorry, Khenti. Yeah, they're yummy. Em, how old would you say the Freeman sisters are?"

Emily followed her gaze to see the Freeman sister squeal tires down Main Street. "They've gotta be, like, at least sixty or so. Seriously grandma old."

"Have you ever in your life seen grown women fight like that in public?" Mercy asked.

"Never."

"As I said before: something feels wrong." Khenti kept his voice low so that the families eating at the red-and-white-checkered tables couldn't hear them.

"Well, yeah, grown folks hitting each other in the middle of Main Street is definitely wrong," said Emily.

"It is more than that," continued Khenti between sips of his float. "I spent almost the entire day outside with Xena. We walked a lot, visited your Norse tree, followed that little path through the fields. That all felt right. But this"—he gestured out at Main Street— "doesn't feel anything like that. It reminds me of the banyan tree— death and decomposition and darkness. It is as if your town has been cursed, or more precisely, hexed."

"Oh, shit!" Emily leaned forward and whispered across Khenti. "Mag, could there be another witch out there with power like you two? She could be jealous of you and H, or whatever, and she's hexed Goodeville?"

Mercy snorted. "There aren't any other witches out there who are powerful like Hunter and me."

Emily's dark brows arched up. "Egotistical much? I thought we had that talk already?"

Mercy wanted to tell Em she was being ridiculous—that she wasn't being egotistical. She was just being accurate, but her best friend's words came back to her: . . . *you only thought about* you. *And the problem is you've been doing a lot of that lately.* Mercy blew out a long breath. "You're right, Em. I don't know for sure if H and I are the only powerful witches in this world. I shouldn't assume. That's more of a question for Xena."

"Do all witches know what you told me about hexes?" Khenti asked after he drained the last of his float. "That they come back on the witch threefold?"

Mercy nodded. "Yeah, I would assume so. It's common knowledge to anyone who chooses The Path."

"Then there must be other witches in this world," said Khenti.

"Well, yeah, there are, but I don't know of any who can tap into the ley line power," said Mercy. "But you know what would be worse than a rogue witch? If whatever killed Mrs. Stoll is also affecting the town."

"Even worse than that," Emily added. "What if the sick trees are literally making the town sick, too?"

"Oh, no! You could be right. Before I went to Khenti's world I saw two grown men fighting at the park. I thought it was strange, but then what with everything that happened I forgot about it." She pushed her float away, not wanting to add fizz to her already gurgling stomach. "What if the trees being sick have made the town super susceptible to whatever came through the gate?"

"That would be like a double hex, right?" said Emily.

"Yeah, it would."

"And that would be really bad," Khenti said.

"Incredibly bad," agreed Mercy.

"Okay, here you go, Hunter! Hot pies for you and four salads." Mr. Mitchell handed the pizza boxes to Khenti. "Your young man can carry this for you. Now, you three be careful out there. Seems patience is running thin. Probably just a big spring thunderstorm brewing, but still."

"Thanks, Mr. Mitchell. And you're right. There is definitely a storm coming," said Mercy.

———————

"Khenti kitten, are you quite certain you would not like a slice of my pizza? Tuna is delicious." The cat person offered a piece of the tuna-and-cheese pie to Khenti as she smiled magnanimously. "You may have this slice. I have only licked the tiniest part of it."

"Oh. Well. That is generous of you . . ." Khenti's voice trailed off as he gave the glistening cat-spit slice of pie a dubious glance.

Mercy had to stifle a laugh as she saved him. "Xena, Khenti just ate more than half of a large veggie pie by himself and an entire salad. You wouldn't want him to eat too much and feel sick, would you?"

"Oh, no! Eating to excess is terribly uncomfortable. Khenti kitten, I shall share my next pizza with you." From her perch on the back of the couch, Xena reached forward and gave Khenti's shoulder a motherly pat.

"Thank you. That is, uh, considerate of you," said Khenti as he shared an amused look with Mercy, who sat beside him (on the regular couch cushions, where people usually sat).

Xena turned her attention to Emily, who sat on the other side of the couch nibbling her own pizza slice. "Emily kitten? Would you like to partake?"

Emily's dark eyes went wide. "Oh, no, thank you, Xena. I'm super full, too. Maybe next time."

"I shall ask sooner next time so that you will not be overly full," Xena said.

"Oh, uh, goodie," said Em, who had not been done with her slice, but as Xena noisily licked the cheesy tuna from her pizza she placed her own half-eaten slice carefully back on her plate and shoved it onto the coffee table.

"We need to talk about the trees," said Hunter as she put her empty plate on the coffee table by Emily's. She was sitting on the floor using the recliner Jax always sat in as a backrest. Behind her, Jax was still eating—and was unusually quiet.

"Yeah, now that I'm not starving I agree," said Mercy, adding her empty plate to the coffee table pile.

"Yes, kittens, what did you discover?" asked Xena as she began to thoroughly lick her fingers.

"The tree's sick." Hunter and Mercy spoke at the same time.

"Bloody hell!" said Mercy. "The Japanese tree isn't healed?"

Hunter stifled a yawn and then picked at her thumbnail. "Nope. And worse than that, it was super obvious whatever killed Mrs. Stoll came from the Japanese Underworld. It actually left a slime trail." She shuddered. "It was disgusting, right, Jax?"

Jax nodded and spoke around a bite of pizza. "Yeah, there was a tunnellike hole at the base of the tree and disgusting goopy stuff all over."

Hunter picked up the telling. "The goopy stuff led to the creek. Whatever kind of creature it is, it's definitely attracted to water. And Mrs. Stoll was killed at Goode Lake . . ." Her shoulders drooped before she tightened her ponytail. "The spell Amphitrite gave me—the one from the book—definitely did not work. I'm really sorry."

"Hey, that's not your fault. Amphitrite used you," Mercy said, then sighed. "But this really sucks because not only is the banyan tree super sick, but something is going on in town—something bad."

"That is not good news. Not good news at all." Xena manically licked the slice of pizza she'd offered to Khenti.

"Could whatever escaped from the Japanese Underworld be affecting the town?" Jax's golden-brown skin suddenly looked sallow.

"Yes." Khenti spoke so definitively everyone turned to look at him. "We know a water creature killed the woman at the lake. Mercy, you said the humidity in the air was unusual, correct?"

"Yeah, it gets humid here, but not until summer," said Mercy.

"After what we witnessed downtown today it is obvious that

something is affecting the townsfolk, and the unusual moisture in the air might mean that something is a creature allied with water."

Hunter leaned forward. "What do you mean?"

"It was *bonkers*!" Emily said as she wiped pizza grease from her hands on a napkin. "Adults—like, people older than my mom—were fighting. In public."

"While the air was practically dripping with water," added Mercy.

Jax's brow furrowed as he shook his head. "Wait, you don't mean fist fighting, do you?"

"Totally," said Emily.

"Yeah, and that's not all. People were yelling at each other. You know the Freeman sisters?" Mercy said.

"The two old women who have lived together forever down by the school?" Hunter said as Jax nodded.

"Right. They were literally screaming at each other. In front of everyone," said Mercy.

"I heard the first sister say something about the second throwing water in her hair," said Khenti. "So, again, a reference that could point to a water creature instigating the town's aggression."

Mercy nodded. "And Mr. Mitchell at the pizza place said he'd had to kick a bunch of people out of the restaurant today."

Emily snorted. "He blamed it on a storm coming, which also is about water."

Jax sat up straighter. "Hey, I swear I smelled water this morning during zero hour when Dillon tried to pick a really stupid fight with me."

"Do you have a list of creatures that might have escaped from the Japanese Underworld and their attributes?" Khenti asked.

Hunter yawned again and rubbed her eyes before answering. "No. We have grimoires from our ancestors that note spells and weather and such, but for hundreds of years the gates have held. There wasn't any reason to make a list of beings that could escape from them because they were contained."

"Grimoires?" Khenti asked.

"A book that witches record spells and other information in," explained Mercy. Then she turned to Xena. "Hey, are we the only witches in the world like us?"

Xena paused midlick. "Goode witches are unique. There are, of course, many others who follow The Path in this world, but I know of no other witches who draw the power of the ley lines into their spellwork. Why do you ask, kitten?"

"Well, Em brought this up, and I think she has a point." Mercy smiled at her best friend. "She—and Khenti—wondered if some other witches might be hexing us, or the town."

"Oh, kitten, were there other witches casting spells in Goodeville I would know it. I would feel their energy. I believe you would as well."

"Well, also, why would another witch hex us?" Jax ran his hand through his hair. "Unless you, or *we,* have done something really wrong."

Mercy noticed that Jax looked unusually tense—and as she leaned against his recliner Hunter shifted restlessly. Both of them seemed exhausted and stressed, especially her sister. *Wonder what's going on between them?*

"Hexing someone is bad news," said Mercy. "It can hurt the witch that casts the spell as badly, if not worse, than whoever she's hexing." *I should know. That's what I did to Khenti's dad and then we ended up in hell . . .* Mercy shook off the thought and continued.

"But we haven't hexed anyone here. All we've done is to try and protect the town. No." Mercy shook her head emphatically. "It's not a hex. It's a monster. A water monster. And all we have to do is figure out what it is, and find it so Khenti can kill it and send it back to its hell where it belongs."

"That is a lot," said Khenti.

"Well, it's a good thing Hunter and I are powerful witches and we have you four to back us up." Mercy sounded a lot more confident than she felt. "Speaking of a powerful witch—H, how 'bout you get out your tarot cards and do some bibbidi-bobbidi-boo-ing? I'm ready to figure out how to take down this new boogey monster before the town tears itself apart."

"Yeah. I can do that." Hunter stood and then stumbled and would've fallen had Jax not caught her elbow.

"Hey, steady there," said Jax.

"H, you okay? You look terrible," said Mercy.

Hunter's lips quirked into a sarcastic half smile. "Thanks a lot, Mag."

"I didn't mean that in a bad way. I just meant I'm worried about you." Mercy spoke hastily—absolutely not wanting to start another fight with her sister.

"Kitten, I do not believe you have grounded yourself properly." Xena spoke up. "The energy you manipulated yesterday was extremely powerful. Are you feeling unusually tired? Is your mind filled with feathers?"

Everyone looked at Xena.

"Feathers?" Hunter asked.

Xena nodded emphatically. "Yes, kitten. Feathers. It is a metaphor for a mind too exhausted to think well—and a rather good metaphor at that. Did you soak in a mineral bath last night?"

"No," said Hunter. "You know I don't like baths. Who wants to sit in warm, dirty water?"

"Well, I quite like it." Xena gave Hunter a perplexed look. "But whether you usually enjoy a lovely bath or not—you should soak yourself in minerals—Epsom salts and magnesium will help. Add lavender oil to be sure you rest well tonight."

"That sounds like a good idea, H," said Mercy.

"Yeah, I'll do that, but maybe I should try to get some answers from my tarot first. A monster that could kill Mrs. Stoll is bad enough. But now it's affecting the whole town. We can't exactly wait for me to bathe." As Hunter spoke she swayed like she was standing on the deck of a ship.

"I know this is not my world, but it is clear that you must rest and regain your strength," said Khenti.

"I agree with Khenti," said Em just as her phone beeped with a text message. She glanced at it and gave the group an apologetic smile. "Sorry, that's Mom. It's late and she's worried. I need to get home."

"Yeah, I need to get going, too." Jax stood and put his hand on Hunter's shoulder. "Hey, rest first—tarot tomorrow."

"Okay. Yeah. I get it. I'll take the bath and go to bed. Tomorrow I'll tarot." Hunter walked to the door with Jax and Emily, who waved over their shoulders at Xena and Mercy and Khenti before going out into the warm spring night and their cars that waited in the driveway. When she turned back, Xena, Khenti, and Mercy were staring at her. "What? Do I have food in my teeth?"

"No! Nothing like that," said Mercy. "It's just that you look really tired, H."

Xena gracefully hopped off the back of the couch and smoothed her wild mane of hair. "Kitten, I shall run a bath for you. I know exactly what to add to it to make quite sure you are properly grounded and will get a good night's sleep."

"Okay. Thanks." Hunter rubbed her eyes again.

Quickly, before Mercy could warn Khenti, Xena bent and licked his cheek. "Good night, lovely Khenti kitten."

His brown eyes widened and he grinned. "Good night, magnificent Goode familiar."

Mercy dodged Xena's lick by pulling the cat person into a hug. "Night, Xena. Love you." She released Xena and met her sister's weary gaze. "Love you, too, H."

"Ditto," said Hunter as she followed Xena slowly up the stairs. Partway up, she stopped and looked back over her shoulder. "You're gonna stay up and research, right?"

"Totally," said Mercy. She smiled. "I'm going to introduce Khenti to the internet."

Hunter's smile didn't reach her eyes. "That sounds fun. 'Night."

"Night-nights," said Mercy. She watched her sister disappear up the stairs before she turned to Khenti. "Are you up for some research?"

"Absolutely. But what is an internet?"

SIXTEEN

Hunter had no intention of taking a bath. She hid at the top of the stairs, around the corner from the bathroom, and waited until Xena turned off the tap and padded out of the room and down the hall, steam trailing behind her like wings, before Hunter dashed to her closed bedroom door and turned the handle.

"Kitten, your bath is all warm and bubbly and ready for you," Xena said from behind Hunter, her slippered human feet as silent as cat paws.

"I'm not a bath person, Xena." Hunter groaned and released the door handle. "It's the human soup of it all. With your hairs and sock fuzz floating around you . . ." She grimaced. "I can ground myself in my room." She pushed open her door, the low *creak* of old hinges punctuating her statement.

Xena narrowed her yellow eyes and tilted her head. "Kitten—"

"I'm fine, Xena. Promise," Hunter said, slipping into her room before the cat person rubbed her all-too-human tongue against her cheek. "I just need to rest."

Satisfied, Xena shrugged out of her fluffy robe, revealing smooth, pinkish-white skin the same color as her soft cat belly. "Mustn't let the warm, bubbly water go to waste." She plucked the robe off the floor, tossed it over her shoulder, and vanished into the bathroom, another ghostly wave of steam rushing from the humid space as she closed the door.

With a sigh, Hunter leaned against her own closed door. She bit her lip, her hand hovering over the lock. She didn't lock her door, not normally, not in this house, and not when she'd stayed in the Ashleys' garage apartment. Had she been better at securing her space, she might still be there. But that didn't mean she needed to lock *this* door. No matter how annoying her sister's past unwelcome, unannounced visits to talk boys or clothes or plants or spells, they had also been a comfort.

Will I ever find comfort in Mercy again?

Hunter backed away from the unlocked door and dropped onto the edge of her bed. She was home. To stay. The thought tugged on her throat, and she stifled a cough. Yes, this was the house she grew up in, and this was the room she'd once painted mauve and then green and finally the deep, unending navy of the night sky. But this house, this room, still held the same coldness it had all those days ago when she'd made her escape, dragging her duffle behind her down to the first floor, the sound of her exit like a body falling down stairs.

I can't stay.

This time, it had nothing to do with her sister. Pushing Mag aside, finding fault with everything she did, holding on to grudges like friendships, had nearly destroyed them both. Hunter wouldn't make the same mistakes again. She also wouldn't stay in a place that hindered her growth. She wouldn't sacrifice herself for the sake of history—just to write in her grimoire that she'd chained herself to Goodeville to keep its people and the Goode magic safe. Mercy could do that. Mercy *would* do that. Hunter didn't have to . . .

She could be free.

A lightness filled her stomach, a balloon swelling with helium, floating up, up, up until she was standing, only tethered to the ground by the shoes on her feet.

"I can leave," she said to the room, to the house, to her god. "I can start over. Go to Chicago. I can do . . ." She pressed her palm over her heart to keep it from beating out of her chest. "I can do whatever I want. I can *go* wherever I want."

She darted to the maple desk that sat under the picture window and dropped onto her chair. Switching on the full moon lamp Mercy had given her last Yule, Hunter opened the top drawer, wiggling it a bit so the old, warped wood wouldn't wedge itself into an impossible-to-close position. An oversized pad of lined neon-pink Post-its sat on top of a stack of completed journals. She picked up the notepad, her fingers sweeping over the top journal, silver crescents pressed into a glittering silver cover. This journal, just like the four beneath, was full, every page covered in ink. But she still had yet to complete her manuscript. She had barely thought about it, much less worked on it, since her mother died.

"That's what I'll do." Again, she spoke to forces bigger than herself. "I'll find a coffee shop in Chicago and finally finish my book."

Stomach warm and filled with joy, she closed the drawer and chose a silver metallic pen the same color as moonlight on water from the holder on her desk. She would get to work planning the rest of her life as soon as she took care of the present, or, at least, the very near future.

1. heal the gates

2. stop the trail of goo creature

3. ~~fix~~ help Kylie/tell the truth/undo the spell

4. identify the trail of goo creature

She chewed on the end of her pen and studied the list, the metallic ink glinting in the light. It was out of order, and a disorganized list was as bad as no list at all.

1. identify the trail of goo creature

2. help Kylie/tell the truth/undo the spell

3. stop the trail of goo creature

4. heal the gates

5. leave Goodeville and start my life

"There." She capped her pen. The satisfaction of having created a succinct tally of to-dos faded as quickly as it had come. The items, while challenging, weren't completely undoable. She could achieve them. She *would* achieve them. She *had to* achieve them. But a part of her didn't want to. Well, not all of them, anyway. There was one she wished she could leave for another time—a high school reunion when a decade had passed and the stresses of life outside of Goodeville High made the past feel like a dream.

Maybe the spell will wear off by then. Maybe Kylie will forgive me. Maybe—

A soft *tink tink tink* against the window drew her attention.

The brown wings of a moth beat against the glass, its fuzzy body tapping the pane, drawn by the yellowish glow of lamplight. It had been pulled to this place, this house, to Hunter, who had switched on the moon light and forever changed the insect's life.

Tink tink.

Hunter had done the same to Kylie—created a new moon for her to follow.

Tink tink tink.

If Hunter left without turning off the light, Kylie, like this moth, would stay in one place, wings fluttering, desperately trying to reach something she could never attain.

Hunter switched off the lamp, and the gentle taps against the glass faded as the insect adjusted and, guided by the light of its true moon, flew up and away from the house.

Her hand drifted to her pendant, her fingertips drawing slow circles against the smooth stone. Tyr had come back to her. Jax had accepted her apology. Mercy had forgiven her. It might be too much to expect Kylie to do the same, but no matter the outcome, Hunter had to do the right thing. She couldn't live with herself in Goodeville or Chicago if she didn't.

She would do it tomorrow. Before then, she would cross off number one.

Hunter went to her pillow, a firm lump at the head of her bed, and slid her hand under the cool fabric until her fingers reached the blue velvet pouch that held her tarot deck. She removed the satchel and poured her cards onto her comforter. Their silver backs seemed to shimmer, reflecting the same phase of the moon beaming down through the cloudy sky. She swept her cards into a neat pile and closed her eyes. She'd spent sleepless nights consulting her tarot. No matter how drained or exhausted she was, the messages from her cards always came through clearly. Well, as clear and direct as tarot cards could be. There was always room for interpretation. Always room for human mistakes.

Hunter settled her right palm against the deck.

Reveal yourself, reveal yourself, reveal yourself. She inwardly repeated her intention until it was all she could hear.

"Reveal yourself!" she commanded.

But there were no sparks of energy or flashes of power fizzling against her skin.

"Reveal yourself!" she repeated.

Again, no magic tingled against her fingertips.

She rolled her amulet between her left fingers as she chewed the inside of her cheek. Even though she couldn't feel it, her magic had to still be there, resting in the depths. If she could only reach it.

Hunter filled her lungs and focused on diving within herself to find the power that coursed through her veins.

Reveal yourself.

She flipped the top card and set it faceup next to the deck. The milky white that had once been a placeholder, a circle of swirling colors until a picture loaded, clear as day, remained cloudy.

Hunter bit the inside of her cheek, closed her eyes, and tried again.

The threads of power like extensions of her veins, her nerves, her very being had vanished. She felt nothing from her tarot. Her eyelids fluttered open as she pressed her fingers to her pendant. It was cool against her skin, not warm or thrumming with power, *her* power.

She picked up the card and squinted at the foggy rectangle.

She was tired. That was all. She tilted her head. Or maybe this was the answer.

Tarot card in hand, Hunter rounded her bed and slowly and quietly opened her door. Her ponytail swung listlessly as she leaned out and peered down the hall at her sister's room. The shadow darkening the thin strip of empty space between the bottom of her door and the wood floor told Hunter exactly what she needed to know. She charged toward the stairs, a sudden burst of laughter reaching her as she neared the bottom.

"H!" Mercy chimed, her cheeks round with giggles.

Khenti hid his final bits of laughter with a cough as he looked up at Hunter, the bright screen of the open laptop reflecting in his brown eyes. "Were we too loud? I'm afraid my technological difficulties have led to much amusement."

Heat crept up Hunter's neck. She felt like she'd walked in on something private. Sure, Mercy and Khenti weren't touching, but touching wasn't always the first step in making a true connection. "No, you two are fine. I just—" She handed the card to Mercy, grimacing at the streaks her sweaty grip left behind. "I wanted to show you this."

Her sister and Khenti huddled around the card, squinting the same way Hunter had when the foggy gray image ceased churning, offering the unreadable haze as answer to her question.

"I know I need to rest. I mean, that's clear from the card, but I wanted to try and give us a head start." Hunter stuffed her clammy hands into her pockets. This had been a terrible idea. She should have waited, asked again after a good night's sleep, instead of stampeding downstairs to flaunt her failings. They were depending on her. This was the absolute best way to get an insight on what plagued Goodeville. After all, it had worked before.

"What is it?" Mercy asked, her brow knitting.

"My tarot. I'm a little disconnected right now." Hunter stroked the end of her ponytail, which hung like a security blanket over her shoulder. "I just wanted you to see that I'm working on getting an answer about whatever's come through the Japanese Gate."

They need me, and I'm useless.

She took the card from Mercy and stared down at the milky white. "I'll try again in the morning."

Mercy and Khenti exchanged a glance, further proof of their deepening connection. Carefully, he turned the laptop to face Hunter. "We have found possibilities."

Mag clasped her hands and nodded, straightening as if ready to deliver a speech. "We're compiling a list."

"Oh." Hunter tucked the card into her back pocket.

They don't need me.

"Guess you've gotten really good at researching," she said, jealousy twisting in her gut.

"Learned from the best." Mercy winked, an overdramatized motion that would have made Hunter laugh had she not felt so defeated.

Khenti spun the computer back around and resumed working,

poking at the keyboard as if his index fingers were two sticks. "Your Google is a powerful sorcerer."

"Search engine," Mercy corrected, leaning into him.

He nodded. "Yes, and its magic is the only kind we require."

"Rest, H," Mercy said, the corners of her bright eyes creasing with a smile. "Khenti and I have all the facts. We'll cross off possibilities until there's only one left. It won't take us long to figure out exactly what's come through the gate."

"You don't need me," Hunter murmured, but Mercy and Khenti were laughing again, pointing at the screen and whispering to each other.

They don't need me. I can leave, and everything will be fine.

The balloon filled again, carrying her up the stairs and back to her room. She had an item of her own to cross off.

SEVENTEEN

Mercy had set her alarm to go off early the next morning, and even though she was tempted to pull the covers over her head and go back to sleep for that extra hour, she didn't. She actually liked research, and she and Khenti had been onto something the night before, until they were both so exhausted that they had to go to bed.

She dressed quickly in her favorite pair of hand-embroidered jeans, a fringed belt, and a V-necked tee that was the same color as her turquoise-blue eyes. Instead of fighting with her hair to act right, Mercy pulled it back in a high ponytail that was more Hunter's style than hers, hurriedly lined her eyes, and brushed on mascara, some lip gloss, and then carried her boots with her as she made her way quietly down the creaky staircase.

Khenti's broad back was the first thing she noticed as she turned the corner to the kitchen and the coffee brewer waiting there to finish waking her.

"Hey, you haven't been researching all night, have you?" Mercy asked as she entered the kitchen nook on silent socked feet.

Khenti jumped from the chair and whirled around, automatically crouching in a defensive stance as he raised his hand to summon his khopesh. Then he blew out a long breath and ran a hand over his face. "Mercy! You startled me."

"Sorry." Mercy lifted her boots. "I was being quiet on purpose because it's early and I didn't want to wake Xena or Hunter. I'll make us a pot of coffee. You look like you need it even more than I do. *Have* you been here all night?"

He sighed heavily as he sat in front of the computer again. "Xena is already awake. She said she was going to hunt for her breakfast."

"Gross," said Mercy.

"She does love those sparrows."

"Yeah, if by *love* you mean *slaughter.*" She shuddered. "I'm just glad she's quit bringing them inside to devour."

Khenti grinned. "She is a fierce huntress." Then he ran his hand wearily across his face again. "And I tried to sleep, but my mind was filled with questions left from our research. When I realized I wasn't going to be able to rest I got up and returned to the *internet.*" He spoke the word reverently. "It is a marvel."

Mercy grinned over her shoulder. "Yeah, you've reminded me how awesome it is. Hard to believe that only, like, twenty years ago we didn't have it. Talk about the Dark Ages." She finished filling the coffee maker, grabbed a carton of eggs, and went to peer at the computer as she rested her hands on Khenti's shoulders. "So, did you figure out which demon is our baddie?" But as Mercy's gaze went to the computer screen she saw that instead of information on Japanese water demons or mosquito-like Hindu monsters, the page was about ancient Egypt.

Khenti put his hands over hers and gave her an apologetic look. "I—um—just wanted to see what it said about my home."

She sat next to him at the little breakfast table. "Hey, that's totally understandable. What'd you find?"

His full lips twitched up at the corners. "Much misinformation."

"Yeah, well, that's probably the biggest problem with the internet."

"It did make me miss my mother even more than I already do," he said softly, his gaze returning to the screen. "Did you know that there is an actual reference to her in your world?"

"What?! No! That's majorly cool!"

Khenti nodded and pointed to the screen. "They have the facts wrong, but that is not surprising. The explorers were trying to piece together information found from thousands of years ago. They say she was the wife of Pharaoh's favorite architect. Actually, she was the daughter of an architect so highly favored by Pharaoh that even the gods took notice—which is how my father met my mother." Khenti touched the screen gently.

"You'll get back to her," said Mercy.

Khenti straightened. "Yes. Yes, I absolutely will—as soon as I aid you and Hunter in the defeat of the monster that is loosed on your village. And I believe I have discovered what that monster could be."

"Oh, yea! Which one?"

Khenti clicked on a page he'd minimized. "This demon seems to be what we're looking for."

Quickly, Mercy read the information. "Hmm, a Nure-Onna. So, a water demon that's really a woman who takes the form of a serpent."

"Yes," Khenti continued. "The information I found says that she lures victims close to her through the cries of a ghostly child she carries—and her preferred victims are women. Her bite is poisonous—it paralyzes the Nure-Onna's prey so that she can easily drink the blood of her victim. It always strikes around or in water and it often sheds its skin, so we need to look for a huge snake's skin, or at least scales. If we find either we can be sure it's a Nure-Onna."

"That's great work, Khenti! Did you find anything about it having the ability to manipulate people's emotions?" Mercy said.

"Not directly, though from the information I read we might infer she can. It states clearly that she draws victims to her by making them believe they hear the cries of an infant."

Mercy nodded slowly. "That seems reasonable. I can't wait to tell Hunter and Xena. Right after school we can go on a snakeskin hunt—which is disgusting, but if that's what we have to do to—"

"Good morning, kittens!" Xena burst into the kitchen nook through the back door—completely naked with glistening scarlet blood spatter on her chin. She hurried to Mercy to hug her, but Mercy backed quickly out of her reach.

"Oh, no no no. You have blood on your face! And you're naked!"

Xena stopped and touched her face until she found the blood, then she began licking her fingers and cleaning herself. Between licks she spoke. "I am not surprised at the blood. My breakfast sparrow was quite feisty this morning. Ridiculous little creatures, but so, so tasty. And of course I am naked. I am always naked when I change into my human skin. Abigail's bathrobe is . . ." She gestured vaguely behind her at the living room. "You don't mind that I am naked, do you, Khenti kitten?"

Khenti grinned up at the cat person. "I am comfortable with your form with or without clothes." He lowered his voice conspiratorially. "We are much less *covered* in my world than yours."

"I'm getting the bathrobe!" Mercy called as she sprinted into the living room to find her mother's soft old bathrobe had been discarded across the couch. She had just grabbed it when Hunter padded down the stairs.

"Xena's naked again?" she asked her twin.

Mercy rolled her eyes. "Come see."

"Well, it definitely won't be the first time." Hunter laughed.

"She's also bloody. Be careful." Mercy followed her sister back to the kitchen.

"Mercy Anne Goode." Xena fisted her hands on her ample hips.

"I am no longer bloody. As always, I am perfectly groomed. Good morning, Hunter."

"'Morning, Xena—'morning, Khenti." Khenti nodded a friendly greeting while Hunter neatly sidestepped Xena's attempt to lick her cheek. "Xena, you have sparrow breath."

Xena beamed a satisfied smile. "Of course I do!"

Mercy tossed the bathrobe to her familiar. "Coffee is almost ready and I thought I'd scramble a bunch of eggs. *And* Khenti and I think we figured out what the Japanese demon is."

"Oh, that is wonderful news! Tell us!" Xena slid into the bathrobe and then perched beside Khenti on the top of the breakfast table.

While Khenti filled them in on the Nure-Onna, Mercy made breakfast. She was humming softly to herself and loving the feeling of her family being together again when she realized Hunter was unusually quiet. From the stove, Mercy studied her twin. She looked normal and she was being attentive to the monster discussion Khenti and Xena were having, but she wasn't saying hardly anything. Mercy quickly divided the eggs—including some for Xena—spread plant-based butter and Abigail's strawberry jam on the toast, and then carried the plates to the table.

"Xena, you gotta get your butt off the table so we can eat," said Mercy.

"Well, of course, kitten. I know how to eat at a—" Xena coughed as she slid off the table and then plucked something small and spindly out of her mouth. She stared at it for a moment before her yellow eyes flashed and she said, "Ooo! Sparrow claw." She popped it back into her mouth and chewed it loudly as the three humans stared at her. "What?" she asked after she swallowed. "They're crunchy. Like sparrow potato chips."

Khenti covered a laugh with a cough while Mercy and Hunter exchanged a long-suffering look that warmed Mercy's heart. *My twin is back!*

"So, we must go to the sites we know the demon has visited," Xena said as she licked at the scrambled eggs. "And look for scales or discarded serpent skin."

"Yeah," said Mercy. "But I think you should wait until Hunter or I can go with you. Remember the part about the Nure-Onna's bite being super poisonous? And since it's not a straight-up snake—like a rattler or any other poisonous snake around here—we don't have an antitoxin for it."

"You are quite right to remind us. We must be very careful when we battle the demon. I will kill it, but you must not get bitten by it before I do," said Khenti.

"Then what shall we do while the girls are at school today, Khenti kitten? Shall we hunt again? I will be hungry soon. Sparrows are delicious, but not very filling," said Xena after she'd lapped up the last of her eggs.

"Xena, I think you should help Khenti with his research." Mercy spoke quickly before Khenti—who was always polite—said he'd go hunting with the cat. "We can't forget that Khenti is only staying here until he kills the demon. Then he has to go home and figure out how to petition Osiris for the release of his mom from Duat."

"That is so true. Forgive me, Khenti kitten. Of course you must return to rescue your lovely mother. We shall diligently research how to petition Osiris." Xena gave Khenti's shoulder a motherly pat.

"Hunter, what do you think?" Mercy asked her twin.

"About what?"

"About the Nure-Onna." Mercy watched as her twin shrugged.

Hunter moved her eggs around with her fork and didn't look up at Mercy. "I don't know. It's good you two figured out which demon it probably is. I guess we find out for sure after school."

Something was definitely wrong with Hunter, and Mercy had little doubt that it was her fault, which meant it was up to her to fix what was still messed up between them. Quickly, she put the dishes in the sink and then disappeared into the spellwork supply pantry on the far side of the kitchen. She worked methodically, knowing exactly what she'd need. She even wrote a quick spell on a slip of prayer paper. When her basket was loaded she carried it from the pantry and returned to the kitchen nook where Xena and Khenti were having a lively debate about the merits of wearing less clothing. Hunter was still picking at her eggs.

"Hey, uh, H—would you come with me for a sec? There's something I have to do before we leave for school, and I need you to help me." Mercy nodded at the back door.

"Yeah, okay." Hunter stood and followed Mercy out the door. "What's up?" she asked as soon as they were alone.

"Would you come to my greenhouse? It'll be easier in there," Mercy said.

Hunter glanced at the spellwork basket held in the crook of her sister's arm, shrugged, and nodded. Silently the twins made their way across the dewy grass to Mercy's greenhouse. They went in and Mercy flipped on the light, inhaling deeply the scent of green, growing things before she turned to face her sister.

"Hunter, I'm sorry," Mercy said.

Hunter cocked her head. "About?"

"Well, for one"—she held up a finger for each point she counted off—"being so damn selfish that I messed up our relationship. And two—about not being there for you when you needed me most. Three—about running away and, as you said, leaving you to clean up my messes. And four—about not showing you every day how important you are to me, how much I need you, and how much I love you." She met her sister's gaze steadily. "I'm sorry for all of that, Hunter. I really am, and I promise I'm gonna do better."

Hunter didn't say anything for so long that Mercy started to chew her lip and sent a silent prayer to her goddess. *Freya, please don't let me have messed-up things between Hunter and me permanently.*

"Thanks for saying all that. I appreciate it," Hunter said slowly. "But what happened between us wasn't *completely* your fault."

Mercy sighed. "Not completely but *mostly* my fault."

Hunter's lips twitched like she wanted to smile. "True, but I did push you away."

"You had reason to. It was because of me that you and Tyr broke up." Mercy had to brush a tear from her cheek, but she didn't stop apologizing. "I'm really sorry about that, H. Your god is your business. I shoulda never even considered that you reject him."

Hunter looked down then as her fingers found the pendant that had returned to its rightful place in the center of her chest. "Yeah, I should never have rejected him."

Mercy brushed away another tear. "Will you forgive me?"

Slowly, Hunter raised her gaze to her sister's again. "Yes."

"Will you seal it with a spell?"

Hunter's lips did curve up then. "What, like a twin love spell or something?"

Mercy smiled through her tears. "Yeah, definitely."

"Okay, I guess. Seems a good way to start the day," Hunter said, her gaze flicking to Mercy's spellwork basket. "I mean, you have the basket and everything."

"Right? I'll set it up. It's a real quick spell." Mercy moved aside some African violets she'd been propagating to make room on one of the tables. She set down the bottle of essential oils she'd already mixed, brought out two pink pillar candles, a velvet pouch filled with salt, and long, wooden ritual matches—and put everything on the table.

First, Mercy poured a salt pentagram and then began rubbing the essential oil mixture into the candles.

Hunter sniffed. "That smells like citrus with jojoba." Her eyes widened. "That's joy and laughter oil!"

Mercy grinned and nodded. "Yep. Sweet orange, lime, and pink grapefruit mixed with a jojoba oil base. Wanna anoint the other candle?"

"Yeah, sure."

The twins worked companionably side by side and Mercy realized she hadn't felt this content since before their mom died. She kept sneaking looks at her twin and thinking how good it was to just be with her without fighting. *I'll never let anything come between us again—ever!*

When they were done anointing the identical pink pillars they placed them in the center of the salt pentagram. Mercy met her twin's gaze. "Believe it or not, I couldn't find a twin love spell in any grimoire."

"Strange, right?" Hunter said with a grin.

"It's a definite lack in our ancestors' spellwork," agreed Mercy.

"It's weird that we're the only Goode twins ever recorded, don't you think?" Hunter asked.

"If by weird you mean cool and special—then yep," Mercy said. "Anyway, let's light the candles together. Then I made up a twin love spell for us. So, I'll speak the words and then I'll pull up some power from the ley lines and pour it into us. When we're all warm and fuzzy we can blow out the candles together and—ta da!—*twin lurve!*"

Hunter snorted a laugh. "You're a little wild, but okay."

"Wild awesome, right?"

Hunter's smile reached her turquoise-blue eyes. "Right, Mag."

"Okay, let's light the candles and focus our intention on never, ever fighting again." Mercy handed her sister a long ritual match.

"Never, ever," repeated Hunter.

Together, the sisters lit their matches and then touched the flame to the twin wicks, which lit easily. Then Mercy took the slip of prayer paper from her basket and spoke the little spell she'd written just moments before.

> *"When my twin and I fight cool it is not*
> *It's awful, it's sad, it makes me sob and snot.*
> *From today till forever we will not break up—we will not fight*
> *We move forward together in love, always love—and light!"*

Mercy closed her eyes and concentrated on the fat, green river of power that ran endlessly deep in the earth below them; she imagined pulling the ley line warmth up, up, up—into her. The energy responded immediately, and washed into her body through her feet. Mercy opened her eyes and held out her hand, which Hunter took.

> *"Washed new by ley line power*
> *Like a twin lurve shower!"*

She heard Hunter giggle softly at the words of her spell, but her sister gripped her hand tightly. Mercy felt the ley line energy flow through her body, but as it got to her hand, the one clutching Hunter's, it sputtered and like a wave receding from shore, washed away.

"Uh, Mag, I don't feel anything," whispered Hunter.

"I know! I don't understand what's wrong. I can pull the power up from the ley lines, but I can't make it go into you."

"I'll help." Hunter reached over for Mercy's other hand so that they faced each other, gripping both hands. Hunter closed her eyes and concentrated. Her face relaxed visibly as the ley line power responded to her, but when she opened her eyes and stared at her sister, concentrating on sending the warmth to her, she shook her head in exasperation. "Nothing! I can't make it go to you at all."

"Something's wrong. This has only happened to me when I tried to heal one of the trees. Do you think we're too stressed to cast a successful spell?" Mercy had to blink hard to keep from bursting into frustrated tears.

Hunter moved her shoulders. "I don't know, Mag. It doesn't make any sense."

Mercy sighed. "Well, let's just concentrate on twin love and blow out the candles. It's still a spell, even if the ley lines let us down." Together, Mercy and Hunter blew out the candles and then Mercy pulled her sister into a tight hug. "Nothing will ever come between us again. Promise."

"Promise," Hunter echoed.

Still holding hands, the sisters walked back to the house. "Do you feel better?" Mercy asked Hunter.

Hunter glanced at her sister. "Yeah, but that has more to do with what you said to me before the spell than the spell itself."

"What do you mean?"

Hunter stopped and the twins faced each other. "You took responsibility without blame and without being forced into it. Mag, I do believe you're learning and growing."

Mercy sighed. "You mean *finally*."

"No. I mean for real, and that's more important than any messed-up spell."

"Oh. Okay. Good." The twins started walking again—still holding hands.

"Hey, do you think Xena is going to get Khenti to eat a sparrow?" Hunter asked.

"Oh, definitely," Mercy said.

"By the way, I like him," Hunter said.

Mercy stopped just outside the closed back door. "I like him, too, but I'm pretty burned out on relationships after the Kirk disaster, so I'm trying not to jump into anything."

Hunter's eyes sparkled. "*Trying* is the key word in that sentence."

Mercy blew out a long breath. "Yeah. He is smart and kind and sweet."

"And hot?"

Mercy tried unsuccessfully to hide a smile. "Are you asking?"

Hunter's only answer was to raise one arched brow at her twin.

"Yeah, Khenti is definitely hot, which makes it harder every day for me to keep him in the friend zone."

Hunter shrugged. "Well, like Mom used to say, the best relationships begin with friendship."

"I miss her so much," Mercy said.

"Me, too. You think when the veil is thin at Samhain she'll visit?" Hunter asked softly.

"H, I don't think she's ever far from us." Mercy squeezed her sister's hand. "I love you."

"Love you, too, Mag." Hunter dropped her sister's hand and opened the door.

"Kittens! You must hurry or you'll be late for school." Xena fluttered around them, ironically more sparrowlike than a cat.

Just as the twins were heading to the front door, backpacks slung over shoulders and insulated coffee cups in hand, Hunter stopped and turned to Xena. "While you're researching today would you check the old grimoires for references to any Goode witch who might have had trouble channeling the ley line power?"

Mercy turned at the door and nodded. "That's a really good idea, H."

"Kittens, is there something Xena should know?" the familiar asked.

The twins shrugged together and Hunter said, "If everything was working right we'd have the gates sealed and we wouldn't be monster hunting after school today."

"Very true," added Mercy.

"You are absolutely correct. I should have thought of it before. I shall research. Have a lovely day at school, kittens," said Xena. And then she licked their cheeks—quickly—before they could flee.

EIGHTEEN

I mean I love her and appreciate that she cares about us—a lot—but as usual that cat freaked for no reason," Mercy said as Hunter easily snagged a front-row parking spot. "We're early. Like, really early."

"Yeah." Hunter sighed, locked the car doors, and shoved the keys in her backpack. "I should have checked the time. We totally could've had our coffee at home."

"Yep. So annoying." Mercy stopped and jerked her chin at a big, shiny black SUV also parked in the front row. "Hey, that's Tiffany's. Her dad gave it to her as a sweet sixteen present a couple months ago."

Hunter stared. "That costs more than Mom made in a year."

"Right? Range Rover turned Range Whore-ver." Mercy giggled at her own joke.

Hunter didn't giggle. She just looked at her sister.

"What?" Mercy asked.

"We have to stop that," H said firmly.

"Stop what?"

"Stop being bitchy about the cheerleaders just because they're cheerleaders," said Hunter.

"Well, actually, we're being bitchy about them because they're horrible. Remember Em's dad's funeral? They're the worst."

"That doesn't mean we should be like them, Mag. I mean, how are we not as bad as they are if we act like them?"

Mercy snorted. "You mean minus the uniforms and the massive popularity—oh, and the Range Rover?"

Hunter's lips curled up at the corners. "Yeah, minus that stuff." Then she shook her head. "It's not right that we have some ridiculous feud with them. If they don't like us, fine. It's none of our business anyway. Plus, I've gotten to know Kylie and I like her. She's really nice. And you know what Mom would say."

Mercy blew out a long breath and looked down, shoulders bowing. "Abigail would say we have to look at the inside not the outside of people and give everyone a chance. Shit. We gotta stop being mean to them and—" She broke off, bent down, and picked up something shiny that tinkled musically. "Check it out, H!"

Hunter squinted. "Does that pink leather key chain say RANGE ROVER in crystals?"

"Yep." Mercy put her hand over her eyes to block the bright morning sunlight and searched the parking lot. "Isn't that Tiffany over there with Heather heading out back to the stadium?"

Hunter followed her gaze. "Yeah, I think so."

"Well, wanna start acting differently right now?" Mercy held up the key chain, which sparkled intensely.

Hunter shook her head, grinned, and said. "No, but yeah."

"No, but yeah, pretty much sums it up. So, let's go." Side by side, they hurried across the parking lot, easily catching the two girls who were walking slowly as Heather texted.

"Hey, Tiffany?" Mercy called when they were not far behind them. "I think Hunter and I found your keys." She held them up as Tiffany turned.

The head cheerleader's blond hair cascaded perfectly around her shoulders to her mid back and as she turned it floated around her like a gorgeous veil. Her glacier-blue eyes were narrowed, but when she saw her keys she blinked quickly in surprise and looked from Mercy to Hunter.

Beside her, Heather stepped forward as she grinned. "OMG! That's so awesome of you two to find them! We would've been screwed after school without them." She took the keys and tossed them to Tiffany. "Thanks, you two!"

"Um. Yeah. That was really nice of you," said Tiffany with a lot less enthusiasm. Then she focused her cerulean gaze on Hunter. "You haven't talked to Kylie recently, have you?"

Hunter picked her thumbnail. "No. Not since yesterday."

"Why?" Mercy asked.

Tiffany held up her phone like it was a talisman. "I've been texting her since last night about meeting Heather and me before school today to move some equipment because Coach Livingston was, like, super pissed yesterday when Kylie took off from practice."

"Yeah," Heather continued. "We thought it'd put Coach in a good mood if we had the JV field all set up for practice."

"JV field?" Mercy asked. "Why are you practicing out there?"

Heather rolled her brown eyes. "Misogyny. Get this—the football team is in trouble because their coach told our coach his team has an attitude problem, so *we* have to move to the crappy field as their punishment."

"Typical that women are inconvenienced by the asinine actions of men," Hunter grumbled.

"OMG! *Exactly!*" said Heather. "You and I speak the same language." She lifted her fist in the air and pronounced, "SMASH THE PATRIARCHY!"

Hunter's laugh was genuine as she nodded and repeated, "Smash the patriarchy!"

Mercy drew in a deep breath, like she was going to plunge into a

pool of cold water, and then said in a rush, "Hunter and I accidentally got to school early and since Kylie isn't here yet we'll help you
move the equipment. Right, H?"

Hunter shrugged. "Sure."

Heather exchanged a glance with Tiffany, who also shrugged before Heather grinned and said, "That would be awesome. You do
not even know how mean Coach L can be when she's grumpy. She
looks, like, *super* sweet, but she's hiding an alter ego that's more Ursula
than Ariel."

"We'd hate for a sea witch to zap you, so we're happy to help,"
said Mercy as the four of them headed to the equipment storage shed
that sat outside the stadium just before the concession building.

"Wait, is that a thing?" Heather peered, big-eyed from Mercy to
Hunter. "Are there really sea witches?"

Mercy laughed. "Probably, but I wouldn't worry about them. Illinois is definitely not near a sea."

"Yeah, and witches aren't evil," added Hunter. "The truth is any
spellwork we do comes back on us times three—which is a definite
incentive to *not* hex anyone."

Tiffany put in a code to the push-button lock on the equipment
storage shed, but turned to face Hunter and Mercy before she flipped
on the light. "What's a hex?"

"It's like a curse," said Mercy.

Tiffany and Heather exchanged another long look before she continued. "So, let's say *someone* was spreading rumors about you two
cursing or, um, hexing the whole town. Would that mean the bad
stuff would come back on both of you?"

"Yeah. A hex always comes back on the witch who casts it," said
Hunter.

"That's why we almost never hex anyone, and if we do we have to
be super careful about the wording of the hex," said Mercy.

"What do you mean by 'super careful'?" Heather air quoted.

"Well, let's say I was pissed at you," Mercy explained. "And decided to hex you to be too uncoordinated to make the varsity squad at tryouts this year."

Heather gasped. "That would be super mean!"

"Yeah," said Hunter. "It would also make Mercy three times as clumsy as it made you."

"For real?" Tiffany asked.

"Totally," Mercy said. "I'd barely be able to walk up a flight of stairs without tripping."

"Do you see now why that *someone* spreading rumors about us hexing the town or whatever is full of shit?" Hunter said.

"And by *someone* we know you mean Kirk," added Mercy. She shook her head. "I'm really sorry I was ever with him. He's deluded and mean."

"He says you two are real witches," said Tiffany.

Hunter laughed. "That's because we *are* real witches."

"Yeah, and we try hard to live by the real Witches' Rede—our set of rules. The biggest one is *An ye harm none, do what ye will*," Mercy said.

Hunter met Tiffany's gaze. "You don't have to be afraid of us."

Mercy nodded. "Promise."

Tiffany didn't look away from Hunter as she nodded. "Okay. We won't be."

"Do you have any spells that'll help us move heavy, sweat-soaked, disgusting equipment?" Heather asked as she flipped on the light and strode into the musty-smelling little building.

"Sadly, no." Mercy sighed dramatically. "We also don't have little mice that clean our rooms for us or make us clothes."

Heather called from within the shed, "Hey, a bunch of the tumbling pads are missing."

Tiffany followed her inside. "That's weird. We dragged them all back here after practice yesterday. Oh, crap! Do you think Coach Livingston is already here and started setting stuff up?"

"Hey, that's okay," said Mercy, joining the two cheerleaders inside.

"Even if she beat you here you're gonna get some points for helping, right?"

Tiffany blew out a long breath. "I guess. Okay, let's grab these two big pads. They're too heavy for one person to handle, so getting them out there will definitely help Coach."

The twins took one of the big pads and Heather and Tiffany took another—then the four of them dragged the equipment from the shed to the JV practice field.

"Yeah, look," Heather said as she wiped the sweat from her face with the back of her sleeve. "See that pile of smaller tumbling pads over there by the cornfield? Coach has definitely been here."

"Should we put our pads by the others?" Mercy asked.

"Yeah, might as well," said Tiffany. "I wonder where Coach is?"

"Probably in the teachers' lounge drinking coffee." Heather grunted as she and Tiffany flopped their pad next to the smaller ones already resting on the grass.

"Well, I hope this puts her in a better mood," said Mercy as she and Hunter heaved their heavy pad on top of the other one.

"Ugh! What the hell is this crap in the grass?" Tiffany was staring down at her ballet flat, which was smeared with something that looked like snot.

"Gross, Tiff! It's messed up your sparkly flats. Come over here where the grass isn't wet and try to wipe them off." Heather shepherded Tiffany away from the practice pads.

"So nasty!" Tiffany complained as she tried to clean her shoe in the grass. "Like a giant slug trail."

"Mag!" Hunter whispered. "That's the disgusting stuff that was at the Japanese tree."

"Oh, shit!" Mercy stared down at the grass. Softly, she told her sister, "It's a trail. It goes into the field."

"Hey, Tiffany. Mercy and I will pull some leaves off the corn. You can wipe your shoe with them better than just using grass on that gooey stuff," Hunter called to the irate cheerleader.

"Thanks, it's so sticky and yucky it's, like, impossible to get off," whined Tiffany.

Mercy and Hunter quickly followed the slime trail to the edge of the cornfield. As they reached the field Heather joined them.

"OMG, I got some on my shoes, too! My mom is gonna *kill* me if I mess up these Jimmy Choos. She's done nothing but complain about how much they cost since I talked her into buying them for me." She bent and took off one shoe. "I think we should just go to the restroom and wash it off. Whatever this is, it's really nasty and sticky and I don't think these corn leaves are gonna do shit 'cause—" Heather gave the corn a dubious look—and her tawny face went ash pale. She opened and then closed her mouth and made a strangely strangled sound.

"Heather? What's wrong?" Mercy asked.

But Hunter was already turning to peer into the cornfield, even before Heather lifted a trembling hand to point at Coach Livingston's body. She was on her back just inside the edge of the field. Her neck was lacerated with a cut so deep that it had caused her head to tilt oddly. Her open, dead eyes stared vacantly at them.

Heather screamed.

Tiffany ran to the field—and her screams joined Heather's.

At the same moment Mercy and Hunter took a step toward each other. Blindly, they gripped hands.

"Call 911," Mercy told Heather.

"'K-k-kay." Heather's teeth chattered with shock. She started punching numbers into her phone while she and Tiffany backed quickly away from the gruesome sight.

"We'll check to see if she's still alive," said Hunter.

Hand in hand, the twins walked slowly to the fallen coach while Tiffany fell to the ground and sobbed and Heather screamed into her phone at the 911 dispatcher.

"H, she's dead." Mercy clasped her sister's hand like a lifeline.

"I know," Hunter whispered. "Look for sloughed scales or a snakeskin. Quick! Before anyone else gets here."

It didn't take much looking. Just past the coach's feet was a strip of discarded snakeskin, deflated like an enormous, grotesque party balloon.

"We gotta get rid of it!" said Mercy as she glanced at Heather and Tiffany, who had their arms around each other and were sobbing as they carefully averted their eyes from their dead coach.

"Stand right there and be sure to block their view," Hunter said. She strode to the skin, whispering, "Gross! Gross! Gross!" as she picked the huge thing up and threw it as far into the center of the mazelike cornfield as possible. She shuddered and wiped her hand on her jeans when she returned to her sister. "That was disgusting."

"But at least now we know for sure," said Mercy. "It's definitely a Nure-Onna."

Hunter nodded somberly. "Yep. It looks like our demi-god has a snake to kill."

NINETEEN

Filled with fury, Amphitrite tore through the sky and swooped down to the cherry tree, a typhoon striking land. *"You are supposed to be better than the mortals!"* she thundered as the Nure-Onna emerged from her cave. *"They are simple animals, giving in to each craving. I gave you a command—hunt those allied with Hunter Goode and her sister, Mercy. I did not give you leave to kill anyone else!"*

Water droplets hissed in the air around Amphitrite. What good was a weapon if it had no aim?

"Forgive me! For thousands of years, I've been ssstarving," the Nure-Onna hissed, her tongue flicking out to sense the steamy air.

Amphitrite swelled, gathering power from the waters of Sugar Creek. *"And I can send you back without your reward!"*

The great goddess of the sea paused before striking out and killing this creature who could see her, hear her, feel her as if Amphitrite's body still caused the ground to quake beneath her tentacles.

The Nure-Onna's suffering was nothing in comparison to that of Hunter Goode. Laughter like squealing brakes drifted through the rotting branches of the old guardian. To destroy all the witch had to live for and watch the fragile mortal crawl back, begging for an end to her waking nightmare, would be a delicious victory.

"I allowed you to feed when you first arrived in this realm, but you now have a purpose greater than carnage."

The Nure-Onna's thick body tightened, and her tail shook from side to side, the dry leaves crunching in warning.

So many felt as if they could challenge a goddess. Every time they'd been wrong.

"Resist your simple temptations, my pet, and you will reap a great reward." Amphitrite gazed upon her own glowing blue figure reflected in the Nure-Onna's dark eyes and held her hand up to her ear. *"Is that a babe I hear? Calling for his mother?"*

The Nure-Onna's eyes widened and blurred with unshed tears that morphed Amphitrite's image into a swirling azure sea.

The creature's tongue again shot out as the air thickened with moisture, with Amphitrite's false promises, with her lies.

"Get to work, pet. The redhead first." The goddess watched the Nure-Onna slither to the creek and submerge herself in the glistening water. *"Or the cat!"* she called, her words rippling the creek's surface.

There wasn't room in all the oceans of this realm to hold the tears Hunter Goode would shed before Amphitrite finished her revenge.

TWENTY

There'd been too much death and sadness for life in Goodeville to ever be normal again. At least, that's what it felt like to Hunter as she sat drumming her fingers against her study hall desk, watching students roam the halls as directionless as gnats. Some of her peers were grieving, truly grieving, their heart-twisting wails echoing off the metal lockers. But to most, Coach Livingston's death was an excuse, a way to get out of class, find friends, and traipse around campus, or simply pile into a car and leave school completely.

Hunter rolled her mangled pen cap between her teeth as Heather and Tiffany walked by, hand in hand, headed toward the cafeteria where the other half of the sophomore class was at lunch. Tiffany dabbed her cheeks with a wad of tissues that bloomed from between her fingers like the petals of a dahlia. Hunter opened her mouth to call out but thought better of it. What would she say that she hadn't already?

Her fingers fell to her pendant as her thoughts went to the to-do list burning a hole in the pocket of her ripped jeans.

help Kylie/tell the truth/undo the spell

153

She'd intended on completing the second task after school when she could grab Kylie and Jax on their way to their separate practices, perform the undoing spell, and send them on their way. In truth, cheerleading and football practice were supposed to separate the spell from the intense and honest talk with Kylie that she knew her friend deserved. But Hunter no longer had the luxury of waiting for the distraction of cheer practice. The spell had wound itself around Kylie's true emotions, and Hunter wasn't sure what that meant for her friend's ability to sort through her pain and heal in this time of crisis.

Hunter ran her fingertips over the bumpy outline of the rectangular lighter she'd slid into her pocket along with the list.

"Mrs. Macadam!" she blurted, her hand shooting into the air. "I need to go to the, uh, counselor."

Mrs. Macadam's straw-blond curls bounced with a nod. "Take the pass," she said without looking up from the fifth-edition *Teacher's Handbook* she used to hide the most recent Coldwater Creek catalog.

Hunter slipped the pen into her back pocket and scooped her studies into the folder behind the original *WANT* spell, tucking it under her arm as she bolted to the door. She took the plastic cow figurine from its hook and charged into the hall. Years of wear had rubbed bare patches in the cow's black spots, and the name MACADAM had been scrawled so many times in so many different colors that the side of the animal looked tie-dyed.

She smoothed her thumb over a bare spot and focused her intention.

Undo the spell. Undo the spell. Undo the spell.

The mantra echoed through Hunter's thoughts as she opened the door to the cafeteria and surveyed the tables. Heads turned in her direction, glassy eyes boring into her.

"Witch."

The word was spit like a curse. Loud and quiet all at once. Everywhere and nowhere. It had come from their lips, from their thoughts, from the air that swirled around her, alive with the roar of heartbeats that crashed against her eardrums like surging sea waters.

Hunter swallowed. Clutching her pendant for strength, she wound around the tables; crude slurs speared her back, the fall of Caesar had she only been popular. She tightened her grip on her pendant and pushed forward, through the humid air, and toward Kylie's fiery burst of golden-red hair.

The roaring ceased altogether as Hunter reached the far corner of the cafeteria, where Kylie sat sandwiched between Heather and Tiffany, eyes pink and puffy from crying. Jax looked up, a crooked smile on his face as he sat across from the girls, scraping the last bits of pudding from his cup.

"Mag's in the loo," he said, licking a streak of chocolate from his spoon before setting it into the empty cup.

"The *loo*." An attempted grin quaked against Tiffany's lips. "I haven't met any Brits, but I don't think they sound like that."

Jax snorted, and Hunter couldn't help but chuckle. Her sister would most definitely disagree.

Kylie shoved away from the table, sending Jax's empty pudding cup tumbling onto its side, the metal spoon clattering against the table. "I have to go prepare for Coach Livingston's vigil," she bit out. "You coming, Jax?" She swept her hair from her shoulders, and a gust of grapefruit-scented air brushed Hunter's cheeks.

She wished she could go back, choose a different spell, or choose no spell at all. Choose Jax and Kylie and pizza and Call of Duty. Choose peace and contentment and friendship instead of the ravenous need for power that had nearly devoured her life.

But it would all be okay. Hunter would make it okay. She would undo the spell, send the Nure-Onna back from where it came, heal the gates, and then be off. She'd ride the train to Chicago, a crisp and clean *The End* separating Goodeville from the rest of her life.

"Kylie, I need to talk to you," Hunter said, gripping the plastic cow. "You, too, Jax."

Kylie crossed her arms over her chest, wrinkling the cotton T-shirt Hunter knew she had in every color. "Whatever you have to say to us, you can say in front of our friends."

Heather's sallow cheeks reddened as she and Tiffany glanced from Hunter to Kylie and back again.

"I can't. It has to be in private." She picked at a bit of plastic curling up from the cow's weathered snout. "It's important. I need to—"

Jax stood and pushed in his chair, coming to Hunter's rescue the same way he always did. "Let's just go with her, Kylie."

Kylie's hazel eyes narrowed. "You always take her side."

Jax dragged his hand down his cheek. "Look." He let out a puff of air. "I'm going with H. You do what you want."

He swiped his trash from the table and motioned for Hunter to follow as he chucked his mess into the garbage can and walked toward the double doors that led to the courtyard.

Hunter hurried behind, her eyes widening and brows pinching as she sent him covert messages only years of friendship could decipher. She needed Kylie. *They* needed Kylie. The spell couldn't be broken without her.

As Hunter opened her mouth to say as much, a squawk of annoyance erupted behind her.

"This is ridiculous," Kylie seethed, racing past Hunter to catch up with Jax. "And that's the absolute last time you choose her over me." She pushed open the door. It crashed against its stopper and swung back, knocking into Hunter as she hurried through.

Kylie kept speed walking, scolding Jax as she marched through the courtyard and around the back of the gym building where smokers gathered between periods.

"So, what is it?" She stopped and spun around. "What was *sooo* important that you felt you had to take Jax away to talk about?"

Hunter ignored her hammering pulse and locked her trembling knees. "I'm a witch."

Kylie blinked, her mouth opening and closing with an unspoken thought.

"A real one," Jax said, his gaze never leaving Kylie.

"Right." Kylie tented her hands on her hips. "I mean, that's what pretty much everyone is saying. Heather and Tiffany even said that—" Her voice caught, and she cleared her throat, her eyes glossy with tears. "I may hate you, Hunter, but I don't think you and your sister are going around hexing people or cursing them to death."

Hunter's chest tightened. "You hate me?"

She wanted to reach out to Jax, squeeze his hand, and have him tell her that everything would be okay. But everything might not be. She'd done a bad thing. She only hoped it wasn't unforgivable.

Kylie's gaze fell to the ground, which was littered with cigarette butts and vape cartridges. "Yes." She shook her head. "No." Another shake of her head. "I know how I feel about Jax, but everything else . . ." Her hands turned to fists by her side. "It's all foggy."

She inhaled, eyes wide, lips parting with a grin. "You can help. You're a witch. Heather and Tiff said that you don't hurt people, and Emily's told stories about your mom. She helped all sorts of people. She's the whole reason Em's parents fell in love."

Kylie lunged forward and grabbed Hunter's hand. "You'll help me, won't you?"

Tears bit the backs of Hunter's eyes. "I don't always do good things." She couldn't bring herself to look at Kylie or Jax. Instead, she stared at Kylie's hand in hers and wished it would stay there forever. "I put a spell on you. I'm the reason you're foggy. I'm the reason—"

Kylie let go and shuffled backward.

"I can fix it." Hunter took a step forward, and Kylie stiffened. "I can take it all back. I can undo it. I just need your help." She knelt against the cigarette-and plastic-speckled earth, tossed the hall pass aside, and opened her folder. She pulled out the page of spellwork as crisp and dry as a dead leaf and offered it to Kylie. "Take this," she instructed, fishing the lighter from her pocket and holding it up as well. "And this. You'll kneel down, light the page on fire, and Jax will bury the ashes."

"Here?" Jax asked, jabbing an empty cartridge with the toe of his shoe.

"It doesn't have to be deep," Hunter offered, hoping his desire for this to end would outweigh his grumblings.

Jax groaned and kicked the debris aside before kneeling down next to her to scoop away handfuls of loamy dirt.

Kylie stomped her foot. "She put a spell me, and you're just going to dig a hole?"

"She put a spell on us both." Jax wiped his hands on his shorts and looked up at her. "It won't be over until we do this."

Kylie plucked the lighter and the delicate page from Hunter's hands and sank onto the dirty earth. "What do I have to do?"

Hunter dragged her sweaty palms against her jeans. "Light the spell page and drop it into the hole. When it's done burning and the page turns to ash, Jax will cover it."

It wasn't a complicated spell and barely required any magic; more important were fire and earth and the willingness of the people involved. That was also the trouble with undoing a spell—some people didn't want it to end, while others were too far gone to agree.

Kylie narrowed her eyes. "I'm only doing this because I trust Jax."

Hunter had been right. Nothing would ever be the same.

Kylie flicked the lighter and held the flame under the paper. It caught quickly and burned slowly, a magical slowness that cradled the page more than destroyed it. The rippling flames drew Jax and Kylie in like moths. They stared at the page floating between them on a sea of fire, unaware of the world around them.

Hunter stared up at the blue sky, at the icy white moon she knew hung above. *"Erase this spell. Set these two right. Scrub this magic out of sight."*

The flames shot up, devouring the page in an instant. Ash spiraled into the freshly dug hole, a cyclone of regret.

Released from its power, Jax hurriedly covered the remains. "It's over," he whispered, bowing his head.

Kylie drew in a deep, quavering breath, a sob escaping on her exhale. Hunter could already see the clarity returning. The clarity she had taken.

Hunter tucked a stray hair behind her ear. "Kylie, I'm sorry. I—"

Kylie's palm connected with Hunter's cheek.

The sound splintered against her ear as needles scraped her flesh. Hunter sucked in a trembling breath and covered her stinging cheek with her hand.

"There aren't enough apologies in the world, Hunter." Kylie surged to her feet and brushed the grime from her white legs. "This isn't over, but I have my coach and my team to think about. And they are way more deserving of my tears and my time." She swiped a tear from her cheek, leaving a trail of dirt in its wake, before stepping over the buried spell and charging back the way they'd come.

"That was fair." Jax stood and wiped the dirt from his shins. "Love you, H," he said, and jogged after Kylie.

Hunter's vision swirled with tears as she fished the to-do list and pen from her back pocket and drew a line through the second item on her list.

TWENTY-ONE

H ey, Whitfield! Over here!"

Kirk looked around the crowded stadium. It was dusk, but they hadn't turned on the field lights. Kirk guessed the Booster Club mommies wanted the prayer vigil candles they were handing out to look cool in the dark, but it was damn hard to find his friends in the gloom.

"Whitfield!" Derek Burke bellowed again. This time he waved his meaty arms and Kirk saw him.

"Coming!" Kirk shouted. He grabbed a candle from a frowning mommy before he started to make his way to Burke. As he passed a small group of middle-aged women shuffling their way into the stadium, he slowed, especially when he noticed Mrs. Ashley, Jax's Jesus freak mom, clutching her own special candleholder made in the shape of a wooden crucifix—which he thought looked more like someone had set Jesus's head on fire than lit a vigil candle.

"It's just so horrible," said one of the moms.

"It's Satanic, that's what it is," said Mrs. Ashley.

Kirk took advantage of the shadows and moved closer to the group of women.

"Jana, not everything is Satanic." A woman with the same brown skin and dark eyes as overly nice Heather Johnson wiped moisture from her brow and spoke not unkindly to Mrs. Ashley.

Kirk wanted to snort and tell her to get a damn clue, but now at least he knew where her daughter got her disgusting *I'm oh so nice-ness.*

"Latisha, I know you mean well, but you need to listen to me," said Mrs. Ashley firmly. "There is something evil going on in Goodeville, and we're only helping them by not calling them out."

"Them?" Another woman spoke up. Kirk recognized her as Tiffany Wilson's mom.

"Yes, Cathy, *them*. The set of twins in our town who worship Satan," said Mrs. Ashley.

Kirk woulda kissed her if she hadn't been so old and gross. *Now. Now is the time!* Old Mrs. Ashley's words were his cue. He fixed his face into a sad, stricken expression and ran directly into her. "Excuse me, ma'am," he said quickly and then he looked up like he'd just realized who she was. "Mrs. Ashley! I'm real sorry for bumping you. I guess I was too upset about Coach Livingston and wasn't watching where I was going."

Mrs. Ashley's expression was classic Concerned Mom. "Oh, Kirk! That is understandable. Were you close with Ms. Livingston?"

Kirk lifted and dropped his broad shoulders and wiped at a nonexistent tear. "Yeah, kinda. She was pretty cool, and the cheerleaders all said she was a good coach." *This religious freak can help show the town the truth about the Goode bitches.* He stepped closer to Mrs. Ashley and lowered his voice, but not so low that the two listening mommies couldn't still hear him. "Mrs. Ashley, do you know if *they* were there when Coach Livingston was found?"

Of course Kirk already knew the answer to his question. Almost everyone with a pulse at school knew the answer, but he felt compelled to make sure all the nosy mommies knew, too.

"I do know and I was just explaining to my friends that Hunter and Mercy Goode, and the evil with which they traffic, are responsible for the horrible things that have been happening in our good, God-fearing town, but I am having trouble making them listen to me," said Jana Ashley with a hint of righteous anger.

Mrs. Johnson fanned her face. "Look, Jana, my Heather was with the twins when they found Coach Livingston."

"As was my Tiffany," added Mrs. Wilson. "And neither of our girls were involved in any way. To even infer anything else is ridiculous. Both Tiff and poor Heather are traumatized. They aren't even *here* they're so upset."

"That's right, and also why I can't stay long," said Mrs. Johnson. Her hand went into her purse and brought out a tissue with which she dabbed salty sweat from her face. "I had to give Heather *two* of my Xanax to stop her hysteria."

"Excuse me, Mrs. Johnson and Mrs. Wilson, but I really need you to hear Mrs. Ashley and me. We would never think Tiff or Heather had anything to do with hurting anyone." The polite but manipulative words came easily to Kirk—almost as if someone whispered them to him. *Hey, I'm smart. It's just some people who think I'm not 'cause I can kick ass on a football field.* "But the Goode twins are trouble. I know Hunter made it sound like I tried to hit her, and of course everyone believed her because she's just a girl and I'm a big guy. But like I've been trying to make everyone understand, *she* hurt *me*. And Hunter totally knew no one would believe me, which is why she's getting away with it." He held up his injured hand.

"Exactly." Mrs. Ashley nodded vehemently. Her florid face was flushed and sweat dripped down her neck. "Please believe Kirk. I witnessed Hunter trafficking with Satan myself. There was blood *everywhere* in our garage apartment." She shuddered and clutched her candle crucifix more tightly. "Cathy, I heard the twins were helping Tiffany and Heather take equipment to the practice field. But I'm very much confused as to why. We all know the Goode twins do not get along with the cheerleaders."

"Yeah, ladies, please listen to Mrs. Ashley. Hunter and Mercy are *not* friends with Tiff and Heather, so whatever they were doing out there this morning didn't have anything to do with helping your daughters." *They need to keep their daughters away from the twins.* The words washed against him, a tide of hatred and malice. Kirk nodded in agreement with his super smart inner voice. "I know I'm just a kid and all, but I really care about Tiff and Heather and they need to stay away from those witches."

Mrs. Johnson sighed heavily. "Kirk, Coach Livingston's throat was torn open and her blood was drained."

"That is definitely part of a Satanic ritual!" Spittle flew from Jana Ashley's lips like salty rain.

"Well, whether it has to do with Satan or not," Mrs. Johnson continued in a reasonable voice, "it certainly is difficult to believe that two sixteen-year-old girls could do something so gruesome and then pretend innocence so well that they hung around the crime scene and helped our daughters move equipment."

Kirk lifted his injured hand again. "As hard to believe as the fact that sixteen-year-old Hunter Goode broke all five of my fingers?" *They're caring mothers. Make them listen.* "Hey, I know you're real good moms, and you'll do the best thing for your daughters."

Mrs. Johnson frowned at Kirk, and then dabbed her face with the back of her hand. "It's really hot and humid out here tonight. I don't think I'm going to wait for the principal to lead the prayer. I need to get home to Heather, but be assured, I will consider all that you have said."

"I will be sure to say a prayer for you and for Heather," said Mrs. Ashley as Mrs. Johnson walked quickly away.

"Mrs. Ashley, Mrs. Wilson, I swear on Jesus's cross that I'm telling you the truth. I didn't break my hand hitting the bathroom mirror—and Hunter and Mercy are Satan's witches." Kirk wiped away another pretend tear and stared at Jax's gullible mom beseechingly.

"Oh, honey, I believe you!" Mrs. Ashley pulled him into a one-armed mom hug—with the other hand she still clutched her crucifix candle.

"You know, I am starting to wonder about those twins," said Tiffany's mom slowly. "Jana, I've never known you to lie."

"As God is my witness I never tell untruths," Jana said quickly.

Mrs. Wilson nodded as she fanned herself with the vigil's hastily put together program of events. "Yes. It is odd that the twins are connected to almost all of the deaths in town. I never liked Abigail Goode. She was such a loner. Always acting superior to everyone else, even after she had those girls out of wedlock. Like Latisha, I am going to carefully consider what you two have told us tonight."

"You are showing great wisdom and discernment," said Mrs. Ashley.

Mrs. Wilson patted her flawless blond hair into place. "You know, Jana, I *am* going to speak with my husband about the Goode twins. Bob and his friends will know what to do. If those girls have any responsibility at all for these deaths they must be stopped and held accountable."

"It is always wise to get our husbands' opinions," agreed Jana. "The Bible made them our leaders for a very good reason."

"Exactly," echoed Mrs. Wilson. "It is awfully humid out here tonight. I believe I should go home to Tiffany."

"I shall pray for you and for your lovely daughter," said Jana. She gave Cathy Wilson a hug. "Please don't hesitate to call me if you need anything—*especially* after you speak with Bob about this."

"Oh, I will." Mrs. Wilson smiled at Kirk before turning away and said, "Young man, I appreciate your tenacity."

"As do I," said Mrs. Ashley after her friend left. "But more than that I appreciate your righteous indignation. *For the wrath of God is revealed from heaven against all ungodliness and unrighteousness of men, who by their unrighteousness suppress the truth,*" she quoted, nodding to herself in agreement with the verse. "Romans 1:18."

"I'm just so glad you believe me." Kirk wiped another pretend tear away, though it was just sweat. *Shit. I wish it would just rain.* He mentally shook himself and continued to manipulate gullible Mrs. Ashley. "I hope you don't mind if I tell you something kinda personal." Kirk shuffled his feet and looked down as he swallowed audibly.

"You may tell me anything," said Mrs. Ashley, moving closer to him.

"Sometimes it's really hard not having a mom anymore."

"Oh, honey, I'll always be here for you." Mrs. Ashley pulled him into another one-armed hug, but she let him go quickly to wipe real tears from her cheeks. "Now, come with me, my sweet boy. Let us pray together for poor Coach Livingston, and then I must tell you more about why I believe what you have been telling everyone about the Goode twins. God has touched me and through His wisdom He has shown me more than the truth you have been speaking."

With an effort, Kirk kept himself from laughing as Mrs. Ashley threaded her arm through his and began to tell him about the voice of God.

TWENTY-TWO

Nure-Onna's need to complete Amphitrite's command and claim her reward would not allow her to rest. The two tastes of blood had awakened more of her memories. She could now remember the scent of her son's hair—the way his soft, perfect skin had felt—the weight of him in her arms. He had been so handsome. So trusting. Unlike his Samurai father, he had loved her completely. He had not cared that she was only a beautiful servant. Even as she had taken him under the glassy surface of the ocean surrounding Kyushu, he had simply clung to her. He'd hardly struggled. Together they had let the peaceful turquoise waters close over their heads.

We were supposed to be together forever! I saved him from being taken from me! He is not in the World of Darkness, but the goddess knows where he rests! Amphitrite gave me her word. If I obey her she will return my child to me. So I will obey her.

Resolutely, Nure-Onna slithered from the offal-scented slime hole that bridged worlds and followed her moist trail to the creek. It was dusk, but that did not matter. She had not depended upon her eyesight for thousands of years. Her tongue flicked out to taste the humid night air—and in it she found traces of the ocean goddess, as well as another scent. One that was much less familiar, but no less distinct.

Feline.

Could that feline be the large Goode familiar the goddess had commanded she target? Eagerly, Nure-Onna entered the creek. Cloaked by darkness, she swam powerfully along the surface, her forked tongue following the scent of her prey.

"Hurry, you fool!"

Nure-Onna had been so focused on the scent trail of the feline that she hadn't noticed the ocean spray that drifted down from above. Startled, she looked up to see the diaphanous form of Amphitrite hovering in the night sky, stars showing through her body like crystalized sea salt.

"I come!" hissed Nure-Onna.

"Well, be quick about it! The cat is a swift huntress. She will strike soon and then be off!"

"Yesssss, I hear and obey," said Nure-Onna.

"The cat is there, under the willows by the bank ahead. You need not kill her. Actually, I command you do not kill her. Simply wound her. I prefer she make her way back to the witches. Hunter Goode shall begin to understand that she is being hunted. Move swiftly, demon! That is, if you want to see your infant again."

Nure-Onna did not waste time replying. The weeping trees were just ahead. Their branches, like long, slender fingers, stroked the surface of the creek. Before she reached them, Nure-Onna left the creek. Silently, she glided over the soft, spring grass, drawn by the sharp scent of the feline. On her belly the enormous serpent passed under the trailing boughs and stopped to allow her limited vision to become accustomed to the shadows under the tree's canopy.

There, crouched at the base of the trunk, was a large black-tan-and-white feline who had the long ear tufts the goddess had described. The cat was staring up into the branches of the tree, tail twitching with concentration.

Slowly, Nure-Onna slithered forward. Within touching distance of the cat she raised herself and held her hands before her like claws. She had planned on biting the creature, paralyzing it and draining it of blood just before it died, but the goddess had commanded it live—so instead Nure-Onna would use her purposefully filthy claws to rake the feline. The creature could live, but only just.

Suddenly, the cat whirled around. Her yellow eyes went huge and round, and her spine arched as she yowled dangerously at Nure-Onna.

The serpent was not used to prey that fought back, and she hesitated before striking the cat.

"What are you doing, you brainless snake? Attack her!"

The cat's gaze went skyward—and her yellow eyes slitted as she hissed at the goddess.

Amphitrite's words worked like a goad on Nure-Onna. While the cat was still looking up, she lunged at it, raking her pointed fingernails along her shoulder.

Above them, the goddess laughed and clapped as salt water made the air heavy. The cat screamed in pain, but then she surprised Nure-Onna again. Instead of streaking off into the night, the feline launched herself at Nure-Onna. She was all claws and outrage as she clung to the snake's torso, ripping and tearing at her soft underside.

Nure-Onna shrieked and bared her poisonous fangs, preparing to bite the creature.

"Do not kill her!"

The goddess's command made Nure-Onna falter, which allowed the cat to leap away and disappear into the darkness. Sobbing quietly, Nure-Onna touched the scratches that crisscrossed her pale stomach. Precious blood trickled down her skin and she caught it with her hand, lapping it from her palm.

"I shall leave you now. You did well tonight. Next time leave your den

earlier. I want that redhead, or the boy, or the brown girl called Emily killed. Sooner rather than later. I grow impatient."

"Yesssss, goddess," she said softly, still licking blood from her hands. But Amphitrite had already gone, leaving Nure-Onna to return to the soothing waters of the creek and make her way slowly back to the World of Darkness.

TWENTY-THREE

Mercy flopped down on the couch beside Khenti. "I'm so glad it's Friday. Today sucked majorly. Everyone except the cheerleaders were so weird. I mean, serious staring and whispering."

Hunter joined them from the kitchen with two big bowls of popcorn. She gave one to Mercy, and then Hunter took the second bowl and sat cross-legged with it in her lap in the recliner that was Jax's favorite. She glanced around before asking, "Hey, Khenti, where did you say Xena went?"

"She said something about doing some night-bird hunting. I reminded her to change into her cat form before she left," said Khenti around a mouthful of popcorn. "She promised she would not be gone long." He put his arm around Mercy and added, "I am sorry your day was difficult. The death of a coach must have been a terrible shock to the school, as well as to the town," said Khenti as Mercy snuggled into him.

"Yeah, but it's not like Hunter and I killed her."

Khenti frowned. "Of course you did not kill her. Your village must know that."

"Our town isn't thinking clearly," said Hunter after swallowing a mouthful of popcorn. "I overheard enough of the gossip to know some of them actually blame us."

"It's Kirk." Mercy snarled his name. "That jerk is spreading so much shit about us, the local farmers should hire him to fertilize their fields."

"It has to be more than just him, though," said Hunter. "It has to be the Nure-Onna. Rational adults don't blame sixteen-year-olds for murders unless there's other stuff going on."

"I totally agree," said Mercy. "So, now that we found its skin . . ." Mercy paused and the twins shivered in unison. "We know it's definitely a Nure-Onna. Do we know how to kill it?" She and Hunter turned to look expectantly at Khenti.

The demi-god smiled. "Yes, I believe we do. It is rather simple, really. It is a snake. We kill it as we would any other snake. We cut off its head."

"And you're sure that'll work?" Hunter asked.

"I feel confident it will kill the demon," said Khenti. "I have dealt with many demons in my world, and when they manifest in a form that is tied to the earth—like a viper—they always have some of the same weaknesses as the mundane forms they mimic. As your familiar pointed out so accurately when we researched earlier today— vipers are easily killed by removing their heads—and my khopesh is an excellent weapon for that."

"H, I think it's gonna work. Plus, we get to go all Buffy on the demon!" Mercy grinned at her twin.

Hunter smiled back at her and quoted, "'First lesson—stick 'em with the pointy end,' said Buffy."

"Yaaasss!" laughed Mercy.

"What is a buffy?" asked Khenti.

Utterly speechless, Hunter and Mercy stared at him.

Khenti looked carefully at each of them. "What have I said?"

Instead of answering him, Mercy turned to Hunter. "That cat had him watching those garbage reality shows instead of educating him on Buffy Summers!"

"That's a serious fail on Xena's part. Serious." Hunter shook her head.

"We're gonna have a talk with that cat when she gets back," said Mercy. "*The Bachelorette* instead of *Buffy*? No. Bloody hell no."

"A Buffy is a person? On the television?" Khenti asked.

"Buffy is more than a person," said Mercy. "She's iconic. She kicked ass—vampire ass, demon ass—didn't matter what it was as long as it was a big bad. We're gonna make like Buffy and kick that viper's ass." She paused and her gaze returned to her twin. "Ohmygoddess, H! You were going all Dark Willow!"

"That's ridiculous," said Hunter.

Khenti rubbed his brow. "Is Dark Willow another name for Buffy?"

"No!" said the twins together.

"Hey, Mag." Hunter's eyes glittered mischievously. "Maybe I was kinda Dark Willow, but you were *definitely* Cordelia."

Mercy narrowed her eyes at her sister. "Before season three Cordelia or Cordelia in *Angel*?"

Hunter grinned. "Prior to season three Cordy. Definitely."

Khenti sighed. "I am very confused."

"Tonight you start watching *Buffy*," Mercy said solemnly. "You can't go back to your world without knowledge of the Scooby Gang."

"We have the entire DVD collection," said Hunter smugly. "You've got some bingeing to do."

"Oooh! And we already have popcorn! Plus, *Buffy* is a perfect antidote to the awfulness at school," said Mercy, sitting straight up and bouncing a little on the couch cushions. It was so great to feel *normal* for a little while—so great to be with her sister and Khenti and laugh, eat popcorn, and talk about something as ordinary as Buffy.

Then Mercy deflated. "But first we have to figure out how to catch the Nure-Onna. I wish that damn cat would come home." She looked at Khenti. "Did you two have any ideas about that?"

Khenti shrugged his broad shoulders. "I assume that we would simply wait at the Japanese tree for the creature to emerge."

"That sounds like too much defense and not enough offense, plus that means we'd basically have to stake out the site," said Hunter. "That could draw the attention of people, and the town is already hating on us. We don't need them asking questions and watching us." Hunter picked at her thumbnail.

"And we don't know if the Nure-Onna returned to the Japanese Underworld, or if it's still in this world," said Mercy. She turned to Khenti. "Do you have any idea how long it can stay in this world before it dies?"

Khenti shook his head. "I would have to know how old it is. Remember, the older a creature is, the longer it can remain here without having to take on another body. My guess, though, is that the demon is old. The references we found to the thing drawing victims to it through the cries of a ghostly infant were ancient."

"Waaaait, I have an idea!" Mercy said. "But Xena will have to help."

"Xena?" Hunter's brows went up. "What can she—" Hunter's words broke off at the painful screeching of squealing tires that seemed to come from right outside the house. "What the—?" She stood and began to walk to the big picture window to peek out at what sounded like a major accident, when Khenti suddenly launched himself off the couch.

"Get down!" he shouted. He knocked Hunter to the floor and covered her with his body as something flew through the picture window, shattering it and raining glass shards all over them. The thing hit the wall behind the couch, where it broke a framed original of their mother's favorite painting of Athena.

Khenti was instantly on his feet. He checked Hunter first. "Are you wounded?"

"No. I don't think so," said Hunter as she picked a shard of glass from her hair.

"Ohmygoddess! W-what the b-bloody hell?" Mercy's voice shook with adrenaline. "She stood and started toward the pile of Khenti, Hunter, and glass that lay in the center of the living room.

Khenti held up his hand, palm out. "Stay back, Mercy! No one move! There's glass everywhere! I shall return!" Then he jumped through the broken window as he summoned his khopesh.

"Khenti's right, Mag. There's glass everywhere. Stay there." Hunter, who still had her shoes on, walked shakily to the couch. Carefully, she used one of the decorative pillows to brush glass from the cushions before she sat beside her twin and studied her. "Are you cut? Bleeding? Hurt?"

Mercy shook her head. Tiny glass fragments rained from her dark hair. "I don't think I'm hurt. What the hell happened?"

Hunter looked behind the couch. "The thing that came through the window is back there. Hang on. I'll get it." Hunter carefully circled around the couch and picked up something. "It's a fucking brick!" The words exploded from her.

"What?! How can that even be a thing?" Mercy was shaking her head back and forth, back and forth.

"There's something written on a piece of paper tied to it. Hang on." Hunter wiped pieces of glass from the brick and then untied the twine holding the sheet of paper. She lifted it and held it so that Mercy could read the Bible quote written forcefully in black Sharpie:

Exodus 22:18—Thou shalt not suffer a witch to live.

Mercy's stomach rolled with nausea as she tried to comprehend the hatred and bigotry that one sentence represented.

The front door opened and Khenti came in, still holding his khopesh—which disappeared when he tossed it into the air. "I could not capture them. Their vehicle moved too fast for even me to catch."

"Did you see it, or was it too dark?" asked Mercy.

Khenti blew out a long, frustrated breath. "It was too dark for me to see many details, especially as they had their lights off. But it wasn't like the vehicles you, Emily, and Jax drive. It was bigger and the back was different."

Hunter took her phone from her pocket, tapped it, and then turned it so Khenti could see the screen. "Like this?"

Khenti's forehead furrowed as he studied the picture of a truck. "Yes. I believe it was much the same shape and size, but as I said, it was so dark I could not see the color."

"Half the football team has trucks," said Mercy. "Show him a Jeep like Kirk's."

Hunter nodded as she joined Mercy on the couch again. "Good idea." She went back to tapping on her phone, then showed Khenti a picture of a red Jeep.

Khenti shook his head. "No, the rear part of it was like what you called a truck."

"Kirk is a dangerous douchebag," said Mercy. "But when it comes to self-preservation he's smart. He's probably behind this, so no way would he drive his own vehicle."

"You're right, Mag. He instigates and thinks he can escape the consequences of his douchebaggery," said Hunter.

Khenti looked around the glass-littered living room angrily. "I can bring the consequences to him."

"That would be great, but we really need to handle this the right way—the legal way," said Mercy. "Kirk has already proven that he's violent and dangerous. Deputy Carter knows he has a vendetta against us. I'm calling the sheriff's office."

"Now?" Hunter asked.

"Absolutely. Maybe they can catch Kirk and his football buddies carrying around bricks." Mercy took her phone from her pocket, quickly looked up the sheriff's department number, and called it.

It only rang once when a familiar, perky voice answered. "Goodeville sheriff's department, this is Trish! How may I help you?"

"Hi Trish, this is Mercy Goode." She tried hard, but couldn't help that her voice sounded shaky—probably because she felt so shaky. "Someone just threw a brick through our living room window. It had a threatening Bible verse attached to it."

There was a long pause and then Trish asked in a flat, emotionless voice, "Was anyone hurt?"

"No, but there's glass everywhere," said Mercy.

"Did anyone see who did it?" Trish's tone didn't change.

"No. Well, my friend saw that it was a truck, but it's dark and—"

Trish interrupted. "If you didn't see who did it and no one was hurt, what is it you expect the deputy to do?"

Mercy paused, shocked at the coldness in Trish. She knew Trish. Everyone in Goodeville did. She was a nice older lady who cried at dog movies. And now she couldn't be bothered to care about what had just happened to them? Mercy was too surprised to be truly angry. Instead her stomach hurt and she felt confused. "I, um, expect Deputy Carter to come by and make a report, and then see if he can find who vandalized and threatened us."

There was another long pause. "I'll leave him a note about it. I'd say you could see him in church and talk with him, but you Goode twins don't go to church, do you?"

Then the line went dead.

Slowly, Mercy put her phone back in her pocket.

"What happened?" Hunter asked.

"They hate us. The town hates us, and they're not going to help us. At all," said Mercy.

The sound of the back door slamming open had Mercy and Hunter jumping and Khenti lifting his hand to call his khopesh. Xena staggered into the living room. Naked except for the blood that dripped from several lacerations on her shoulder, she stood at the entry of the living room, swaying drunkenly.

"Xena! Oh, goddess!" Mercy shrieked.

The cat person focused her wide, yellow eyes on Mercy. She was panting so hard she was difficult to understand. "Kitten! It was terrible! The snake! Amphitrite! They . . ." She paused. Her face drained of color, and with a boneless grace, Xena fell to the floor.

TWENTY FOUR

"I really think you should go back to bed." Mercy hovered around Xena, who was lounging on the couch, wrapped in Abigail's bathrobe, lapping cocoa from a big mug. There was an empty plate of scrambled eggs on the coffee table in front of her. Khenti had boarded up the picture window and after cleaning and dressing Xena's wounds and putting the cat to bed, Mercy and Hunter had joined him to sweep the glass from the living room.

"Kitten, do stop worrying. I told you I have divine recovery powers. I slept quite soundly last night and feel almost myself this morning." Xena put the empty mug with her discarded plate and sighed contentedly.

Khenti joined them at the couch. He smiled at Xena. "You do seem well today. Shall we change the dressing on your wounds?"

"There is no need." Xena shrugged her shoulder out of the bathrobe to expose newly healed pink lines where bleeding lacerations had been the night before. Mercy bent closer, studying the wounds.

"Xena! These are so, so much better!"

"Yes, of course. Your Xena is much more difficult to kill than that

179

horrid snake imagined." She paused and shuddered. "And that water goddess." The cat person hissed softly before continuing. "She is an abomination!"

Mercy sat beside Xena. "Do you feel up to telling us what happened?"

"Oh, yes, kitten. I do apologize for how uncommunicative I was last night. What happened was quite a shock and I had to focus on healing myself."

Mercy took Xena's hand. "You really scared us."

"Yes, all of us," Khenti echoed.

"Well, I have returned to myself now and will be just fine." Xena gazed around the room. "Where is Hunter?"

"She said she had to talk to Kylie." Mercy shrugged. "She'll meet us at the Japanese tree later to help trap and kill that bloody awful snake. But first you have to tell us what happened."

"Should I not wait for Hunter kitten?"

"She said what she had to talk to Kylie about was really important," said Mercy.

Xena raised her dark, perfect brows. "More important than this?"

"Hunter said it couldn't wait, and I absolutely trust her," Mercy said firmly and then her lips tilted up. "Of course her absence means you'll have to retell your story. Do you mind?"

"It was a magnificent battle and well worth the retelling." Xena shook back her mane of hair and launched into her tale. "I had tracked a whip-poor-will to that lovely little cluster of weeping willow trees by the creek, and was just about to pounce when . . ." Xena paused as she studied Khenti. "I have just begun, but you look quite confused, Khenti kitten."

"I would not wish to interrupt you," he said quickly.

Xena waved a hand dismissively. "Oh, kitten, you may ask me anything."

"I was just wondering why you were not hunting your favorite prey, sparrow."

"Because they are all tucked away in their little nests at night. Whip-poor-wills are nocturnal—like cats—and their song makes them easy to track. Though they are not as delicious as my juicy little sparrows. But, no matter, I tracked the bird to a willow tree and was readying myself to silently scale the trunk and devour my pre-bedtime snack when the snake was suddenly there!" Xena shivered and Mercy tightened her grip on the cat person's hand. "The horrid snake demon raked its filthy claws across my shoulder. Well, that did not stop me! I pounced!" Xena lifted the hand Mercy was not holding to show that her usually perfectly manicured fingernails were jagged and broken.

"Xena! Your poor nails!" Mercy stroked her familiar's hands and shook her head. "I just hate that you were attacked, and I'm so glad you got away."

Xena's smile was feral. "Not before wounding the snake. I clawed her soft belly over and over as the viper shrieked and above us Amphitrite watched gleefully."

"You mentioned the goddess's name last night right before you passed out," said Mercy. "Are you telling us Hunter's banishment spell has somehow been undone?"

"No, I do not believe so. The goddess was not in physical form. I could see the sky through her wet body." The cat paused to shiver delicately again. "I have been going over Hunter's banishment spell, and I think that the transparency of the goddess's body proves it worked. Our kitten did, indeed, banish the goddess from this realm—but it only banished her physical presence and not her essence—her spirit."

"Xena, this is super important." Mercy spoke quickly. "Right before you saw the goddess did you notice the air getting damper? Or did you maybe smell the sea or rain?"

"Yes, kitten, I do remember thinking how humid the night had become," said Xena.

"Shit! That's it! The Nure-Onna hasn't been messing with the town!" Mercy stood and paced. "It's Amphitrite! Think about it.

We've all felt the weird humidity, especially when we watched people fighting downtown the other night. That damn goddess has been poisoning the town against us."

"I agree. It all makes sense now," said Khenti.

"Amphitrite is trying to cause Hunter harm," said Xena. "She and the Nure-Onna are working together. Well, that is not entirely accurate. From what I heard and saw last night, the Nure-Onna is under Amphitrite's command."

"So we shall prepare to battle a goddess today as well as a demon snake," Khenti said darkly. "My khopesh and I are ready!"

"Wait, if Amphitrite doesn't have a body how can we battle her?" asked Mercy.

"She cannot harm us physically without corporeal form," said Xena. "Which is why she needs the Nure-Onna."

"So get rid of the snake and we get rid of the goddess?" said Mercy.

"Perhaps . . ." Xena said slowly.

"Hey, how did you get away from the Nure-Onna?" Mercy asked.

Xena's smile was cat-licking-cream satisfaction. "Oh, kitten, the same way I healed myself. You do know I am more than a simple feline, do you not?"

Mercy laughed and leaned forward to hug her familiar. "I totally know you're magic! Hey, speaking of—now that you're feeling so much better we could really use your help killing the Nure-Onna."

Xena's yellow eyes flashed with anger. "I would love to sink my claws into that snake again!" Then she deflated and her eyes went soft. "But kitten, there are limits to even my powers. Our Khenti kitten must vanquish the horrid snake."

"Oh, no! I didn't mean that we want you to fight the Nure-Onna again!" Mercy said.

"No, you must stay well away from its poison fangs," added Khenti. "I will deliver the killing blow."

"Then what do you mean, kitten?"

"Well, you know that whole thing about how yowling cats sound like crying babies?" Mercy asked.

"Yes," said Khenti as Xena answered with a resounding, "No!"

Mercy forced herself not to laugh at Xena's offended expression. "Okay, so maybe cats don't sound *exactly* like crying babies, but do you think you could *try* to sound enough like one to fool the demon into checking you out?"

Xena licked her fingers and smoothed back her hair. "I suppose if it would help my kittens I could try, though I was very much hoping my help involved my claws. Where shall I yowl?"

"From the Japanese tree," said Mercy. "You'd be key in drawing the Nure-Onna to us, *and* you'd be using your claws to climb the tree. The rest of us can hide in the cornfield with Khenti, who will be ready to jump out and cut its head off—whether it's coming or going from the Underworld."

"Yes," Xena said. "I could do that."

"Awesome, Xena! That sounds like it would work." Mercy turned to Khenti. "What do you think?"

"I think it is a good plan," said Khenti. "I look forward to cleaving its head from its body."

"When do we leave?" Xena asked.

"Hunter said to give her an hour or so. She'll text us when she's on her way to the cherry tree, so—" Mercy's words were cut off by a knock on the front door.

Khenti was up and moving in one breath—his hand lifted to summon his khopesh. He peered through the peephole and relaxed before opening the door.

"Oh. My. God." Emily walked in, staring from the boarded-up window to the brick with the Bible verse that sat on the end table. She strode to the table and picked up the sheet of paper with the black words EXODUS 22:18—THOU SHALT NOT SUFFER A WITCH TO LIVE printed on it. She shook her head. "Why do assholes like this always use the Bible to justify their crappy actions? Like, did they just skip the whole part about loving your neighbor as yourself? Not to mention the whole forgiveness part?"

Mercy snorted. "I'm not in a very forgiving mood today."

"Emily, kitten, the Nure-Onna attacked me last night!" Xena said.

"What?! Are you okay?" Em rushed to the cat person and hugged her gently.

"I shall be just fine." Xena patted Emily's head before she licked her cheek affectionately. "I am already well enough to play a key role in the trapping of the Nure-Onna."

Emily turned to look at Khenti and Mercy. "We're killing a snake today?"

"We?" Mercy asked.

"Hell, yes, *we!* Technically, I know Khenti has to kill it, but we'll be there to be his backup. Nothing messes with Xena and gets away with it," Emily said firmly before she took the cat person's face between her hands and licked her—right on her nose. "Did that make it all better?"

Xena smiled. "Indeed, kitten. Thank you ever so."

"You're welcome," Emily said. "Now, tell me the plan and how I can help."

TWENTY-FIVE

Hunter avoided Kylie's hazel gaze and poked at the mound of cold fries, soggy with ketchup. She would be happy if she never again had to step foot in Shake It. The retro diner she used to visit for salty fries, dairy-free milkshakes, and friendly conversation had been bulldozed by the real world. She now came to the diner for huge helpings of *doing the right thing* chased with *cleaning up her messes*. It made her feel better and worse all at the same time. Kind of like exercising.

"You owe me a conversation," Kylie said, crashing through Hunter's internal pity party. "And, at the very least, a real apology."

"Last time I apologized, you slapped me." Hunter pressed her palm against her cheek with the memory.

Kylie crossed her arms over her chest. "You deserved it."

"I know," Hunter said, picking at her jagged thumbnail. "I am sorry, Kylie. Really. I—"

"We could have been friends," Kylie blurted, her eyes welling with tears. "We could have been—" Grapefruit splashed against Hunter's senses as Kylie shook her head. "You destroyed everything."

185

Hunter was back where she'd been the last time she'd sat in this sticky booth—hoping that she was still a good person, still deserving of friendship—but this time . . . Her heart squeezed and a sob bubbled up her throat. There was a universe out there in which she hadn't made such bad decisions. A time and place where she and Kylie were . . . *something*.

"We can still be friends," she offered, a smile tugging on her lips.

"We can't." Kylie blinked, and her tears were gone for good. "You did this. You changed who I was. You made me a mess and then you just stood there while I begged you for help."

I didn't mean to.

The words wouldn't leave Hunter's mouth. It wasn't a lie. Not exactly. But it also wasn't the truth.

"I didn't think about what would happen to you or to Jax." The words hung between them like the blade of a guillotine.

Kylie's eyes widened with disbelief, sorrow, pain.

Hunter pressed forward. There was no use in holding back now. Not after what she'd already done. "I wanted the power from the spell. That's the only thing I could think about."

Kylie wrapped her arms tighter around her middle, all traces of vulnerability and sadness wiped from her face. "You ruined everything, Hunter. You know that, right? Now we can never be friends."

Slice.

The blade fell, beheading their relationship. It was a corpse between them; a dead, rotting thing that would take years to stitch back together. Even if Hunter could, it would never be the same.

The bell over the entrance chimed, and Hunter felt Jax's presence before she looked up. He was a warm blanket, a bear hug, a sanctuary. Their friendship had changed, too. It wasn't gone, slayed by Hunter's sharp-edged lies, but it wasn't like it had been. It was brittle and soft. A stale saltine dunked in soup. Whether or not he said it, she was on probation.

As he neared the table, Hunter offered him a sad smile before turning her attention to the wooden bench on the other side of the window. A newspaper sat in the middle of the empty seat. Its pages fluttered in the breeze, the headlines blurring into a black cloud as Hunter's eyes filled with tears.

Sit next to me. Choose me. Choose me.

"Please." Her whisper struck the window and slid down the glass like rain. She wiped her eyes and blinked back the rest of her tears as she dragged her gaze from the world outside Shake It to her plate of untouched fries.

Choose me. Choose me. Choose me.

The laminate squeaked as Jax sat next to her, his weight squishing the foam padding, pulling her in. Had they not been in public, she would have let herself sag against him, pressed her damp cheeks into his shoulder, and thanked him for knowing her, for loving her, especially when she didn't love herself.

Hunter had won a tiny battle when Jax had chosen to sit next to her. Not a battle against Kylie. One against the world, this uncomfortable place she'd created and could not escape. But the victory would be short lived. She couldn't celebrate until everything was crossed off her list.

"You good, Kyles?" Jax asked, frowning as he plucked a limp fry from Hunter's plate.

"I will be." She offered him a half smile, relaxing for the first time since she'd joined Hunter in the booth. "Thanks, by the way, for earlier. Everything you said . . ." Another soft smile. "You're a good guy, Jax."

Hunter dragged her pendant back and forth along its rope cord. "I'm glad you two are okay."

Jax popped the floppy fry into his mouth. "Like old times."

Hunter hiked one shoulder. "Except that Kylie and I aren't friends anymore."

Kylie's smile faltered. "Don't say it like that."

"Say it like what?" Hunter asked as Jax reached in front of her for another mushy fry.

"All, *I killed your puppy* sort of sad."

Hunter frowned. "You did kill my puppy," she said, their beheaded friendship twitching in front of her. "I like you, Kylie. I want to be friends. I want you in my life."

Kylie shook her head, her strawberry-blond hair brushing her shoulders. "I can't, Hunter. Not right now."

"*But . . .*" Jax drew out around a mouthful of fry.

Hunter and Kylie exchanged a confused glance before blinking up at him.

Kylie's thin brows lifted. "But what?"

"*But maybe . . .*"

"*Maybe?*" Hunter parroted, pushing the plate of fries in front of him.

He licked a blob of ketchup off his finger before looking from Kylie to Hunter and back again. "*But maybe some . . .*"

Kylie held up her hand. "I get it, Jax. But no. There's no *maybe someday.* What Hunter did is serious. I didn't deserve it. Neither did you." She crossed her arms back over her chest. A position, Hunter was learning, that meant Kylie's decision was firmly in place.

"You two have history. You've been best friends forever. Hunter has earned your love and respect, but she hasn't earned mine. All I know about H is that she's manipulative and rates power over friendship, so what she wants right now doesn't matter."

Hunter swallowed. She'd taken Jax and her sister for granted. She'd been horrible to both of them, and as much as she feared their ire and rejection, somewhere deep down she knew they wouldn't leave her out in the cold. Eventually, after probation or awkwardness, they would welcome her back, hold her close, tell her they loved her and that they'd never fight again. But Kylie wasn't family. And Hunter had made sure she never would be.

Jax leaned forward and rested his elbows on the table. "If you knew everything that happened—"

"I know enough."

A cloud covered the sun, plunging the trio into a dull gray that described the mood better than words.

Hunter's phone chimed, a small break in the tension that gathered in the booth like a storm.

> H! K, E, X, and I r going to the tree. We need you! "In every generation, there is a Chosen One!" (It's us!)

Hunter sent a quick reply before clearing her throat. "Still up for that project at the cherry tree?"

Jax stiffened. "Yeah, totally," he said, brushing off his hands and scooting out of the booth.

"I'll drive." The scent of fresh-picked citrus floated around them as Kylie stood and swept her hair into a loose bun. "Top down, of course."

Jax halted mid-scoot and stared wide-eyed at Hunter. "She can't." His gaze snapped up to Kylie. "You can't."

She shrugged. "This is clearly a witch thing, and you said yourself that I would feel differently about what happened with Hunter if I knew what was going on. Well, here's my chance," she said, sliding her purse strap over her shoulder.

"You can't, Kylie," Hunter began as she followed Jax out of the booth. "It might not be safe."

"You know, being told I can't do something has never actually stopped me." She folded her arms over her chest, and Hunter felt her odds of success plummet. "And, not sure if you've noticed, but living in Goodeville isn't exactly the safest anymore, either. At least this way, I'll know what's going on and be better able to protect myself."

Hunter opened her mouth to reply, but Kylie spun on her heels and marched toward the door.

"Knowledge is power, H," she called, waving her keys in the air like a carrot. "Meet you at the car."

"Well." Jax tossed up his hands as he followed Kylie to the exit. "At least she didn't slap you. Again."

TWENTY-SIX

"Gross, gross, gross, gross, gross!" Emily wrinkled her nose as she followed Mercy, Khenti, and Xena through the dying boughs of the weeping cherry tree. "I thought the banyan tree was nasty, but this one is worse."

Mercy looked over her shoulder at her best friend. "I don't think it smells as bad."

"It doesn't. But the banyan didn't have that." Emily gagged as she pointed to the moist, dark hole that was a rotting, open mouth at the base of the tree. "I mean, seriously. That is disgusting."

"Em, maybe you should wait in the car. You know, like our getaway driver," said Mercy.

Emily's dark curls bounced as she shook her head. "I'm not waiting way back there with the car. You might need me." She patted her little Mansur Gavriel crossbody that looked like a cloud. "I brought my pepper-spray gun. Plus, I wouldn't miss Xena's performance."

Xena, who was wearing only Abigail's fluffy bathrobe, put her arm around Emily and licked her quickly on the cheek. "Thank you, kitten!"

"Okay, you can stay, but you're gonna hide and when the Nure-Onna shows up you *do not* do anything to it," Mercy said sternly. "You don't go near it. You don't call any attention to yourself. You're strictly on the defense. Actually, the plan is that none of us except Khenti are gonna attack it. He's the one with the sharp, pointy thing, the demi-god-ness, and the skillz."

Emily wiped her cheek and sighed. "I hear ya. I'm just here as backup. You been bingeing *Buffy* again?"

Khenti grinned. "We have! I began it last night! It is excellent."

Em nodded thoughtfully. "Yep. *Buffy* transcends worlds."

"That is exactly what Mag and Hunter and I thought!" Xena exclaimed and moved toward Emily again, but Em, still rubbing her check, sidestepped the cat person.

"Xena, you and Em stay back there for a sec. We'll check things out at the tree," said Mercy.

While Xena and Emily remained on the fringes, standing just within the long, shriveled boughs that used to be so thick and verdant that she and Hunter pretended they were stage curtains, Mercy strode to the tree with Khenti beside her.

"Will this tree make you sick as well?" Khenti asked her softly.

"It has before, but I'm ready for it." She rubbed her hands together nervously. "Still, I think I should try to give it a ley line boost, and then see if I can get it to communicate with me like the banyan did. It'd be good to know if the Nure-Onna is in there"—she pointed at the gaping maw of a hole—"or out here."

Khenti nodded. "I shall remain beside you just in case you need your hair held."

"Thanks. I hope I don't puke, but still—thanks. Okay, here goes." Mercy pressed her palms against the rough bark of the tree. "Hello there. You feeling any better today?"

The tree's response was sluggish. Yeah, Mercy felt nauseous, but she'd expected that and she shoved the sick feeling away from her and into the ground. What worried her more was the numbness that began to creep into her palms and crawl up her arms.

Mercy closed her eyes and reached down, down, down into the fertile earth to find the pulsing green ley line that flowed with emerald power deep below. She tapped into the familiar energy and pulled it up into her body. It answered willingly, chasing the numbness away from her hands and arms. Then Mercy imagined she was nothing but a conduit, a human garden hose that was attached to a massive source she directed through her body and into the sick tree.

And just like that—in the space of a single heartbeat—the hose kinked. The power fizzled down to a drip, drip, drip of almost nothing. But Mercy knew that even almost nothing could help the tree, so she pressed her palms more firmly against it, and with everything in her she willed the power to pour into the tree. It was only after her arms started to shake and she could feel sweat dampening her hair that she staggered back.

Khenti was there, taking her arm and steadying her. "Do you need water?"

She wiped her sweaty forehead with the back of her hand and leaned against Khenti, grateful for his solid presence. "No. I'm pretty good. The power from the ley line will barely move from me to the tree, which means I get to keep most of it. So, even though I'm sweaty and it's really hard to keep trying to force it into the tree, I'm fine. Now I'm gonna try to see if she'll communicate with me."

Mercy drew a deep breath and then pressed her hands against the skin of the tree again. "Hi, old friend. I'm sorry you're sick and I hope I helped—if just a little." She waited and felt the tree's sickness deep in her belly, but the numbness in her hands and arms did not return. Taking that as an excellent sign, Mercy continued. "I know something disgusting has come through you. I even know what it is." She paused and in her mind she envisioned the most detailed picture of a Nure-Onna that she and Khenti had found on the internet. "It's this thing called a Nure-Onna. It doesn't belong here, so we're going to get rid of it. Can you tell me if it's come through that hole recently?"

She waited with her hands firmly against the bark, but all she could sense was a vague feeling of discomfort radiating from the dank hole. What overshadowed everything was the sickness that lodged deeply within the tree, pulling all of its energy and attention inward. Mercy sighed and patted the tree. "Thank you for trying."

"Kitten, could it not tell you anything?" Xena called from behind them.

Mercy and Khenti rejoined Xena and Emily as she explained. "No. It's like if I was super sick and then I stubbed my toe. I'd mostly just feel super sick with an annoyingly sore toe. That's what the hole feels like to the tree. It's too distracted by feeling awful and struggling to stay alive. It's really not registering much of anything else."

"Shall we pour a salt circle around the tree for protection?" Xena asked.

"No, we can't because we don't know whether the Nure-Onna is inside there or outside here," said Mercy.

Emily shivered. "Which isn't creepy at all!"

"Em, are you *sure* you don't want to wait at the—"

"Mag? Xena? Hello?"

Mercy parted the ropelike branches, grimacing as dead leaves drifted to the ground around her. "In here, H!"

Hunter joined them and went to Xena, touching the shoulder of Abigail's bathrobe gently. "Hey, are you okay? Shouldn't you be in bed? Or at the vet clinic or something?"

Xena's laughter was musical. "Vet clinic? Oh, kitten! No, no, no. I have all the healing I need in here." She touched the place over her heart. "And I am just fine. Ask Mercy and Khenti kitten."

Hunter's gaze went to her twin. Mercy shrugged. "What looked like horrible gashes last night are almost completely gone today." Then Mercy blinked in surprise at Kylie, who walked through the branches beside Jax and joined them, gazing around with open curiosity.

Before Mercy could ask WTF, Hunter said, "She knows we're real witches."

Kylie fisted her hands on her hips and frowned. "Mostly because your sister zapped Jax and me with a spell."

"Huh?" Mercy looked from Kylie to her sister.

Hunter picked at her thumbnail. "I undid it. Yesterday."

"Too little too late," said Kylie. "Anyway, Jax said if I knew more about the witchy part of you two I'd be more understanding about your sister turning me into a defective Stepford."

Xena narrowed her yellow eyes at Kylie. "Well, kitten, I could be wrong, but by the tone of your voice and your posture I would say that you are not actually here to be understanding."

Kylie tilted her head and studied Xena. "Who are you and why are you wearing a bathrobe?"

"I am Xena, of course, and I wear only this bathrobe because, kitten, clothes are an abomination."

"Kylie, Xena is Mercy's familiar," Hunter said quickly.

"What's that?" asked Kylie.

"It is an extremely important being who attaches to a witch—or a family of witches," said Xena. "And who are you?"

"She's my friend," said Jax. "Hi, Xena. Hi, Khenti."

"Khenti?" Kylie studied him with open curiosity. "Are you another familiar?"

Khenti met Mercy's gaze. His dark eyes sparkled with humor and he shrugged.

Mercy snorted a laugh. "Not hardly. Khenti isn't from here. He's just visiting." She turned to her sister. "May I have a word with you? *In private.*"

Hunter blew out a long sigh. "No need. Jax and I filled Kylie in on the way here. She already knows about the Nure-Onna and what we're doing."

Mercy squeezed the bridge of her nose, unsuccessfully trying to stave off a headache. "Okay, I'm gonna trust that you had a real good reason for that." She turned to Kylie. "The Nure-Onna is danger-ous. It has killed at least two people—including your cheerleading coach. It attacked Xena last night. This isn't a game. Its bite is deadly. I need you to stay completely quiet and away from this tree—*no matter what happens*. Do you understand?"

Kylie's bravado deflated with her shoulders. "Yeah, I hear you."

"Okay, let's get this over with. No telling how long we'll have to wait," said Mercy. "Are you ready, Xena?"

"Kitten, you should know by now that I was born ready. Behold my magnificent acting ability!" Xena untied Abigail Goode's fuzzy flowered bathrobe and with a grand flourish tossed it to Emily. Completely naked, the long, pink ridges of the newly healed battle wounds were all that marked her flawless skin. Proudly, Xena shook back her thick hair and as the five *kittens* watched she lifted both hands dramatically over her head and spoke words that reverberated with power. *"To mine own form be true!"*

There was a flash of light and then Xena was nowhere. In her place was a huge Maine coon with truly impressive fur; long, dark tufts of ear hair; big, white fluffy paws; and long, pink scars decorat-ing her shoulder and part of her back.

As Xena trotted to the tree Kylie made a strangled sound and stag-gered back against Jax, who put his arm comfortingly around her. "What the actual fuck just happened?"

"It's okay. That's just Xena. Cats make really good witches' famil-iars," Jax explained.

Kylie's face was the color of curdled milk. "But, but, but—she was just a person."

"Actually, no," said Mercy. "She's never really a person. She's a cat who can take human form when she needs to. Hey, are you okay?"

"I'm not sure," said Kylie. "I may need a minute."

"Maybe you and Jax should go back to the car," said Hunter, though not unkindly.

"The Nure-Onna is poisonous. Its bite is deadly. I have to stay," said Jax.

"If Jax stays then I stay." Kylie's hands were back on her hips.

"Bloody hell," Mercy muttered. "Fine. We're all going to hide in the cornfield now and wait for Xena to lure the Nure-Onna. When it gets here, Khenti is going to kill it. H and I will be Khenti's backup."

"And the rest of us will be your backup." Emily patted her cross-body.

"Em. Seriously. The rest of you will stay in the bloody cornfield. If that thing gets away from us you run like hell to the car." Mercy looked from Emily to Jax and then Kylie. "Get inside the car. Lock the doors. And drive out of here."

"I'm not leaving you guys alone with a snake demon," said Emily.

"Its bite will kill you," Khenti said. "We will not be able to save you." Mercy nodded. "What Khenti said."

"What if it bites *you*?" Emily looked like she was on the verge of tears.

"Khenti won't let it," said Mercy. "Plus, Hunter and I have magic. Do any of you?"

Jax, Kylie, and Emily exchanged nervous glances as they shook their heads.

Hunter stepped forward. "Then you need to listen to Mag. If this goes wrong—you get out. We'll handle the Nure-Onna."

From the tree there came a soft, mewing sound.

Mercy looked over her shoulder. "Hang on, Xena. Wait until we're hidden and then start." She turned back to the group. "Em, you, Jax, and Kylie see that clump of willows over there between the creek and the cornfield?" They looked and nodded. "You three hide under the willow branches."

"It'll be hard to see what's going on from there," said Jax.

"Yeah, that's the point," said Hunter. "If it's hard for you to see—then it'll be hard for you to *be seen*. Plus, you have an easy escape back to where we left the car from there."

"Where are you going to be?" Jax asked Hunter.

"With Khenti and me over there." Mercy pointed. "Where the creek comes closest to the cherry tree. The Nure-Onna is most dangerous in or around water, so if she's already out here somewhere and Xena's calls draw her to the tree, logically she'll leave the water there."

Khenti nodded. "And if she's in the Underworld she will come out of the hole at the base of the tree. When I attack her she will head for the water."

"And we'll be there to stop her," said Hunter.

"Though I plan on cutting off her head before it comes to that," Khenti said grimly. He lifted his hand and called, "Khopesh!" Instantly the long, curved sword appeared in his hand, glittering dangerously.

"Shit. I may puke," said Kylie.

"Kylie, I like you and all," said Mercy. "But you should leave."

"No! We already settled that!" Kylie insisted. "I just need to breathe and process all of this." She made a sweeping motion, which included Khenti, the tree, and Xena. "I need a minute. But I'll be safe. In the cornfield near the clump of willows where you want us to hide."

Jax nodded. "That's understandable. I'll come with you."

Kylie held up her hand like a stop sign. "I can't breathe and process with company—that's why I'm going back there"—she jerked her chin at the cornfield—*"alone."*

Before anyone could say anything else, Kylie marched away from them, disappearing into the tall, green stalks.

"Jax, you're responsible for her," said Mercy. "But she should *not* be here."

"I know! I know! I just thought . . ." Jax's words trailed off and he ran his hand through his dark curls.

"It's my fault," said Hunter quietly. "I messed up."

Mercy looked at her sister. H definitely was stressed—and she was sad. Whatever spell her sister had cast on Kylie and Jax . . . "Oh, bugger! No . . . Tell me it wasn't a love spell!"

Hunter sighed and stared at her feet. "I can't tell you that. But the spell absolutely has been broken." She met her sister's gaze. "I told you I messed up."

Mercy's sigh mirrored her twin's. "Well, I can't judge you. I've done my share of messing up lately, too." She thought about how she'd hexed Khenti's dad—but this definitely wasn't the time to mention it to H. Instead she said, "I wish Abigail was here."

"Me, too, Mag," said Hunter.

"Meow?" came from the tree.

"Okay, Xena! We're hiding now! As soon as you can't see us you can start," Mercy called to her familiar who was perched high in the sick tree. "Em, Jax, be careful."

Emily nodded. "We will, and I'll help Jax keep an eye on Kylie—as soon as she breathes and takes her moment."

As Mercy, Khenti, and Hunter went toward the sound of water, Jax reached out and snagged Hunter's arm. He pulled her into a hug. "Don't let that thing bite you."

Hunter briefly clung to him and then she stepped out of his arms. "I'm not planning on it."

Jax and Emily disappeared into the cornfield. Mercy could see the stalks rippling like a green sea as the two of them made their way to the three willows grouped together—a tree oasis in the corn.

She, Hunter, and Khenti walked past the tree and into the cornfield that narrowed to just a few rows between the easement where the cherry tree was situated and the bend in Sugar Creek.

"There." Khenti's voice was hushed. "See the slime trail?"

Mercy shuddered. "*Sooooo* nasty."

Hunter nodded. "Yeah, and imagine how nasty the thing is to leave so much of that gooey crap wherever . . ." She paused and walked a few feet ahead of them and out of the cornfield to point down at something. "Yeah. It's definitely a giant snake."

Mercy and Khenti joined her by the creek. Discarded on the bank was an entire snakeskin.

Mercy kept her voice low. "Oh, Freya! That thing has to be at least ten feet long." She turned to face her sister, speaking quickly. "Okay, you have to hear what Xena told us this morning. She saw Amphitrite last night when the Nure-Onna attacked her."

Hunter blinked in shock and shook her head. "No! That's impossible. I got rid of her."

"You banished her body," Khenti explained. "Xena said the goddess was insubstantial."

"Shit! So, I got rid of her body but her spirit is still around here, causing . . ." Hunter's voice trailed off as she worried her thumbnail and then her eyes widened and words burst from her. "It's her not the damn snake! Amphitrite has been fucking floating around whispering crap to the townspeople!"

And that was when Xena began yowling. It was a sound that was definitely very infant-screaming-its-brains-out.

"She's really good at that," Mercy whispered as the three of them retreated back into the field and crouched down to hide behind a cluster of ragweed that mingled with the growing cornstalks.

"It's creepy," said Hunter, being careful to keep her voice low. "Like mixing a screaming baby with fingernails on a chalkboard."

"Xena is doing an excellent job. It should work spectacularly," said Khenti as he gripped his khopesh.

"That cat's ego is going to be bigger than her hair after this," said Mercy.

"I believe it already is," whispered Khenti with a muffled laugh.

Together Mercy and Hunter said, "That cat!"

TWENTY-SEVEN

Nure-Onna slithered into the hole from which the delicious scents of life teased her sensitive nose. It was difficult to wriggle from the tunnel-like opening to the mortal world. *I am bigger than before, when I was starved for blood. But I am also stronger. It is good my body is coated with ichor. That, with the undulations of my powerful form, enable me to move from world to world.*

But Nure-Onna knew she must be careful. As she slithered from the hole in the sick tree to the creek, Nure-Onna reminded herself to remain submerged and near enough to the muddy bottom so that as she swam her mighty serpentine body stirred up the mud, which hid her from any too-curious eyes.

She longed to follow the creek around to the field where she had made her last meal, but the goddess's disappointment with her when she hadn't scented yuzu Kylie again—or any of the young morsels Amphitrite had commanded she kill—was still with her. No, the sea goddess had little patience, though she had been pleased by her attack on the feline the night before.

Nure-Onna turned onto her back and gazed down at her belly. Its

201

smoothness was marred by scarlet slashes, which were sore and wept watery blood. She grimaced and forced herself to ignore the pain. She would return to the lake. It was closer than the field in which she had killed the adult, and it was a bright, sunny day. Surely there would be delicious young people at the lake, enjoying the exquisite sunshine. Surely one of them would be an ally of the goddess's enemy.

Nure-Onna was very disappointed. The lake was as quiet as a tomb. There was only one ancient man fishing from the dock. She swam under the dock and considered tasting of him, but his scent was not delicious, and she was unwilling to risk Amphitrite's wrath on such a dried-up old man.

She would go to the field again. Perhaps the young ones had returned!

She swam from the lake, following the creek that wound past the sick tree that held the tunnel between worlds. She needed only to continue upstream of the tree to the place where the field met the grassy area where the young people had congregated.

Beginning at her neck, Nure-Onna's body undulated in a lateral, wavelike movement that propelled her forward. Her smoothly scaled body lifted the mud again as, with renewed anticipation, she swam quickly, powerfully, *eagerly*.

Though Nure-Onna had to breathe air, she was able to hold her breath for many minutes. She was careful when she surfaced. Typically, she would only allow the top of her head and her nose to rise out of the water. If anyone happened to glance her way, all they would see was a young woman with dark hair swimming in the creek—though she was always quick about surfacing. As she neared the gentle curve in the creek that took it past the ailing cherry tree, Nure-Onna surfaced to fill her lungs.

At first she thought she imagined the citrus scent. It simply could not be yuzu Kylie! It was only Nure-Onna's desire rising from her memory that she smelled. And then she heard it! The young mortal's breathing came in gasps, sending the alluring aroma of sweet, tangy yuzu fruit out on the warm breeze—which carried it to Nure-Onna.

She slowed. Nure-Onna submerged again and slithered beneath the water—silent and deadly—until she came to a part of the creek where the bank met the water with the gentle curve of a woman's back. There Nure-Onna surfaced soundlessly.

And there, like a gift from the gods, was yuzu Kylie! It seemed as if the girl had emerged from the field, a willing sacrifice. *I will honor you by never forgetting the taste of your blood and the scent of your citrus skin.* After vowing to herself to savor every drop of yuzu Kylie, Nure-Onna surged from the creek.

TWENTY-EIGHT

They call it a *bloodcurdling scream*. But when a scream like that explodes in the air, cracking glass and setting off alarms, blood doesn't halt. It doesn't still, congeal, or curdle. It drains away completely. It leaves behind frost, tiny slivers of ice that find their way to the heart and encase it in snow.

Kylie's scream left Hunter bloodless. Her arms and legs were numb, frozen fleshy logs that wouldn't react to the command flashing through her mind.

Run. Run. Run!

And then she was off. Ice thawing into sweat as she raced through the cornstalks toward the scream. Leaves smacked her arms, scraped her cheeks, barbed by her speed and the shrieks that electrified the air.

Behind her, footsteps pounded the earth. The *thwack* of cornstalks striking bodies a dull applause beneath the bloodless screams. Hunter wasn't alone. She, Khenti, and Mercy would kill this beast together.

The cornstalks finally gave way to open air and the clear bank of the cornfield that sloped into Sugar Creek.

205

The Nure-Onna rose out of the water. Its long, black hair slick and wet, dripped rivulets down her bare breasts. Droplets ran along her soft middle, laced with claw marks, that swelled into the thick body of a snake, and a forked tongue slipped past its parted lips as its catlike pupils fixed on Kylie.

"Run!" Hunter shouted, but her scream was swallowed by Kylie's shrieks and the splash of water as the snakelike creature slithered onto shore.

Jax leaned out from the row of corn that bordered the bank, his neck corded with shouts of his own. Emily's body was tucked behind his, only the milky white toes of her shoes visible.

"Get back!" Hunter hollered, motioning for him and Emily to hide.

Xena ran past, her back arched as she hurled herself at the non-magical pair. She pushed her furry body against Jax's legs, forcing him and Emily deeper into the field.

Hunter heard Mercy and Khenti behind her, erupting from the corn and adding to the chaos, their fear and anger a living thing pushing at her back.

The Nure-Onna's thick body rose off the ground, curving, coiling, preparing to strike.

Kylie stood unmoving, her feet glued to the earth like a doll in a diorama.

Hunter charged forward. Her tennis shoes slid in the ichor, and she crashed into Kylie. She wrapped her arms around her ex-friend's waist and pushed her to the ground. The air fled Hunter's lungs as she fell down next to her.

Kylie screamed again, her arms and legs striking the earth in panicked bursts that moved her backward like a crab.

A shadow fell over Hunter as she scrambled to her feet. Slime spread around her, slippery and warm. With each step forward, her feet slid out from under her, bringing her to her hands, a macabre treadmill that kept her legs moving but got her nowhere.

Her pulse roared between her ears, a freight train willing her forward, drowning out Khenti's shouts and the slice of his khopesh through the air.

Hunter's legs burned as they flew out from under her for the hundredth time. Her cheek smacked against the mucous-coated earth, but she wouldn't give up. She flipped onto her back, strings of goo whipping the air as she whirled around.

The Nure-Onna's jaw unhinged, her expression stretching, distorting until Hunter could see only fangs like scythes and the deep, unending dark of the creature's throat.

"Hunter!" Mercy's cry was far away, tinny, a muffled shout down a long hall. And then her sister was there. Mercy stood over Hunter, corn silk hanging from her shoulders like tinsel and the vintage lace panels of her jeans stained with dirt and shiny with ooze.

"Get the bloody fucking hell away from my sister!" Mercy commanded, her dark hair wild around her shoulders.

She was a Valkyrie guarding Hunter, protecting her. Or was she there as an escort to the great life beyond?

The Nure-Onna's tail coiled, tightening against its thick body.

"Mag!" Hunter reached out, her arm slick and glistening with mucous. She grabbed Mercy's jeans and yanked. Hunter wheezed as Mercy's body slammed against her own.

Khenti's howl was beating drums, the strike of a thousand boots against the earth as he leapt at the Nure-Onna. He flew through the air with the ferocity of a lion and brought his khopesh down in one fluid strike.

The Nure-Onna's head slid off, and its body struck out, throwing slimy, silver liquid before it slapped against the ground, withered, and melted into the same slime that coated the earth.

Warm liquid washed down Hunter's arm. *Blood.* Her whole body ached, and she wasn't quite sure where it was coming from.

"Mercy, get up. I'm bleeding."

Her sister didn't move.

"Mag?" Hunter's heart pounded within her chest, vibrating every inch of her body. "Mag? Mag!"

A great roar of crashing ocean waves and a pealing laugh like screeching tires pummeled Hunter's ears as she called to her sister.

Amphitrite was there watching, laughing.

Khenti scrambled to the twins' side, a silver stripe of the Nure-Onna's blood splattered against his face and torso. "Mercy!" He lifted her, and Hunter was able to wriggle out from under her weight.

She squeezed her hands into fists and willed herself not to cry as she crawled next to her sister. The whites of Mercy's eyes showed beneath her half-closed lids, and blood oozed from two deep punctures just beneath her collarbone.

"She'll be fine," Hunter said more to herself than to Khenti. "She'll be fine!" she shouted at the invisible goddess of the sea.

Hunter swallowed back the sob that tightened her throat and stared down at her sister—her best friend in the entire world. "Mercy Anne Goode, you better not die on me!"

And then she took a page out of Kylie's book and slapped her.

TWENTY-NINE

Mercy felt the Nure-Onna's bite. When people say they don't feel anything at first when they're stabbed or shot or what-the-bloody-hell-ever *they lie.* The bite of the Nure-Onna was sharp and deep and it fucking hurt! But not as much as the lava flow of poison that followed it. That had been so painful that Mercy's world had narrowed to a weird gray tunnel and then gone completely black.

It was pain that brought her back to consciousness. Not the pain of another bite wound, but the pain of her sister slapping her—hard.

"Stop!" Mercy thought she'd shouted the word, but it came out as a broken whisper. Her body felt strange—heavy. She could feel her heartbeat—fast and frantic—and it was hard for her to catch her breath.

"Khenti kitten! Put Mercy on the ground over here immediately!" Xena was a naked goddess—her hair was a fierce riot around her face; her eyes blazed yellow—the pink scars bright against her pale skin. "Now! Khenti! There is no time to waste!"

"But don't we have to cut the bite marks and suck the poison out of them?" Somehow Kylie's voice sounded almost normal, though tears were pouring down her chalky face.

"No!" Emily shouted. "That was debunked years ago. We found out in biology class. It does more harm than good. Oh, God! Mercy, please be okay. Please be okay." Em stood not far from where Khenti gently placed Mercy on the grassy ground of the easement, well outside the circumference of the cherry tree. She clutched her hands together so tightly that her tawny knuckles blanched white.

"Mag, can you hear me?" Hunter was there, kneeling beside her in the grass.

"I can hear everything" was what Mercy thought she'd said, but no words managed to escape her mouth. How could they? Her neck felt like it had turned into steel. And, worst of all, her jaw had clenched shut so tightly that there was no way she could say a word. Her heartbeat still hammered in her ears, and then over it all came the sound of laughter—mean, sarcastic laughter.

Mercy's gaze lifted to follow the sound and she could see Amphitrite, transparent and floating above them. Her see-through body was bloated, like a jellyfish, with tentacles where there should be legs and living algae where there should be hair. The goddess was staring at Hunter as she cackled with glee.

"In the air. She's here in the air above us," Mercy thought she spoke the words, but they had no sound. They were only breath and whispers, drowned by pain.

Still laughing, Amphitrite floated over Hunter. Mercy struggled to shout a warning to her sister, but the strange numbness that was filling her body had lodged in her throat—damming her words.

"Mag, please be okay! You're going to be okay!" Hunter sobbed.

No, fool! Your sister will die, and I will laugh over her grave as you mourn her and everyone else you love who I take from you! The goddess gave the Nure-Onna's body a contemptuous look and said, *Useless! Why must I do everything myself?*

With the sound of ocean waves breaking on a rocky shore, Amphitrite disappeared.

"You must move, Hunter." Xena spoke solemnly in a tone that suddenly reminded Mercy very much of Abigail when she was super serious and/or super pissed.

Hunter looked up and must have seen the same thing in Xena's face that Mercy heard in her voice because she wiped tears from her cheeks, nodded, and moved so that the cat person could take her place.

"Here, Xena!" Jax's voice seemed far away. "I have your bathrobe."

"No need, kitten." Xena spoke without taking her gaze from Mercy's face. "I prefer to be skyclad for what must come next."

"W-we have to get her to the hospital in Champaign!" Emily sobbed.

"They cannot help my kitten," said Xena. "But I can help her. I *will* help her." Then Xena touched Mercy's cheek gently and asked, "Do you trust me, kitten?"

Mercy could not speak. She could not even nod her head. She did manage to open her hand, which Xena immediately took. Even though Mercy could feel the paralysis spreading from her chest through her body, she squeezed Xena's hand and in her mind shouted to her familiar, *Yes! I trust you! Always!*

"Excellent. Now, you must relax. Slow your heartbeat. Slow your breathing. I promise you that I will not let you die today, but you must do as I say. Breathe with me, my precious kitten." Xena exaggerated slow, steady breaths—in and out to a count of four.

Mercy willed herself to match her breathing to her familiar, and as she relaxed she felt the terrible paralysis recede—if only slightly.

"Well done, kitten. Well done. I am going to do a little spellwork that will give you even more ease."

Mercy's eyes widened as she thought, *I didn't know you could do spellwork!*

Xena smoothed back her savage mane. "Of course I can cast spells. I have been a witch's familiar for generations. And I shall call upon those generations of powerful, compassionate Goode witches now. Kitten, all you need do is to remain calm and when I tell you, breathe in as deeply as possible." She paused then before she added, "I understand you and the other human kittens do not like cat saliva, which is rather silly because it is quite wonderful and has many healing properties, but I bring it up because soon you will have to ignore your dislike for it."

What?!

Xena sighed and patted her cheek. "Do not worry, kitten. It will not last long. And I will not lick you, though I am quite sure some of my saliva will get on you."

Xena, I don't understand!

Xena waved away Mercy's frantic thoughts. "Trust me. Xena shall fix this."

"How?!" The word exploded from Hunter, who was sobbing by Mercy's feet. "She's dying!"

"Exactly," said Xena. "Which is why I must act quickly. Jax kitten, have my Abigail's bathrobe ready. When I have finished here I believe I shall be rather cold."

"O-okay." Jax's voice shook. He was standing near Hunter, still gripping the bathrobe he'd offered Xena earlier. Kylie stood beside him, sobbing silently. Emily moved to Kylie's other side and took her hand.

"I—I did this!" Kylie spoke through her tears. "I'm so, so sorry!"

"No, Kylie, the Nure-Onna did this," said Emily firmly. "You shouldn't blame yourself."

"Xena, may I help you?" Khenti asked.

"Yes, Khenti kitten. You and Hunter and the other kittens can aid me in this spell. Hunter, take her hand. Lend her your strength."

Hunter wiped her nose with the back of her hand and knelt on the other side of Mercy—across from Xena. She gripped her twin's hand.

"Khenti kitten, be at her feet. Put your hands on her legs. Lend her your strength," said Xena as she briefly met the gazes of the five of them, one at a time. "Everyone—each of you—set your intention, which is that Mercy will be healed. Think about sending her strength and, of course, love. Always love."

Then Xena turned her focus back to Mercy. "Ready yourself, kitten." Xena shook back her hair and raised her arms over her head as if she reached for the spring sun in the flawless azure sky above them. When she spoke, her voice wasn't that of a gentle, loving familiar. It was the voice of a goddess, filled with power and righteous passion.

"Goode witches—long departed from this world, but never truly gone
Hear me now—hear me true—I invoke you, I invoke you, I invoke you!"

A circle of specters suddenly materialized around them, with Xena and Mercy at its centermost point. Mercy couldn't speak or move her head, but she could see the spirits surrounding them. They were all women who danced around them, skyclad like Xena, arms raised joyously. *They're our ancestors, here to help!*

Xena continued as Mercy's gaze remained fixed on the Goode witches who had answered her invocation.

"I am Xena—faithful familiar, beloved by generations who follow The Path
I am Xena—willingly allied to this family
I am Xena—who will not let my kitten die
I call you now—ancestors of Mercy Goode—whose life has just begun

Lend me your power—this day—this very hour
Take from me what I give willingly
My spark of divine immortality
To Mercy Anne Goode I gift life with my breath
And stave off this terrible, untimely death!"

Xena began to glow—so brilliantly that she was even brighter than the dancing spirits. Looking at her made Mercy's eyes water. Medusa-like, her hair lifted around her. Xena's smile was feral. Mercy couldn't look away from this creature she'd known her whole life—though never comprehending the power she could summon.

"Now you must breathe, my precious kitten!" Xena's voice was a thunder-clap.

The magnificent cat person drew in a huge breath before she leaned forward, lifted Mercy tenderly into her arms as if she was an infant, and then the feline familiar bent to completely cover Mercy's nose with her mouth.

Bizarrely, all Mercy could think as Xena's face got closer and closer was *this is like the scary stories of cats stealing the breath from babies . . .*

But Xena didn't take. She gave.

With the sound of a gale force wind Xena exhaled the air from her lungs into Mercy.

Mercy inhaled the air. No, not air—diamonds. It was like glittering, glistening, magical diamonds cascaded into Mercy and then from there, like shooting stars, they exploded throughout her body.

Sensation returned in a rush, which is when Mercy realized *she hadn't been able to feel her body!* Now it was like what happened when she sat on her foot for so long that it fell asleep—then she tried to walk on it and it was nothing but pinpricks. Confused and in pain, Mercy lifted her hands to push Xena's mouth from covering her nose, but her familiar was already gone. She'd collapsed beside her.

"Xena?" Mercy gasped as she tried to reach for the cat person.

"Mag! Don't move! You could still be hurt!" Hunter clutched her hand.

Jax was there with Abigail's robe. He held it out and looked around helplessly. "She said she'd be cold!"

Emily rushed to Xena and took the bathrobe from Jax. She knelt beside the crumpled cat person. "Xena, I have Abigail's robe for you."

"I-is m-my k-k-kitten alive?" Xena spoke through chattering teeth.

"Yes! Xena! I'm here." Mercy reached out and brushed a mass of Xena's hair back from her face.

"Oh, g-g-g-good. Th-there you are, m-my k-k-kitten."

"What do you need?" Mercy said. "What can we do for you?"

"C-c-cold!" Xena managed between chattering teeth.

"Help her, Em!" Mercy cried.

"I am! I am!" Gently, Emily supported Xena as she sat. Em threaded her arms into the bathrobe and wrapped it securely around her. Then, through the bathrobe, Emily rubbed Xena's arms and back and even her legs—trying to force her blood to circulate warmth.

Xena snuggled into the robe, holding it closed all the way to her neck as she shivered, but still she managed to turn so that she could see Mercy. The cat person smiled shakily. "M-my k-kitten lives." She glanced at Khenti. "Y-you m-may h-h-have to c-carry me, K-K-Khenti k-kitten."

"It is my honor to carry a warrior such as you, miraculous familiar Xena," Khenti said.

"We need to get them home," said Hunter. "Mag, do you think you can stand, or should Jax carry you?"

"I can stand," said Mercy. But as she tried to find her feet the earth beneath her pitched and rolled like a boat on a choppy sea and Jax quickly picked her up, gathering her into his arms like she was a child. "Wait!" Mercy panted and looked frantically around them. "Hunter?"

Hunter put her hand on Mercy's shoulder. "I'm right here!"

"Amphitrite was here," Mercy told Hunter as Jax carried her back to Emily's car. Em flanked them, and Khenti brought up the rear with Xena and Kylie, who was still sobbing quietly as she walked at his side. "I could see her. She was laughing and floating over us—laughing at you, H. She's behind all of this."

"You're sure? I didn't see anything, and Xena didn't say anything," said Hunter.

"I'm sure. She's not done messing with us. She said she was going to kill everyone you love."

"No," Hunter said firmly. "She didn't kill you and she's not going to kill anyone else. Don't stress. Just concentrate on healing. We're going to stop her. *I'm* going to stop her."

Behind them, Kylie's sobs verged on hysteria.

"H," Mercy said softly when they reached the cars. "Jax needs to take Kylie home. This has all been too much for her."

Hunter nodded and looked up at her best friend. "Mag is right. We'll ride with Emily. Drive Kylie around until she gets herself together." She opened the door to Em's vintage T-bird and pushed the front seat forward. "Jax, put Mercy in the back. I'll get in with her. Khenti can crawl in beside us after he puts Xena in the front seat."

Mercy managed a half smile at her twin. "You're real bossy."

"Yeah, that's what happens when my sister almost dies; so don't almost die again. Just sit back there and keep breathing," ordered Hunter.

Jax bent and gently put Mercy in the backseat. Then he straightened and pulled Hunter into a tight hug. When he released her Kylie was there beside him. She stared at Hunter through swollen, red eyes.

"I'm sorry. I'm really, really sorry," she said between sobs.

Hunter sighed heavily and then pulled Kylie into a quick hug and murmured, "Like Em said, this wasn't your fault."

When Kylie stepped out of her arms she bent so that she could meet Mercy's gaze. "Please don't die."

Mercy had to force herself to smile, even though she felt too exhausted to make her face move at all. But she nodded and said, "I'll do my best."

Then the two of them were gone and Khenti gently placed Xena in the front passenger's seat before he jogged around to the other side of the car and squeezed in on Mercy's left side. He put his arm around her and Mercy rested her head on his shoulder. She closed her eyes and struggled against sleep.

From somewhere that seemed very distant, she heard Emily close the car door and start up the T-bird. She blasted the heat, turning all the vents to point at Xena. Over the motor sounds, Hunter's voice drifted to Mercy. She opened her eyes to see that her sister was standing outside the passenger's side of the car.

"Xena, what did you do?" Hunter asked.

"Simple, kitten. I gave Mercy the spark of my immortality." Xena had stopped shivering, but she sounded as weak as Mercy felt.

"Thank you, Xena! Thank you!" Hunter burst into loud, snotty tears as she put her arms around Xena and cried into her mother's bathrobe.

Xena patted her back soothingly. "It will be okay, kitten. We shall make it be okay. But now I am quite hungry and very cold. I need food, a hot bath, and a lot of cannabis."

Hunter laughed as she smushed into the backseat on the other side of Mercy. "Are you sure you don't want a sparrow or ten, too?"

As Emily pulled out of the easement, Xena turned her head and caught Hunter's eye. "Well, now, kitten. That would truly be lovely."

During the drive home Mercy could feel Hunter's eyes on her. She could even feel Em's gaze in the rearview mirror, but she was just so, so tired that all she could do was rest her head against Khenti's warm shoulder and hold tightly to Hunter's hand. She was almost asleep when Hunter's voice pulled her wide awake.

"Xena, Mag said she saw Amphitrite back there. Did you see her, too?"

The top of Xena's hair moved as the cat person shook her head. "No, kitten, but I was rather busy working magic to save our Mercy."

"She was there," Mercy said softly.

Khenti held her a little tighter. "I scented the ocean and thought I heard laughter, but I, too, was rather distracted."

"She was there," Mercy insisted.

"It's okay! We believe you," Hunter said hastily. "I just wonder why no one else could see her. Do you know why, Xena?"

"I might," Xena said and then added quickly, "but it is something I must consider, and right now I am entirely too cold and tired."

"Right. Okay. Yeah, we can figure it out later," said Hunter.

The rest of the short drive was spent in silence as Mercy stared at the back of Xena's head and wondered why the cat didn't sound as if she was telling the whole truth, and nothing but the truth . . .

Emily parked as close to the porch as she could, and then Khenti unfurled from the backseat, taking Mercy's arm and guiding her out as well.

Mercy stood for a moment. She forced a smile. "I can walk." She took a step and her knees turned into Slinkys. She would've fallen had Khenti not caught her. "Sorry," she muttered into his shoulder as he carried her up the porch steps.

"There is no need to be sorry. You are as fierce a warrior as your familiar," Khenti said.

"Xena!" Mercy peered over his shoulder. "She's not doing great, either."

"I shall return for her, but first, magnificent Green Witch and Gate Guardian, you need to be a potato couch," he said, opening the door and striding toward their couch.

Mercy actually giggled. "You mean a couch potato. A potato couch would not be very comfortable, even if we baked it first."

Khenti deposited her tenderly on the couch, kissed her on her forehead, and then smiled down at her. "Ah, I see my mistake."

From behind them Emily and Hunter entered the house. Xena

was between them so they could wrap their arms around her waist and support her wobbly steps.

"H, please bring her here." Mercy patted the cushion beside her.

They guided Xena to the couch so that she sat beside Mercy. She curled up next to her kitten and began licking her hands and smoothing back her untamable hair.

Hunter, Emily, and Khenti hovered around them.

Xena paused her grooming and looked at the trio. "Shall Xena now starve?"

"Oh, shit!" Hunter said. "No! Just tell me what you want and I'll get it for you."

"Yeah." Emily nodded so hard her dark curls bounced around her face wildly. "I can, like, go get one of your nasty tuna pizzas for you—extra tuna, of course."

"That would be almost as lovely as several plump, newly decapitated sparrows," said Xena. "My Mercy must have sustenance, too, and quickly."

Just the thought of sparrows and tuna pizza had Mercy's stomach churning. "I'm not sure I can eat anything."

"Soup!" Hunter almost shouted, then she cleared her throat and began again in a less manic tone. "I'll look in Mom's recipe book for how to make her—"

"Special soupy-bloupy!" Mercy said with her sister. Mag's grin was authentic. "That sounds perfect, H."

Xena frowned. "There is no meat in that soup. At all. I know. I often complained about it to my dearest Abigail."

"What if H adds tuna to your bowl?" asked Emily.

"Emily kitten, that does sound quite delicious. I wonder why my Abigail never thought to offer to do that?"

Mercy and Hunter exchanged a look that telegraphed *because that's so nasty!* Mercy laughed, but then she coughed so much that she gagged. H was beside her, patting her back.

"Em! Get Mag some water!" Hunter said. "And grab the first-aid box from just inside the pantry door. We need to clean up those puncture wounds."

"On it!" Emily disappeared into the kitchen.

Then Hunter turned to Khenti. "Go up to Mag's room. Somewhere around her bed you'll find a big T-shirt that has WHAT KIND OF ASSHOLE EATS A LAMB printed on it. We gotta get her out of those gooey, bloody clothes and then clean her wounds."

"I shall in just a moment." Khenti knelt before Mercy, who was still coughing and gagging, and took her hands in his. "Remember what Xena told you earlier? Slow your breathing. Match your breath with mine."

Mercy clung to his hands and gasped for air, then she slowed her gasps to mimic Khenti's. When Emily sprinted from the kitchen with a glass of water she gulped it as Khenti hurried up the stairs to her bedroom and returned almost instantly carrying her oversized sleep shirt.

"Better, kitten?" Xena asked, touching her cheek softly.

Mercy met her gaze. "Xena, am I really healed?"

Xena smoothed Mercy's hair back from her clammy face. "My spark of immortality kept you from death—and it paused the spread of the poison. You will live, though I cannot tell you for how long. You still carry the Nure-Onna's toxin within you, but do not fret, my precious kitten, your sister and I will discover how to cure you permanently."

"But what happens to *you* now?" Mercy asked.

Xena shrugged. "Now I am simply a mortal feline. I can still shift my form. That is something imprinted into my soul. But I shall live the normal lifespan of a magnificent Maine coon who will someday frolic in the Summerlands with all of her Goode kittens, including—eventually—you."

"Oh, Xena! No! I don't want you to die!" Tears spilled down Mercy's cheeks.

Xena wiped away Mercy's tears and then licked her fingers. "Not to worry, kitten. I do not intend on dying for many years."

"Khenti, turn your back," ordered Hunter. He instantly complied, and she and Emily carefully helped Mercy out of her vintage tee.

"Oh, bloody hell. My cool Pat Benatar shirt is totally ruined." Mercy grimaced as they pulled the sticky, ripped tee over her head.

"I'll order you another one," said Hunter. "Promise."

"Wow! That's amazing!" Emily bent to get a closer look at the Nure-Onna's bite.

"Amazing and gross?" Mercy asked without looking down at herself.

"No!" Hunter said. "Amazing and healed!" She turned to Xena and hugged her tightly again.

Xena stroked Hunter's hair but said nothing.

Mercy looked down. Just below her clavicle were two bubblegum-pink scars. They were each about the size of a quarter and raised. Slowly, Mercy's trembling fingers touched them.

"Do they hurt?" Hunter asked softly.

Mercy nodded. "Yeah, but not bad. More like bruises than bites."

"Here are some alcohol wipes for that—um—snake yuck on you." Emily tore open the pouches and handed the wipes to Mercy, who quickly cleaned herself before stiffly slipping out of her jeans and putting on her sleep shirt.

"You can turn around now, Khenti," Mercy said before she shifted so that she could face Xena. "These words don't seem enough, but thank you. I love you." Then Mercy kissed Xena, first on each cheek, then her forehead, and finally softly on her lips—just like Abigail used to kiss them.

Xena's yellow eyes filled with tears. "Oh, my precious kitten, you are most welcome."

"Please live a really long time." Mercy gripped Xena's hand.

"Do not worry for me. I am healthy and vibrant and shall live quite a long life." Xena's gaze shifted to Hunter. "Unless I first starve to death."

"Ohmygoddess! Okay! I'm making the soup!" Hunter said.

"I'll add the tuna!" said Emily.

"And I shall remain by the side of my two favorite warriors," said Khenti. "Should I put in the next *Buffy* DVD?"

As one, Xena, Mercy, Hunter, and Emily said a resounding, "Yes!"

THIRTY

Hunter couldn't focus on making soup or sit on the couch next to friends and family and watch *Buffy* like it was any other evening. Like they hadn't just come face-to-face with another monster and a vengeful sea goddess. A goddess that wanted Hunter's head on a spike and no doubt caused Mercy's impending death. Instead, she stood in the kitchen, staring through bleary eyes at the bag of rice and carton of no-chicken broth she'd mindlessly taken from the pantry and set next to the stove.

You will live, though I cannot tell you for how long.

Xena's words were on repeat, forcing Hunter to the brink of tears. The familiar had healed Mercy but only temporarily.

How long was *how long*? Twenty years? Twenty days? Would her sister collapse on the floor, writhing in pain, overtaken by the Nure-Onna's poison in twenty minutes?

Hunter turned on the faucet and cupped her hands beneath the cool stream. She splashed her face and imagined that she was back at Goode Lake before her birthday celebration, before the death of her mom and the horror of Polyphemus. Before Amphitrite and the hungry spellbook and bloody hands and lost lives. Before this day with the Nure-Onna. Before . . .

Another cold splash.

If only there was a spell to go back. If only her magic worked as it should.

"Xena!" Hunter shouted, drying her face with a kitchen towel.

The familiar padded into the kitchen, Abigail's bathrobe wrapped around her like a cloud. "I do not smell soup." She paused, the heart-shaped end of her nose twitching as she sniffed the air. "Or my delicious albacore tuna."

Hunter fisted her hands by her side and marched to the pantry.

Food?! Mercy was dying and a goddess was on the loose and all anyone wanted was food!

She swiped a can of tuna from the shelf and thrust it in Xena's direction. Her golden eyes flicked down to the can and back up at Hunter. "I became a mortal being, but I do still have standards."

Tears flooded Hunter's eyes, and she pressed the back of her hand against her lips to keep from crying out.

"Hunter?" Xena rushed to her side and wrapped a weak, trembling arm around Hunter's heaving shoulders. "What is it, kitten?"

Hunter doubled over, her heart an anchor sinking her to the floor. "You said Mag would die," she managed to choke out between hushed sobs. "That you don't know when, but—" The can of tuna slipped from her grasp and clattered onto the floor.

"You two need help?" Emily's voice came from the living room followed by Mercy's shout of "Try not to burn down the house, H. We've definitely had enough close calls for one day."

"We are well, kittens!" Xena squeezed Hunter a bit tighter as she called back. "Your Xena just foolishly tried to open her own can of tuna!" She pulled Hunter close. "We will not speak about this right now," she whispered, each word clipped, a sharp gust against Hunter's cheek. "Not when only a wall separates us from your sister, who is struggling to survive." She helped Hunter to her feet. "Dry your eyes. Make soup. Have a meal with Mercy."

It could be your last.

The words Xena didn't say hung in the air like smoke—a signal of the fire. A symptom of its damage.

Without her sister, would Hunter become ungrounded, float up to the heavens, and give in to the anguish that had already begun to shadow her heart?

Without my sister . . .

Hunter ripped the corner of her jagged fingernail, wincing as it tore into her nail bed.

No, that couldn't be her world.

"We have to try to do something!" Hunter kicked the tuna can as she spun back toward the open pantry and its shelves of spellwork tools. It shot across the floor and hit the baseboard with a *thwack*.

Xena stilled, her limbs tense, ready to pounce on whoever dared come check on them.

Hunter scrubbed her wet cheeks with the bottom of her shirt as she, too, waited.

Laughter erupted from the living room and both Hunter and Xena relaxed.

"We have to try," she repeated, her tone less insistent and panicked as fear and adrenaline ebbed and anger and sadness took their place.

Xena shook her head. It was a slight gesture that Hunter would have missed if not for the faint sway of the cat person's fluffy mane. "You know as well as I that no tincture or potion from this realm can rid Mercy of the poison from another. We can only purge these creatures from Goodeville, but we cannot undo what they have done."

"I might not be able to undo it, but I can make Amphitrite pay." Hunter's voice was dry gravel, crunchy and rough. "She's the reason this happened. She's the reason the Nure-Onna was here." Heat surged through her chest, rushed down her arms, and flooded her fingertips. "She has to be! Why else would she have been there?"

Hunter's spell had only bound the goddess's body, not her soul, her essence, the core of her power. But what Hunter couldn't bind, she would do anything to destroy. After all, without Mercy, her heart was gone from Goodeville.

Hunter pulled the folded to-do list from her pocket. The quiet night at her desk when she'd written it seemed like a lifetime ago. Since then, she'd carried the note around with her but hadn't had time to review it or feel the satisfaction of eliminating two of the remaining three items. Defeating the Nure-Onna wasn't something worth celebrating. Her next victory, if she survived it, wouldn't be, either. And then there was number four:

4) heal the gates

Without full use of her magic, Hunter had as good a chance of healing the gates as she did of saving her sister.

She rubbed her thumb along the thin edge of the Post-it. Maybe this list was never meant to be completed. She wadded up the note and tossed it at the open garbage pail. She missed. The paper hit the side of the silver canister and dropped onto the floor. She didn't need a list. She needed a plan.

"Hunter . . ."

She needed magic.

"Hunter . . ."

Xena's tone reminded Hunter of her mom—of all she'd lost, still had to lose, and all she'd found. The magic within her was dark and light, whole and fractured. It scared her and freed her and made her fully alive. She was one half of a Goode witch. One half of the magic that flowed through her ancestresses' veins flowed through hers, too. One half of—

"Oh, shit." Hunter groaned and dropped her face into her hands. "We're each only half." Her hands muffled her groan. "Why didn't I see it before?"

"Hunter!" Xena hissed.

Hunter peeked between her fingers. Had she eaten, she would have barfed.

"No, no, no, no, no, no, no," she repeated as she dashed past Xena and out of the kitchen.

Mercy, Khenti, and Emily stared at her as she rushed into the living room on trembling legs.

"I—" Hunter choked on the words, realization crystalizing as the past few weeks flashed behind her eyes. "I'm the Chosen One."

Hunter burst into tears while the *Buffy* credits rolled and the vampire slayer's theme song blared from the speakers.

THIRTY-ONE

The front door creaked, and the screen slammed shut as Jax entered, swirls of dark hair sticking up from his scalp like they used to before he'd learned the wonders of styling gel. "I come bearing tacos," he said, lifting a swollen takeout bag. "I even remembered to get fish."

Hunter blinked at him, her face hot with tears.

The smile slipped from his lips, and he dropped his arm, the bag hanging from his fingers like a pendulum.

"I did something weird." Hunter sniffled.

Mercy cleared her throat and picked up her bottle of water off the coffee table. She shook with the slight movements and water splashed out of the uncapped mouth. "Aren't you always doing something weird?" A weak smile twitched against her lips and dark bags settled beneath her eyes like shadowed crescent moons. "How does that make you the Chosen One?" she asked, leaning back against Khenti as if she could stay conscious, stay alive, through touch alone.

Hunter ignored how pale Mercy was, almost translucent, veins like blue tributaries beneath her skin, and motioned toward the kitchen.

Xena's nose wrinkled with a sniff as she stared at the proof only she and Hunter had witnessed. "Don't make Mercy get up. Call it out." She wiggled her long fingers as if she, too, had the power to summon it.

Hunter hooked her finger and signaled for the evidence to join her in the living room.

The crinkled, fluorescent-pink wad of paper stretched its thin legs and peeked out from behind the trash can.

"Come on." She sighed.

With a sound like nails tapping glass, her magically animated to-do list scampered out to Hunter's side.

"This is my list," Hunter said over the symphony of gasps that erupted from Jax, Khenti, Mercy, and Emily. "Apparently, I wasn't finished with it, and it refused to be thrown away." She stared down at the magical, spiderlike creature skittering over her shoes.

A splattering like a ripe melon smacking dry earth echoed from the couch. Hunter went cold, but this time her legs did as she commanded. She rushed to Mercy's side as Khenti guided her back against a mound of pillows. Her now-empty bottle of water rolled along the floor in its own puddle.

"I'll get some towels," Jax said, setting down the bag of food.

"Yeah." Emily sprang up from the couch. "I'll help." Her eyes were glossy with tears as she and Jax gave the Post-it creature a wide berth and hurried past Hunter and into the kitchen.

What happened? Hunter couldn't force herself to ask. She didn't want to know.

"The poison." Khenti looked up at her, his gaze searching. For what, she didn't know. "It—"

"It bloody hurt!" Mercy forced through clenched teeth.

Hunter rounded the coffee table and took Xena's hand as she knelt in front of her sister. Xena's grip tightened, willing Hunter to be brave, lending her the strength to do so.

With a deep inhale, Hunter shook out her free hand, forcing it not to tremble as she reached for the neck of Mercy's oversized tee. There should be scars beneath the cotton, two pink peony buds blooming against Mercy's white skin.

She squeezed Xena's hand as she hooked her fingers over the cotton collar. Yes, her sister was dying. But not right now. Hunter wasn't ready.

She still has time. She still has time. She still has time.

Hunter pulled down the fabric. Red lines like cat scratches shot out from the pink scars. Around them, crimson speckles painted Mercy's skin. The poison was spreading, wrapping around her blood vessels and squeezing until they popped.

Hunter bit the sides of her tongue. She would stay even and calm. She could grieve later, *away* from Mercy. Right now, her sister needed her to be strong.

"How much does it hurt? On a scale of one to ten," Hunter asked. Their mother used to ask the same thing. Hunter wasn't sure what Abigail used to do with the information (hell, she didn't know what she would do with it), but the question alone used to make her feel better. And that's really all she could do for her sister.

Mercy released a deep, pent-up breath. "It's better now." A weak smile curved her lips. "About a four."

Xena glided her thumb back and forth across Hunter's hand. The encouragement was just what she needed.

"You should call me Dr. Hunter," she said, gently smoothing Mercy's collar to its original position. "I mean, obviously."

Mercy's laugh was bells chiming—a celebration of life. It was the best thing Hunter had ever heard. "You haven't even prescribed anything."

"I was getting there." Hunter wrinkled her forehead and chewed the inside of her cheek as she thought about what their mother would have done. "A poultice!" she shouted, extending her index finger.

Mercy grimaced. "You are the absolute worst at making poultices." Her brow knit and her frown deepened. "The last one you made smelled like pee."

Hunter's mouth gaped. Her poultice-making skills were just as good as Mag's. "You have no room to talk, Miss Magic Cat Pee Tea."

Mercy sucked in a breath. "I will have you know that my teas are very therapeutic."

Khenti made a choking sound, and both Hunter and Mercy erupted into giggles.

It was almost like old times. Almost.

Mercy placed her palm over her scars, her smile fading. "I'm worried, H."

Hunter swallowed. "Me, too."

Emily and Jax shuffled back into the room, tentative smiles stretching each of their faces.

"I have supplies," Jax said, holding out a stack of dish towels.

"And I found this." Emily shook a bottle of pills and squinted down at the label. "I'm pretty sure it's Advil, but it looks super old." She scratched the back of her head. "Do pills really expire though?"

Hunter got up from her spot and held her hand out for the bottle. The ghostly outline of an A and a few numbers were printed on the torn and faded label. The Goodes didn't tend to use pharmaceuticals, so she wasn't surprised that their only bottle of whatever it was was probably older than she was.

"I have no idea what this is, but it looks ancient." She handed the bottle back to Jax before heading to the kitchen. "I'm going to make a poultice, and it's going to be wonderful!" she called over her shoulder.

She walked straight to the pantry, stepped inside, and closed the door. She needed a few moments alone, a few moments to figure out her future.

"It doesn't matter," she finally said to the rows of canned tomatoes on the shelf in front of her. "As long as I take out Amphitrite, it doesn't matter what happens to me."

But what if I fail?

Hunter gripped her pendant, hoping for a sign. None came. Her fate was up to her.

She swallowed and exhaled a deep breath between pursed lips.

"'Cowards die many times before their deaths.'" She whispered the Shakespearian quote aloud. "'The valiant never taste of death but once.'"

Plan made, Hunter sank to the floor between bins of onions and potatoes, drew her legs into her chest, and cried for her sister.

THIRTY-TWO

Seriously. After the tacos I feel better." Mercy swayed only slightly as she stood next to the couch. When her gaze met her sister's, she added, "And the poultice, of course. The Mighty Poultice."

"I told you I could make a poultice," said Hunter as she paused the current episode of *Buffy*. "It made you feel better, and it doesn't come without additional perks. You'll thank me when your hair is super thick and shiny."

"The hair on her head or the hair under her arms, kitten?" Xena asked with a glint in her yellow eyes.

Hunter frowned at the cat person. "Weren't you on your way to soak in a bath?"

"Soon, kitten, soon. Right now I must finish this Samhain episode of *Buffy*. It is my second favorite—after the musical, of course," said Xena.

"The one real bright spot in that disastrous season," muttered Hunter.

Mercy cleared her throat, pulling the focus back to her. "I'm going to go out to my greenhouse. Being around my plants is good for me, and I need some quiet time with Freya. She always feels close to me out there."

"Shall I carry you?" Khenti asked from the couch.

"No, I'll walk really slow. But thanks."

"Here. Take this." Hunter grabbed Mercy's phone from the coffee table. "If you start feeling worse *at all* text me."

"Thanks, H." Mercy smiled as she took the offered phone.

"Or if you feel weak text me and Khenti can come out and carry you back inside," added Hunter. "Basically, do not exert yourself. We're here for you, Mag. We'll help."

Mercy met her sister's Caribbean-blue gaze. Tears made Hunter's eyes swim. She looked pale and worried—and Mercy wanted to go to her and curl up beside her and be normal—binge one episode of *Buffy* after another until she totally forgot snakebites and poison and the terrible numbness that was so, so much worse than pain.

But she couldn't. She needed her goddess. Mercy had to know the truth.

"Don't worry, H. If I feel bad at all I'll text and then sit on my butt and wait for someone to schlep me back here." With a massive effort she grinned at Hunter. "But if you *really* want to make me feel better you'll get online and order me another Pat Benatar tee."

"You know they're hard to find *and* expensive, right?" Hunter said.

"Just hit it with your best shot," Mercy quipped before heading—slowly—to the back door. On the way through the kitchen she took a short detour to the pantry to get a chalice and fill it with red wine before she slipped outside.

"You're not funny!" Hunter's voice trailed after her—along with giggles from Jax and Em—and *who is this Benatar person* from Khenti.

It was one of those warm, fragrant spring nights in Illinois that made the backyard a waking dream. The lilac bushes that clustered like eager girls all dressed in their violet finery perfumed Mercy's slow walk to the greenhouse with the scent of her childhood. She hadn't lied to Hunter and the rest of them. She did feel better after she ate—better, but not stronger. Actually, she *felt* very little.

Her hand lifted to touch the poultice that covered the raised scars through her shirt. Her fingers could feel the ridges of the snakebite and she could definitely smell the nasty poultice, but she couldn't feel her fingers. Mercy prodded around her chest. She had no feeling in about a dinner plate–sized circumference around the bite wounds. Her stomach tightened with fear. *Am I dying?*

Mercy thought about her death as she made her way to her sanctuary. *Would it really be so bad? I'd see Abigail again.* Just thinking about seeing her mom lifted her heart. She wasn't exactly scared of death. She already pretty much knew what dying would feel like—mostly numbness that eventually gave way to blackness. She knew she'd been close to death when Xena had breathed a spark of immortality into her. *No one's saying it, but that's why I could suddenly see Amphitrite—because I was so close to death.* Drifting away to the Summerlands would be easy. *Maybe I'm still close to death . . .*

Leaving Hunter wouldn't be easy. Grief washed through Mercy as she considered how broken her twin would be. They'd just made up! And Mercy was all Hunter had left. Well, Mercy and Xena, but now Xena had an expiration date, too.

And Em. She'd just lost her dad. It would be horrible for Emily to lose her best friend, too.

Xena . . . Mercy didn't want to think about how broken her familiar would be without her—and she wasn't inflating her importance to the cat person. Freya had gifted them with their bond. Mercy already knew how devastated Xena had been to lose her precious Abigail. What would happen to the cat if she had to say good-bye to Mercy, too?

Feeling the weight of love and grief and loss pressing down on her like the hand of a giant, Mercy opened the door to her greenhouse. She didn't turn on the light. She didn't need to. She could close her eyes and still find everything she needed by scent and touch and memory. She walked down the center row, flanked by green and growing things, and the hand that weighed her down eased a little.

Mercy went to the small altar she kept at the far end of the structure. It wasn't a spellwork altar. It was just a simple little shrine on a wooden strip Abigail had instructed be built as a window ledge. On it Mercy honored her goddess, Freya. There was a tall red prayer candle she'd hand-poured with Abigail and scented with apple and cinnamon. She placed the chalice of wine in front of the candle. Beside the candle was a little bronze chariot that was pulled by two big forest cats. Mercy smiled and touched each cat gently; they always reminded her of Xena. Resting before the chariot was a single falcon feather—the goddess's favorite bird. To the side of the ledge was a box of wooden matches, decorated with a fat, red apple.

Moving stiffly, Mercy dragged a stool over to the altar. She had to sit quickly, as her vision rippled and dizziness pulsed with her labored heartbeat. She didn't panic, though. Mercy pretended that Xena and Khenti and Hunter were with her, telling her to concentrate on her breathing—to still herself, to ground herself. She breathed slowly, deeply, in and out to a count of four until the room stopped swimming. Then Mercy reached for the box of matches. She lit one and touched it to the ready wick, which flamed willingly.

Mercy closed her eyes and concentrated on the ley lines beneath her. She could feel them, pulsing emerald and moss, lime and fern deep underground. Their energy was her lifeblood. She focused on that energy, and for the first time felt it beating in tandem with her heart. Mercy called to that energy, willing it to pour into her body.

It answered sluggishly, more sticky tar than readily flowing water. She could feel its warmth and power, pulsing just out of her reach. Mercy drew another deep breath and on her exhale spoke.

"I am Mercy Goode, Green Witch, daughter of the magnificent Kitchen Witch Abigail Goode, sister to the powerful Cosmic Witch Hunter Goode. As is my birthright, I draw you to me and ask that you lend me your strength to invoke my goddess, Freya—Mistress of Cats, Goddess of Love and Fertility, Divine Earth Goddess, Fierce War Goddess, She to whom I have dedicated my Path. Aid me in reaching my Freya because I have no strength left to call Her. So mote it be."

Nothing happened. Not one thing. Mercy could still feel the ley line power. If she closed her eyes she could even see it—fat and green and strong. But for the first time in her life, it wouldn't come to her.

Mercy's shoulders slumped. She covered her face with her hands and a sob escaped her lips. "I don't understand," she whispered brokenly. "What have I done wrong?"

Wrong, my precious Green Witch? I would say what you have done is more unusual than wrong.

With a gasp, Mercy looked up to see her goddess hovering before her. Freya wore a bright red dress that was covered in forest cats embroidered in glistening silver thread. Around her shoulders rested a cloak of falcon feathers that moved in a preternatural wind as if there were thousands of wings that kept the goddess aloft. And around her neck was the famous Brísingamen, a silver torque encrusted with jewels that glistened with an otherworldly beauty.

Tears spilled down Mercy's pallid cheeks. "Freya! Thank you for hearing me! Thank you for coming to me!"

Freya's smile was gentle. *You are mine, Mercy Goode. I always hear you—especially as you near death.*

Dread made Mercy's tears fall faster, and she wiped at them, willing them to stop. "S-so I'm dying?"

You already knew that when you summoned me, young witch, said the goddess.

Mercy swallowed several times and blinked until her vision cleared and her tears completely dried. She took a deep breath. *Be brave! Be strong!* "Am I going to die because my magic won't work? Is that why I can't heal?"

No, dear one. You die because of the poison in your body. Xena's attempt to save you was valiant, but she knew it was temporary. The Nure-Onna's bite is deadly. Not even a goddess can change that.

Mercy nodded slowly as the truth seeped through her veins. "I'm not sorry. It was going to kill Hunter."

Yes, said the goddess.

Mercy met Freya's cornflower-blue gaze. "There is nothing I can do to stop my death."

Though Mercy didn't frame it as a question, her goddess answered. *No, there is nothing you can do.*

"How—how long do I have?"

You know that answer, dear one, said the goddess.

"So, not long." Mercy drew in another long, shaky breath. "Will my mom be there with you to welcome me to the Summerlands?"

Yes, dear one, Abigail Goode and I will happily welcome you to the Summerlands. Your mother will braid flowers into your hair and you will feast at the table with your ancestresses, who will rejoice at your arrival. The goddess paused. *But there is something you must know first.*

Mercy's stomach tightened. "Is it something terrible?"

The goddess's full lips twitched, like she might almost smile. *Yes, I believe* terrible *is an appropriate word for it—though it is not an insurmountable terror. Do you recall Upuant, Father of Khenti Amenti, and the demi-god you hexed in the Egyptian Underworld?*

For a moment Mercy was too shocked to speak, and then she stuttered. "Y-yeah. I remember him. He was awful to Khenti. He totally deserved to be hexed."

The goddess cocked her head to the side, causing her golden hair to wash around her waist. *Did he? Or did your anger cause you to meddle in another world and another family?*

"I thought it was the right thing to do!"

Freya's eyes flashed. *Speak the truth to your goddess!*

Mercy cringed and had to look away from Freya's anger. When she spoke her voice was small and hesitant. "I was really mad. Upuant hurt Khenti for no reason. I just—I just wanted to do something to help."

To help or to punish? Search your heart, Green Witch, and answer with honesty.

Mercy deflated. "I wanted to punish him."

Freya nodded. *Which you did, and by doing so you bound your soul to the hex.*

Mercy fought against the tears that stung her nose like bees. "Do I go to a hell now?"

You would, indeed, have to enter Niflheim, Land of Mist and World of the Dead, until the hex runs its course—which could be rather a long time, as Upuant is a demi-god and extremely long-lived, as well as the type of being who does not easily learn from his mistakes.

Mercy pushed her hair back behind her ears with a trembling hand. "I understand. I'll take my punishment."

There is an alternative, said the goddess.

Hope fluttered around in Mercy's stomach, so breathless and desperate that she thought she might puke. "Whatever it is, if I can I'll do it."

It is quite simple, really. At any time before you breathe your last breath, simply call my name thrice and then speak your sister's full name thrice as well. By doing that you will be asking that I release your soul from being bound to the hex, but in turn the binding shall shift to your sister. I will honor your request and allow you to enter the Summerlands.

Mercy stared at her goddess. "But what happens to Hunter?"

That depends upon how long Upuant lives. The hex will run its course and be broken at his death. Or, of course, should he atone for his mistakes, then that, too, would break the hex and free your sister's soul—just as either would free you from Niflheim.

Mercy blurted the first question that came to her mind. "How long do demi-gods live?"

Freya shrugged smooth, porcelain shoulders. *Upuant has lived for several millennia. Unless a more powerful being destroys him, he could live for several more millennia.*

"So, definitely longer than a human lifespan," Mercy muttered.

Again, the goddess's lips twitched. *Yes.*

"I have a terrible choice to make!"

Hexes are terrible things, Mercy Anne Goode, especially in the hands of a powerful, angry witch. Her expression softened. *Choose wisely, my Green Witch. Niflheim is unpleasant.*

The giant's hand of grief and guilt returned to press down on Mercy. "I've made a lot of mistakes."

Yes, but it is difficult to learn without making mistakes, said Freya.

Mercy sighed. "Well, yeah, but I was supposed to have a bunch of years for that kind of learning."

Life often surprises me. I shall look forward to your decision. Know that, wherever you are, whatever you choose—you will always be favored by me. Now fare thee well, my dear one. The goddess lifted her arms and the cloak of falcon feathers rippled.

"Freya, would you tell my mom that I love her, please?"

Freya smiled. *I shall, indeed, young witch. But like me, Abigail Goode has never doubted your love. We have only, occasionally, doubted your judgment.* Then the cloak of feathers exploded, leaving a magnificent falcon who soared up through the roof of the greenhouse and disappeared into the stars.

Mercy blew out the candle and with heavy feet made her way wearily through the night-damp grass to the back door of her home. She paused there, invisible in the velvet darkness, as she looked through the glass door into her brightly lit house. She could hear the murmur of the television and Khenti's distant laughter, echoed by Emily and Jax. Hunter walked from the living room through the breakfast nook and into the kitchen, where Mercy watched her open the fridge and cupboards, pulling out coconut milk, cocoa, and marshmallows for hot chocolate. Mercy didn't realize she was crying until tears soaked her shirt.

She didn't bother to wipe her cheeks.

"Xena, I need you in here!" Hunter called.

Xena hurried into the kitchen. Color had returned to the cat person's cheeks, and her mass of hair looked almost neat. She perched on the edge of the counter. "Yes, kitten?"

Hunter put down the bag of marshmallows and faced Xena. It was then that Mercy saw that her sister was crying, too—silently, steadily.

"Oh, sweet kitten . . ." Xena held her arms out and Hunter stepped into them.

"Is she really dying?" Hunter sobbed.

Xena stroked Hunter's hair. "Yes, kitten. Our Mercy is dying."

Mercy must have made a noise because Hunter pulled out of Xena's arms and hurried to the door. She opened it and stared at Mercy, who wasn't really sure what to do.

"Oh, Mag. I—I didn't know you were there!"

Mercy stepped into the room and the twins came together, clinging to each other.

"I'm sorry you heard that!" Hunter spoke between sobs. "I'm so sorry!"

Mercy held tightly to her twin. "I already knew, H. I already knew . . ." She drew a deep breath. "But now I also know what I have to do."

Hunter stepped back and wiped her face with her sleeve. "What does that mean?"

"It's just that I talked with Freya. She's who told me I'm dying. You don't need to worry about anything. It's going to be okay. I promise." Mercy hugged her sister again and Xena joined them, putting her arms around her two girls.

"It is good that the goddess is with you, my precious kitten. Freya will be near you from now on. I, too, can feel her watching presence," said Xena.

"Is all well?" Khenti approached them slowly from the living room, his brown eyes dark with concern.

243

Mercy studied his kind face. Her heart seemed to clench. She didn't want to leave him, either. She held out her hand and Khenti took it. "Well, I've been better, but everything will be okay. Eventually."

"Would you like to continue watching *Buffy,* or is there something else you'd rather do?" Khenti asked.

She could feel her sister's worried gaze, as well as how closely her familiar watched her. *What do I want to do? I don't have much time . . .* And that's when Mercy realized she was exactly where she wanted to be, with the people she loved most in this world. She wanted to say good-bye to each of them in her own way in the time she had left. She smiled and squeezed Khenti's hand. "I want to watch *Buffy* with all of you, drink hot cocoa, and eat popcorn that is way too buttery."

"Done!" said Hunter, who kissed Mercy noisily on her tear-streaked cheek.

"That sounds like a lovely evening." Xena licked Mercy's other cheek. "You may want to wash your face first, though, kitten. You're rather salty." Xena tossed her hair and walked toward the living room, calling, "Emily kitten! Get out the next *Buffy* DVD and call your mother. You shall spend the night and we all shall binge! I certainly hope you brought the medication that suppresses the effects of my mighty dander. I would not want you to . . ." Her voice faded out of their hearing.

Together Mercy and Hunter shared a look as they said, "That cat."

THIRTY-THREE

I'm here and I brought Mr. Peppermint Schnapps with me. Who wants a shot?" Kirk lifted the large bottle he'd *borrowed* from his dad's liquor cabinet to a rousing round of cheers. His smile was self-satisfied as he made his way from the Goode Lake parking lot to the little beach next to the dock, where most of the varsity football team was already halfway through a PBR keg. There was a big bonfire burning by the water. Several of the pom squad girls—less cool than cheerleaders, but at least their uniforms were butt-showing short—were sitting on blankets near the water.

"Whitfield! Bring that bottle over here." Derek Burke waved him over to a group of guys hanging at the keg.

Like a returning war hero, Kirk sauntered to his men, who all turned to welcome him. The weirdness from practice when old man Coach kicked him out had been washed away by beer and short attention spans. He was, once again, their leader.

"Um, did anyone bring any wine coolers?" From the beach where the pom girls dangled their bare toes into the water, their captain, a blue-eyed brunette whose nickname was Kitty—like a damn cat—frowned at him.

"Like I'm *anyone*?" Kirk said sarcastically.

Kitty rolled her eyes. "Whatever, Whitfield. I was just asking. That beer is *not* cold and peppermint schnapps is nasty."

"That's for sure," echoed several of the other pom girls as they nodded in agreement and looked bored.

Bitches—every one of them. Like my old man says, nothing is ever enough for a complaining woman.

"Sorry, Your Highness," Kirk said. "I didn't realize PBR and schnapps weren't good enough for you."

Kitty looked him up and down before saying, "That doesn't surprise me."

There are drugs in the Jeep, Kirk's subconscious whispered wise words to him. "Well, *Kitty*." He exaggerated her nickname. "How 'bout a little oxy? Got a fistful of it in my Jeep. Perks from my battle wounds." He lifted his cast-swathed hand.

Kitty's perfect nose wrinkled. "Eww. Oxy is, like, *super* addictive."

A redhead named Colleen, who had just moved to Goodeville the summer before, spoke up. "Yeah, my mom's a doctor. Opioid addiction is no joke. It kills. And, ugh! Why is it suddenly so humid out here? I can practically taste water in the air."

"Right?" Kitty lifted her hair from her neck and sighed. "This weather is terrible for my hair." She shifted her frown to Kirk. "Whitfield, we do not do oxy."

You weren't being serious, his wise subconscious shouted at him.

Kirk raised his hands. "Hey, don't shoot the messenger. Plus, I was just kidding."

Kitty rolled her eyes again. "Not funny, Whitfield. Coach Livingston *was just killed!* We're all upset and your stupid jokes do not help."

Kirk swiped an almost full plastic cup of beer from Jarod Frazier's hand. As it sloshed onto the ground he strode to the pom girls. "Hey, sorry. I didn't mean anything. Me and my team are here for you ladies. Things are definitely not normal in this town and we'll protect you."

"Damn right!" Derek high-fived Jarod and the rest of the team shouted in agreement.

Kitty snorted. "Yeah? Who'll protect us from you?"

The other pom girls laughed and Kirk felt heat rising up his neck. *They need to listen to me!* "I'm not the one you need to worry about."

"Really?" Kitty said. "My mom says a man who hits a woman is dangerous, and actually no man at all."

Kirk forced himself to unclench his jaw. No way was he going to let that bitch see that she got to him. "Good thing that I've never hit a woman."

"Only because Hunter Goode knows how to duck," Colleen muttered as she flipped her long, reddish curls over her shoulders and frowned at him.

"That witch knows a lot more than how to duck." Kirk ground the words through his teeth. "She knows what's wrong with this town—and it's her and her slut of a sister."

"Okay, let's go ladies." Kitty stood and brushed nonexistent dirt off her long, tanned legs. "We're not listening to this slut-shaming garbage."

"Wait! The party's just gettin' started!" Dillon Sanders looked dejected. "Hey, I know! Let's skinny-dip! It's dark." He waggled his eyebrows at the girls. "And we sorta promise we won't look while you strip down and jump in the water, right, guys?"

"Yeah!" his friends shouted.

"That would sound much more appealing if we had wine coolers," said Kitty. "Thanks, but no thanks. We're bored. So, time to go."

Kirk was trying to figure out how to stop them without pissing them off more, when his phone bleeped with a text message. He pulled it out of his pocket and his lips tilted up as he read:

Dearest Kirk, The Christians of this town are meeting at the park. We will march from there to the Goode house in protest of their Satanic connection. Because you are a great leader of young men, and like-minded with me in our battle against the Devil, I would like you and your friends to join us. I hope you can make it. Love in Christ, Mrs. Ashley.

That's it! Something the girls will find interesting. And a great opportunity to help the town get rid of those Goode bitches.

Kirk grinned at Kitty and let his inner voice guide him. "Shame you're leaving, but so are me and the guys. We're gonna go have some real fun."

"Real fun?" Colleen asked. "Like what?"

"Well, remember last year when we TP'd the Freeman sisters' house and put Vaseline on all their doorknobs?" Kirk said.

Kitty lifted on shoulder. "Yeah, I remember."

"Do you also remember hiding in the bushes and laughing our asses off when those two old women came out on their porch and freaked?" Kirk pantomimed an old woman gasping in shock. Then, still in character, he ran in place as he mimicked one of the Freeman sisters. "'Oh, you kids! I'll get you kids!'"

Kitty giggled softly. "She didn't have a bra on and she jiggled like a giant Jell-O mold."

"Right?" Kirk beamed his most charming smile at her. "Just good clean fun—especially 'cause we used toilet paper."

"So, what do you have in mind?" asked Kitty.

"Welllll . . ." He drew out the word and continued to smile his best harmless smile. "I just heard about a big gathering that's going on at the park. I promise you—it will *not* be boring."

"Gathering? What kind of gathering?" asked Colleen.

Kirk shrugged and lied smoothly. "Not one hundred percent sure. Service is crap out here. But everyone is gonna be there 'cause it has something to do with all the murders going on, and that's gotta be more fun than TP-ing an old woman's house." His gaze met Derek's. "Hey man, how 'bout you and me and the guys pile into that monster truck of yours and head to the park to check out what's going on?"

As usual, his wingman didn't let him down. "Hell yes!"

Kirk stood a little taller as his men looked at him expectantly. His gaze moved to Kitty and the girls. "You coming?"

"I don't know. A lot of crazy stuff has happened lately," said Kitty.

Kirk's expression flattened. "If you're too scared, don't go."

Kitty's blue eyes narrowed. "Actually, I do kinda want to check out what's going on."

"Me, too," said Colleen, and the rest of the pom girls echoed her. "Yeah, seriously. We stick together."

Kirk's grin was victorious. "Good choice." He turned to Derek Burke, his best friend and the center of the Mustang's football team—a team Kirk was determined to rejoin, no matter what that out-of-touch coach said. "Ready, Burke?"

"You better believe it!" Derek's face was bright pink from beer and standing too close to the bonfire.

"Awesome! You drive. I'll meet you at your truck as soon as I grab some stuff from the Jeep."

"Yaaasss!" Derek tossed his empty cup into the fire. Six other guys, including Jarod Frazier and Dillon Sanders, did the same. Whooping and shouting, the football players and the less enthusiastic pom squad tossed aside their cups and headed to Burke's big black Dodge Ram.

Kirk jogged to his Jeep, popped the glove box, and took out the switchblade he liked to keep there for emergencies. He tucked that into his pocket. He started to turn away, thought better of it, and went back to the glove box. He took the bottle of oxycodone, opened it, and shoved a couple pills in his mouth, swallowing them dry, like a real man. Then he jogged to Derek's truck.

The bed was full of the pom squad smushed between football

players. Kirk nodded and winked at his men before climbing into the cab with Derek. "To the park!" he commanded Burke, and gravel flew as they sped from the lake's parking lot.

———

As Derek pulled into Goode Park he sent Kirk a sideways, questioning look. "Hey, dude, this isn't a gathering. It's a bunch of church mommies making signs." He jerked his chin toward the bed of the truck. "Those pom girls will definitely *not* be impressed by church mommies."

Burke parked the truck beside a gray minivan that proclaimed GOODEVILLE UNITED BAPTIST CHURCH on its side with a giant cross. Kirk turned in his seat and snorted. "These church moms are gonna take care of our twin bitch witch problem."

Burke's forehead wrinkled in confusion. "But I thought you did that last night when you threw that brick through their window."

"Dude! Be quiet! The poms don't need to know about that and neither do those mommies. All I did was warn the twins." He pointed at the group of middle-aged women who had cardboard signs and craft supplies spread out over several picnic benches. "They're gonna *actually* run them out of town."

Burke blinked slowly and then he smiled. "Seriously? That will be fun to watch."

"Seriously," Kirk said. "Let's go make nice with the mommies so we can have a front-row seat when shit starts to really go down."

Kirk bounded out of the truck, jogged around back, and opened the tailgate. He reached out his hand and grinned at Kitty. "Need help down? For some of us, chivalry isn't dead."

Kitty made a little scoffing noise, but she took his hand—as did the rest of the pom girls. Then she turned to peer at the cluster of women and signs. "What is that?"

"A lot more than it looks like," said Kirk mysteriously.

"Kirk! Over here!" Mrs. Ashley waved her arms over her head, flabby arm flesh wobbling like a turkey neck.

"What does Mrs. Ashley want?" Colleen asked.

"Don't know," said Kirk. "But it'd be real rude not to go over there." He strode toward the group of women, resisting the urge to look back—and then breathing a long sigh of relief when he heard the group following him.

"Kirk, it is so lovely to see you again." Mrs. Ashley pulled him into a mom hug before releasing him to point at the almost completed signs. "What do you think?"

Kirk studied the signs. They all said versions of BEGONE SATAN, CHOOSE TO REPENT, JESUS SAVES, and, his personal favorite, JESUS IS TRUE LOVE. That one almost made him laugh. He let his amusement beam from the smile he turned on Mrs. Ashley. "I think these are great!"

"Um, hi, Mrs. Ashley," Kitty said as she stared at the signs. "These are nice and all, but what are they for?"

Jana dabbed at the salty sweat that beaded her face and her brows lifted. "Why, Katherine, they are for Jesus and against Satan. If that isn't clear, perhaps we should see you in church more often."

Kitty frowned. "I didn't mean that. I meant what are you going to do with them?"

Beside Jana, Mrs. Ritter spoke up. "We are going to march down Main Street straight to that nest of sin that is the Goode house and demand those two girls reject Satan once and for all!"

"Seriously?" Kitty said. Then she fanned herself with her hands. "Well, you better hurry because it definitely feels like it's gonna let loose with some rain pretty soon."

"Yes, the weather has certainly been strange." Mrs. Ashley lifted one of the smaller cardboard signs that said JESUS SAVES and fanned herself. "It was lovely and cool, and then that suddenly changed. No matter. That just means we need to work faster. Come on, Katherine." Mrs. Ashley's eyes skewed the other pom girls and football players. "And the rest of you. We need your help to get this done before the rain starts." When no one moved, she made little shooing motions with her hands and narrowed her eyes at them, her voice taking on a mean edge. "I said we need your help. I did *not* ask."

"Yes, ma'am," the kids muttered and shuffled to the tables filled with fat Magic Markers and cardboard.

Kirk wiped a hand across his moist brow and joined them. *Stay close. Remind them of the sins of the Goode sisters . . .* Like waves crashing on the shore, Kirk's wise inner voice whispered to him over and over and over . . .

THIRTY-FOUR

Mercy readied herself to begin her good-byes. She didn't need to look at her wound and the streaks of red spreading from it like a deadly spider's web to know her time was getting shorter and shorter. She could feel it—or, more accurately, Mercy couldn't feel much of anything, and as the numbness in her body increased her strength decreased.

I have to say good-bye to them, and then I just have one more thing to do. Freya will understand—so will Abigail. But Hunter won't. At least she won't until later . . .

A warm finger lifted her chin and she looked up at Khenti. She was snuggled against him, and when she met his gaze she saw worry there, along with compassion. He spoke softly so that only she could hear him over the current episode of *Buffy*. "You seem very far away."

Mercy drew a deep breath, attempting to also draw strength within her numb body. "I need to talk to you, but privately."

Khenti nodded, cleared his throat, and raised his voice. "Mercy would like to get some air. Could you pause this most excellent episode?"

Jax, who had arrived with pizza, nodded from his favorite recliner and bumped Hunter with his knee. She was sitting on a big pillow on the floor, leaning back against his legs. "H, you've got the remote. Pause it for Mag."

"No, you guys go ahead and keep watching. I'm just going to take a little walk with Khenti. I won't be gone long," said Mercy as Khenti helped her stand.

"Are you sure?" Hunter asked.

"Totally," said Mercy.

"Kitten, shall I get you a sweater? You should not catch a chill." Xena started to rise from her perch on the arm of the couch, but Mercy's words halted her.

"It's okay. I'm not cold."

Khenti put his arm securely around Mercy. "And should our Green Witch get chilled I will bring her right back inside."

"Okay, but don't wait until she's too cold," said Emily. She chewed her lip and stared at Mercy.

"I shall take great care with her," said Khenti as Mercy motioned toward the front door. She was glad Khenti's arm was around her. She could lean on him without everyone else knowing that she was actually leaning on him, and for a moment it was like Mercy was just going for a walk with her new boyfriend.

Boyfriend? Well, I guess I don't have time to go slow after all . . .

Outside they paused on the wide front porch. Mercy had planned on going for a walk with Khenti. The night was soft with spring—not too hot, not too cold—and the air was perfumed with green, growing things, but she could feel her energy waning. *My time is almost gone.* The thought had her stomach tightening, and her thoughts skittered away from her looming death. *Focus on now.*

"Can we sit on the porch swing instead of walking?" Mercy asked Khenti softly.

"Of course." He led her to the porch swing.

Mercy sat beside him within the circle of his arm. He felt warm and strong and filled with life. She envied him so, so much.

"It's time for you to leave," she said and felt surprise jolt through his body.

"I would prefer to stay until the end," he said somberly. "Unless you truly do not want me here."

She turned within his embrace so that she could look into his eyes. "I do want you here, but I am almost at the end."

His face paled. "So soon?"

She nodded and then cleared her throat and continued. "I need to ask you something. A favor."

"You may ask me anything. If it is in my power to grant it, I will."

Mercy drew another deep breath. "I was wondering—would you mind if I joined you in the Egyptian Underworld?"

Khenti blinked several times in surprise. "I would not mind at all, but would you not rather be in the Summerlands with your mother, your goddess, and your ancestresses?"

"Well, yeah, but it's complicated. Remember that I hexed your dad?"

Khenti nodded and his lips quirked up at the edges. "Yes, that I will never forget. But I must deal with my father. You cannot help me with that."

"Oh, no. Sorry. I'm not trying to do some ridiculous white savior thing. I mean, please. I'm not even capable of saving myself. And I don't want you to think I'm being a sticky-booger girlfriend and following you home like a lost little puppy," she said.

His smile widened. "Girlfriend?"

For a second Mercy was almost glad of the poison coursing through her body because it kept her cheeks pale—instead of flaming red. "I know we were going slow, but I'm kinda running out of time and also I honestly really like you. As more than a friend. I want you to know that, but also I want you to know that if I do come to your Underworld that doesn't mean you're stuck with me forever."

Khenti touched her cheek. "I like you as more than a friend, too. And I would never feel as if I was stuck with you. If we are together and more than friends that would be wonderful, but our friendship will stay strong—whether we decide we truly want more or not." He paused before continuing. "I am not him," Khenti said firmly. "Unlike the foolish boy who used and hurt you, I truly see you, Green Witch Mercy."

"What do you see?"

"I see your strength and the ferocity with which you love. If someday I may be granted that ferocious love *that* would, indeed, be a gift beyond value." Khenti smoothed back her hair from her face. "But I will be there for you. Always." He bent slowly, giving her time to turn away.

Mercy did not turn away.

Their lips met and she was filled with a delicious swirl of desire— that just as quickly faded and was replaced by dizzying weakness. Reluctantly, she broke the kiss and then rested her head against his chest.

The front door opened and Emily stuck her head out. "Mag, you gotta check out Buffy's hair. I do not know what the hell happened, but it looks like a newscaster's hair helmet." Then her fawn cheeks pinkened. "Oh, sorry! I didn't mean to interrupt."

Mercy turned and smiled at her best friend. "You didn't. I was just going to ask Khenti to go get you." She met Khenti's gaze. "Could you give Em and me a minute?"

"Of course." He kissed her softly and stood. As he and Emily passed each other, Khenti touched her shoulder gently. "Just call if you need me."

Em bit her lip, but nodded. She sat next to Mercy on the swing and put her arm around her best friend. With a sigh, Mercy leaned wearily against her. "Hey, are you cold?" Emily asked. "Should I get a blanket or something?"

"No, I'm fine."

"Does it hurt?" Emily said softly as she stroked her hair.

Mercy sighed. "No, not at all. It's weird, though, because I can't feel some of my body."

Emily stifled a sob and had to clear her throat before she could speak again. "It's going to be okay. Hunter is an amazing witch and Xena is, like, the best familiar in the world and totally filled with magic. They'll figure out how to save you. I'm sure of it."

Mercy said nothing. *I can't make Emily understand what I'm going to do. I can't even really say good-bye because she'd try to stop me. They'd all try to stop me—especially Hunter.* But she knew what she had to do. And Mercy had to make this as easy for Emily—for the rest of them—as possible.

"Em, thank you for being my bestie." It was getting more and more difficult for her to speak, but Mercy had to. She had to try to say something that would comfort Emily after this was all over.

"You don't have to thank me for that. We've been besties for ages."

"That's true, and we're going to be best friends forever. I mean it, Em. You and I will always be friends. No matter what. No matter where you are. No matter where I am," said Mercy. "I've been thinking about how much you like witchy stuff."

"Hey, sorry about that," Em said quickly. "I never meant to appropriate."

"No, it's not that. I think it's nice. I've been meaning to tell you that. There's no reason you can't help with spellwork and can't learn the Witches' Rede. So, um, until I'm better I'll bet H and Xena can start teaching you some basics."

"Really? Oh, Mag! I would fucking love that!" Emily clamped a hand over her mouth. "Oops. I shouldn't have said *fuck*. That was inappropriate. Was that inappropriate?"

"Well, I prefer British cuss words, but to each her own." Mercy's laugh turned into a cough that left her fighting for air as Emily held her tightly.

"You have to get well. You *have* to," said Emily through tears.

"I'm going. To be. Okay. Promise," said Mercy between gulps of air. "You'll be. Okay. Too, Em. I know it."

The door to the porch burst open and Hunter stepped out, holding a shovel like it was a wooden stake and she was part of the Scooby Gang headed to a graveyard.

"I know what I have to do! We're ending this. Get in the car. I'm gonna kill a goddess!"

———

Hunter craned her neck around from the driver's seat to look at Mercy, who was sandwiched between Khenti and Emily in the backseat of the Camry. "Mag, I really didn't mean for you to come. I was just going to take care of this while you rested and watched *Buffy*."

Mercy forced her numb lips to smile. "No bloody way I'm going to miss this."

"I don't know. You look really pale, Mag." Jax peered over the front seat at Mercy, his eyes bright with worry.

Xena, who was wrapped in Abigail's bathrobe and perched on Jax's lap, patted the top of his head as if he really was a kitten. "Do not worry, Jax. We shall all look after Mercy."

"Well, I'm not staying home, so let's go. Call it a last request if you have to," said Mercy.

Emily rounded on her. "Don't say that! You're going to be *fine*." Then she leaned forward. "H, maybe when you take out Amphitrite you could snag some of her goddess magic and use it to cure Mercy!"

Hunter's turquoise-blue eyes went to Mercy. The twins shared a look that only the two of them could translate. It was them against the world again—as it should always be—and they would protect their friends from sorrow as long as possible. Hunter nodded quickly before she turned her gaze to Emily.

"That's a great idea, Em! I'll definitely keep it in mind." Hunter put the Camry into gear and headed toward the heart of Goodeville.

"Kitten, where exactly are we going?" Xena asked.

"To the park. That's where I buried the Amphitrite poppet at the palms. I'm digging it up and then we're going to take it to the Greek tree where I'll summon that sea hag and be rid of her once and for all."

"Good thing it's late," said Emily. "There shouldn't be anyone at the park to see you dig up that creepy thing."

Hunter turned onto the narrow street that wound through the neighborhood surrounding the park as she said, "Yeah, well, I don't really give a shit about who sees me doing—" Her words broke off as the park came into view.

"That does not look like a deserted park," said Khenti.

"What the bloody hell is going on out there?" Mercy leaned into Khenti as she stared at the park.

"Oh, shit! That's my mom and her Bible study group!" Jax said.

"And Kirk with some of his football buddies. They're with your mom, Jax," said Hunter. "This looks bad."

"Kitten, turn around. We can retrieve your poppet another time. I do not like how this feels," said Xena.

"Yeah, I agree. I'll get us out of here." Hunter pulled into the parking lot, and put the Camry into reverse to back out onto the street.

"Hunter, wait!" Mercy grabbed her sister's shoulder. "She's here! Amphitrite! She's at the park!"

"What? Where?" Hunter looked frantically at the artificially lit park.

"There. The goddess is hovering over Jax's mother and their group at those picnic tables," said Xena solemnly.

Hunter put the car into park. "Then I'm not going anywhere." She turned and looked at her sister. "Stay here." Her eyes swept the car. "All of you. I'm going to get the poppet and end her. Now."

"In front of all these people?" Mercy shook her head. "No, H. You can't."

"Mag, what I can't do is continue to allow that sea hag to poison

259

our town. She's already poisoned you! How many more people have to die because she is completely batshit and vindictive and in need of more couples therapy than money can buy? No. Stay here. I'm the Chosen One. I'm doing this." Shovel in hand, Hunter opened the door. She didn't so much as glance at the group of people, but walked quickly and purposefully toward the cluster of doum palms.

"The goddess sees her." Khenti's voice was steel.

Mercy's gaze went to Amphitrite. Khenti was right. The goddess's bloated, dripping head had swiveled as if she was a demented sea owl and she stared at Hunter. Then her insubstantial body drifted down, closer to the group of people at the picnic tables. Mercy could see her mouth move and didn't need to hear what she said to understand what the goddess was doing.

The people stirred restlessly. They lifted cardboard signs from the tables and as one they turned to look at Hunter.

It was then that Mercy saw what was written on the signs, and her stomach felt sick.

"Open the door. Let me out!" she said.

Khenti quickly did so, helping her to stagger from the car.

"Come back, kitten! You must not overexert yourself!" Xena had crawled from Jax's lap and her face was pale with worry as she spoke through the open window.

"Look at the people. They're going after Hunter. Amphitrite is influencing them. We have to help Hunter!" As Mercy spoke she stumbled from the parking lot to the grass and fell to her knees.

Khenti was beside her in an instant. "How can I help you?"

"Just hang on a sec. I'm going to try to pull energy from the ley lines or I'll be totally useless." Mercy pressed her hands and knees into the grassy earth. She closed her eyes and sent a silent prayer to her goddess. *Freya, I know my time is almost up—and I know you're listening to me. Grant one last request from your faithful Green Witch. Let me draw enough power to help Hunter. Please, I beg it of you!* Eyes still closed, Mercy shifted her concentration from Freya to the ley lines. She could feel them, thick and powerful, beneath her. They hummed with energy. Mercy tapped into them and completely opened herself as she beseeched, *"By right of blood I ask you to fill me, Green Witch Mercy Goode, daughter of Kitchen Witch Abigail Goode, sister of Cosmic Witch Hunter Goode. By right of my ancestry I ask you to fill me. By right of a dying wish granted to one who follows The Path—fill me, strengthen me so that I may help my sister claim victory over She who would destroy those beloved to us witches three! So I have spoken. So mote it be."*

Mercy gasped as warmth rushed into her besieged body. There was pain, too. Terrible pain. But it was worth it. She gritted her teeth against the agony. Khenti's hand rested on her shoulder.

"I am here. You can do this," he said.

"As am I, my kitten." Xena was there, beside her in the grass.

"We're all here, Mag," said Emily.

"You've got this," said Jax.

Mercy drew a deep breath. She could feel her body and the energy of the earth. It hummed through her like she was a conduit for an electric current. She stood without dizziness and tossed back her hair. "That's better."

"Just in time, kitten." Xena pointed across the park at the Bible group that had picked up their signs and marched angrily toward Hunter, who had just reached the palms. Above them, Amphitrite floated. Her transparent tentacles reached down to stroke Jana Ashley, who led the group with Kirk beside her.

"Witch! Your reckoning has come!" Mrs. Ashley shouted.

THIRTY-FIVE

"Let's go!" Mercy strode into the park, followed by three of the four beings who meant the most to her in this world. As she hurried after the mob closing in on Hunter, she remained connected to the earth and the fat, pulsing lines of power that were—temporarily—lending her strength.

"Shall I summon my khopesh?" Khenti asked from Mercy's side.

"Definitely," Mercy said. "I don't want you to have to use it on the townspeople, though."

"I shall brandish it and intimidate them," said Khenti.

"I'll try to talk my mom out of whatever she's up to," said Jax.

Mercy didn't spare him a glance. Her focus remained on the ley lines and the power that sustained her. "Jax, she's under the influence of Amphitrite. Don't be shocked if she won't listen to you."

"Or even turns against you, sweet Jax kitten." Xena jogged to keep up with them.

"You guys, this is reminding me way too much of the *kill the beast* scene from *Beauty and the Beast*." Emily panted as she hurried with them.

"We need to cut that group off before they get to Hunter," said Mercy. "Khenti! I can't get there in time, but you can. Run! Stand in front of them and summon your khopesh. Don't let them get past you!"

"Gladly," said Khenti before he raced forward.

"I'll go with him!" Jax rushed after the demi-god.

Xena wrapped her arm through Mercy's. "Are you well, my kitten?"

"Freya is letting me borrow energy from the ley lines. It won't last."

"I can help, too!" Emily went to Mercy's other side and took her arm. "I'm not a real witch, but I understand intent and focus. And right now I'm totally focused on the intent of stopping this mob."

Mercy nodded. "You help. Both of you help." Her gaze went to her sister. She could just make her out in the deep shadows of the tree. She was on her knees by the trunk of the centermost palm. *Good, she's digging up the poppet. I just need to buy her time.* She looked from Hunter to the hovering goddess and her stomach tightened. Amphitrite had outdistanced her mob and was heading toward Hunter.

No, bloody fucking hell no! You are not getting my sister.

"Halt!" Khenti's voice, filled with the power of a demi-god, was a clarion call across the park. The mob staggered to a stop.

"Hurry! Help me get to the front of that mob! We need to pull that sea bitch's attention away from Hunter!" said Mercy.

"We've got you." Emily nodded at Xena, then they held Mercy so tightly that her feet barely touched the ground as they raced around the mob.

At the head of the crowd, Khenti faced Jana and Kirk, his scythe-shaped weapon held up and ready. Jana's eyes fixed on her son. Kirk's did not leave the khopesh until Mercy rushed to join them, then his expression changed from wide-eyed surprise to a disdainful sneer.

"Good. You're both here. You can both face the consequences of your Satan worshipping." Kirk's words were as sharp as Khenti's sword.

"Oh, shut up, Kirk." Mercy shook free of Xena and Emily and stepped forward, directly in front of Kirk. "You know this is all a lie. You know Hunter and I don't even believe in Satan, let alone worship him." She moved her gaze to Jax's mom. "Mrs. Ashley, I'm sorry you've been misled by Kirk, but ask your son. He knows the truth."

"Mom, Kirk has major issues with the twins and they have nothing to do with Satan. Hunter and Mercy are not devil worshippers. I promise." Jax held up his hands, imploring his mother to believe him.

Jana's brow furrowed as she studied her son. "Jax, honey, I know you are just being a faithful friend, but I'm afraid you have been mistaken about the twins." She began with kindness, but as rain started to fall from the sky—rain that carried the scent of the ocean—her expression hardened and her voice went sharp. "Go home, son. You do not belong here. I am about the Lord's business."

"Yeah, Ashley. Go home," Kirk sneered.

The mob behind them stirred angrily, echoing Jana's words. *Get out! Go home! Leave!*

Mercy licked her lips and tasted salt and fish, seaweed and sand. She looked up. Amphitrite had left Hunter and was floating above the mob. She met Mercy's gaze and smiled, showing pointed shark's teeth. *They are witches! They are evil! Drown them! Drown them! Drown them!*

"Mrs. Ashley." Emily took a step forward. "Please listen to Jax. Mercy is my best friend. I would know if she was into Satan. She isn't. Neither is Hunter. I promise."

Jana's gaze turned to Emily.

Drown them! Drown them! Drown them!

"Emily, do you know how they used to judge whether someone was a witch or not?" Mrs. Ashley's voice echoed as if she spoke underwater. She didn't wait for Emily to respond. "They would tie a rock around their neck and drop them in a lake. If they drowned they were innocent and absolved of any evil. If they did not drown, they were proven to be a consort of Satan and hung."

"That was, indeed, the method used centuries ago, before humanity knew better," said Xena. "It was monstrous. Jana Ashley, do you truly wish to be a monster?"

"Stop the witches!" Amphitrite shrieked from above them.

"It takes a monster to defeat Satan!" Jana shouted as she brandished the gold crucifix that dangled from around her neck.

"Yes! Yes! Yes! Use my power—the power of your Lord—as righteous anger!" Amphitrite goaded from above, filling the air with salt and sea.

"Get the twins! We will take them to Goode Lake, where they will be judged! The Lord is with us!" With otherworldly strength, Jana reached out and grabbed Mercy's arm. "I've got this one! Get the other!"

The mob pressed forward and spilled around Mercy, carrying Emily and Xena with it. Khenti lifted his khopesh and shouted, "Halt! I do not wish to harm you, but I shall not let you take the twins!"

Above them, Amphitrite cackled with delight.

Mercy saw it all happening. The people—pom girls, football players, and Bible group moms—were completely under the influence of Amphitrite. Khenti could stop them, but he would have to hurt them. Maybe kill some of them. And then what? How would Hunter live in this town—in this world?

Mercy bowed her head and ignored everything around her. She blocked out Mrs. Ashley's viselike grip on her arm, the shouts of the mob, Xena's screams, and Emily's terrified cries. Mercy tapped into the ley lines one more time. *"Come to me—power times three—earth's power, I call to thee—so that we might defeat this hag from the sea! Come to me! Come to me! Come to me! So mote it be!"*

Heat surged into Mercy from below. She'd never felt such power. She laughed at the joy of it.

"You should be bowing and praying to the Lord Jesus to save your soul." Jana speared Mercy with invective as she increased the painful grip on her arm. "But I know to whom you pray—and he has horns, not a crown of thorns!"

Filled with strength, Mercy lifted her head and opened her eyes to stare at Mrs. Ashley.

Jana gasped and loosed Mercy's arm as she staggered back, clutching her crucifix. "Your eyes glow with the deceiver's powers! Get thee behind me, Satan!"

Mercy grinned. "If only you knew how ironic that is. Mrs. Ashley, it is you who are being deceived." Then Mercy lifted her arms and concentrated on pulling the ley line power up through her body and into her hands.

Jana shrieked. "You glow with the green of envy! The green of evil!"

Mercy ignored her. Instead she spoke simple spellworks words. *"Stop any who wish us harm. Encircled by mighty earth's arms. They may hear, they may see—but they may* not *hurt Hunter, Xena, Khenti, Jax, Em or me! So mote it be!"* Mercy hurled the power of the earth's ley lines at the mob. It expanded to form a green bubble that enfolded all of them, holding the mob in place like a giant Jell-O mold that only opened in front of Mercy's group. It was a barrier to the rest of them, trapping them and keeping them from Hunter.

Mercy had a moment of sublime relief before her body betrayed her. The borrowed ley line power had spilled from her as she cast the spell, and she collapsed to the ground as Amphitrite's shrieks filled the air with water and wrath.

THIRTY-SIX

Hunter shoveled a final scoop of dirt from the wet earth around the doum palm and threw it and the shovel to the side before dropping to her knees and clawing at the trench for the poppet. Her fingers struck the mushy, wet doll, and she pulled it from the dirt. It glowed the turquoise blue of the Aegean Sea and dripped with the same salty waters.

Hunter frantically tore at the ropes, releasing the knots she tied that had bound Amphitrite's body but not her power. With the mob behind her, there was no way Hunter could make it back to the car, much less to the olive tree. If she was going to end Amphitrite's reign of terror, she had to end it now.

As Hunter struggled to release the final knot, a loud *boom* sounded and a flash of emerald lit the park. Gripping the poppet, she spun around.

"Mag!" Hunter fought back a swell of tears as her twin collapsed onto the wet grass, her skin a sickly green in the light of the magical barrier she'd cast around the snarling mob.

"You'll pay for what you did to my sister," Hunter growled to the invisible Amphitrite and yanked on the end of the rope. It unraveled, freeing the poppet and dropping to the ground like a dead snake.

A snarl creased Hunter's face as the sea goddess materialized before her. "Welcome back."

Amphitrite shook out her brown hair, releasing a current of salt-tinged air that stung Hunter's cheeks. *"I never left."* She stretched her long, blue arms overhead and rolled her slender neck as if stepping out of a small car after a long journey. *"It's really a shame that you don't know the difference between binding the body of a goddess from doing harm in this realm and banishing her completely. The space between the two is vast."*

"It's funny that you mention the vastness of space. I carry that power within me, and you made the mistake of sending your minion to poison my sister. Now my magic is free." Hunter unclenched her hands, and blue flames licked up her fingertips.

"I wouldn't, if I were you."

Goose bumps peaked against Hunter's arms, and behind her, Emily screamed.

Hunter whirled around. Beside Emily, Jax listed from right to left, a strand of kelp swaying in the hypnotic pulse of ocean waves.

More wails sounded as members of the crowd began to sway in unison with Jax.

"Mortals, such spongey creatures, yet you cannot survive in water. However, water is the elixir of life and makes up nearly your entire body. Did you know that, Witch? That mortal blood is mostly water?"

With a snap of the sea goddess's fingers, blood seeped from Jax's pores. It slid down his face, rained from his fingertips, and bloomed against his white T-shirt in tie-dyed bursts of cherry and crimson.

Scarlet mottled the corners of Hunter's vision. She didn't need to hear the shrieks to know the same was happening to members of her town.

Emily's cries ceased as she, too, began swaying and blood spurted from her pores like juice from a lemon.

Hunter rushed to her friends. She gripped Jax's bloody shoulders and shook him. No response. His stare remained vacant, his eyes unblinking. Emily was next. Her curls had lifted from her shoulders and floated around her head in an unseen current. Hunter pressed her own blood-streaked hand against Emily's cheek. "I'll fix this. Just hold on." She reached for Jax's hand and held it tight as she spun around to face Amphitrite.

"Let them go!" she shouted, fire burning within her chest. Beside her, Xena shook off Abigail's bathrobe. There was a flash of light and then the huge cat arched her back and hissed as she stalked toward the goddess.

"Admirable but tedious." Amphitrite held out her arm, spraying water at Xena with the strength of a fire hose.

"Xena!" Hunter shouted as the cat flew back toward Khenti and Mercy, shaking arms still outstretched and eyes pinched shut in concentration as she continued to siphon Khenti's energy for her spell.

"When will you learn to ignore the unimportant?" Amphitrite blinked slowly as she studied her long, glowing fingers still dripping with water. *"Come with me, Witch, and I'll release your friends."* Water sprayed as she returned her hand to the folds of her shimmering skirts and leveled her gaze on Hunter. *"Unfortunately, there's nothing I can do for your poor sister."* Her frown was a mocking pout that hacked at Hunter's heart. *"But, to show that I have truly forgiven you for your blasphemy, I'll put an end to this mess with the townsfolk."* She motioned to the mob. No longer screaming to end Hunter's life, they now needed to save their own.

Hunter straightened her shoulders and lifted her chin. "I would sooner rot in Hel than walk one foot by your side."

Amphitrite's throat bobbed with a tight swallow. *"I have offered you more than—"*

"Wait. Shut up." Realization sprouted a smile against Hunter's lips. "You need me."

Amphitrite floated forward, a neon-green trail as slimy as a sea slug in her wake. "Need *is such a strong word.*"

"Then leave," Hunter said, holding her ground.

"Over and over I have been betrayed." The sea goddess wrinkled her thin nose. *"And betrayal is a nasty companion, but one that is easily slayed by revenge. I want my revenge."* Amphitrite tossed back her hair, and Hunter grimaced as salt water splashed her face. *"Come with me, and I'll make sure your end is swift."*

"It's not this realm's fault your husband can't keep it in his pants," Hunter said, blinking the salt water from her eyes.

Amphitrite's jaw ticked, and her skin flashed an array of Las Vegas neon.

Behind Hunter, Jax and Emily gurgled.

"Your friends don't seem to have much time." Amphitrite's man-eating smile returned. *"Face it, Witch. Only the power of a goddess can save them."* Her gaze roamed over Jax and Emily before drifting to the crowd.

The pentagram carved into Hunter's core tingled with power, with a plan, with the energy that came from trusting herself. "You're absolutely right." She closed the distance between them, rolling her pendant between her bloody fingers. It heated as magic bubbled within her stomach, surged up her throat, and weaponized her tongue.

"I knew you'd see the light, young Witch."

Hunter returned Amphitrite's ghoulish grin with one of her own as she reached out and clapped her hands onto glowing blue shoulders. The goddess's cry was the shriek of owls as her skin bubbled and hissed beneath Hunter's palms and the magic of the banishment spell she'd carved into her flesh. Hunter ran her bloody hands over Amphitrite's chest, water seeping from the boiled skin she left in her wake.

"Release me!" Amphitrite cried as Hunter pressed her palms over the sea goddess's heart, salt water spurting between her fingers, pink

with the blood of Jax and Emily. *"Release me, Witch!"* Amphitrite clawed at Hunter's cheeks, her arms, her torso. Each strike was a bursting water balloon drenching Hunter's skin.

"You first!" Hunter shouted as she drew a bloody pentagram against the sea goddess's steaming chest. "Begone, Amphitrite! I call upon the strength of this mortal blood, the blood of the people of Goodeville and their ancestors, to banish you. I banish you from this town. I banish you from this earth." Heat swelled in Hunter's fingertips as she reached into the chest of the goddess who'd nearly turned her magic dark. "Begone, Amphitrite!" She flexed her fingers, the points of a star aflame with the magic of the universe.

"You have no power here!"

Amphitrite's wail hatched beneath Hunter's flesh and clawed its way to the surface, flaying her skin as the goddess of the sea burst into steam, an azure cloud that rocketed toward the heavens.

A booming clap of thunder and a blazing flash of cerulean lit the night as the misty blue exploded against the blanket of stars. A new constellation. A twinkling blue pentagram winked down at Hunter, the only proof that Amphitrite, sea goddess and scorned wife of Poseidon, had ever sought revenge on the people of this realm.

Hunter's stomach tingled, and she lifted her shirt. The ropy scar receded, melting into her body and leaving behind pale white skin. Her heart hammered between her ears as she spun around and raced to Jax, Emily, and a wet, disgruntled Xena. She collided into them, ignoring Emily's objections, Jax's squirms, and Xena's meows as she scooped up the cat, wrapped her free arm around her friends, and squeezed.

"You're alive." She breathed, finally taking a step back. The blood that had trailed down their skin had vanished as quickly as her scar.

Jax smoothed down his clean white tee. "Zero thanks to that sea monster," he called after Hunter as she dashed toward Mercy.

The green orb had dissipated, leaving the townspeople able to act on their own thoughts and opinions for the first time in days.

"Hunter saved us . . ."

"There was a monster . . ."

"Hunter Goode shot that creature into the sky . . ."

"She's a good witch. Like Glenda . . ."

The whispers swirled around Hunter as she wound through the townspeople slowly making their way from the park.

"They know my name." A spark of joy flickered in her chest before being buried by the sight of Kirk Whitfield.

"This isn't over!" he growled, his chest heaving with frantic inhales.

Hunter's veins buzzed with untapped magic. "It so is."

Jana strode over, eyes pink-rimmed and puffy with tears. "Kirk, it's time to set down the torch." She clutched the gold crucifix dangling from her neck. "I fear we were led astray by a false prophet."

"She's a witch!" He spat. "We have to—"

Jana placed her hand on his shoulder. "Son, like evil, good comes in many forms."

"But—"

Hunter's fingers twitched with stored magic, but Jana squeezed Kirk's shoulder and guided him toward the parking lot. "Let's get you set up in one of the church's Bible study groups."

Hunter darted around another group heading to their car and finally spotted her sister, surrounded by their friends and their cat-turned-guardian.

"Mercy!" The wail tore out of her as she rushed to close the distance between them.

She can't be dead! She can't be!

THIRTY-SEVEN

Mercy fought back to consciousness through layers of green-tinged darkness as Khenti lifted her into his arms.

"You did well, my Green Witch. So, so well," Khenti murmured to her as he held her carefully and walked to the palms. "I shall always remember your courage."

It was hard—so hard for Mercy to form words—but she had to. "You have to go home now, Khenti."

He nodded, his eyes dark with sadness. "I know. And now you must die."

"It doesn't hurt. It doesn't feel like anything." Mercy looked around them. "Hunter. Where is H?"

"I'm here, Mag!" Hunter rushed to her and took her hand. "We did it! We got rid of the sea hag!"

Mercy's lips twitched up. "You did it. Not me."

Hunter snorted. "Your giant green Jell-O barrier made it all possible."

Then Mercy did actually grin at her twin. "I thought it looked like a Jell-O mold, too."

"Great minds . . ." Hunter returned her grin.

"What do we do now?" Emily said as she and Jax joined them while Khenti gently placed Mercy on the ground near the clump of palms. "Should we cast a circle so you can grab some of the power from Amphitrite and give it to Mercy to cure the poison?"

Mercy saw Hunter exchange a look with Jax that had his eyes filling with tears. Then his gaze met hers and she saw understanding there. She held out her hand and Jax took it, bending close to her. "Be there for Hunter. Don't let her be alone. Promise me," Mercy said softly as she held tightly to her sister's best friend.

"I promise," Jax whispered back to her.

"What does that mean?" Emily's voice had risen several octaves. "Hunter, what does she mean? You're going to fix her now, right? That was the plan."

In human form, swathed in Abigail's grass-stained bathrobe, Xena limped to them and put her arm around Emily. "Oh, kitten, our Mercy is beyond even Hunter's power to save."

"No! That can't be true!" Emily's frantic gaze went from Xena to Hunter. "You just killed a goddess! You can save Mercy!"

"Em." Mercy's voice had faded to a whisper. "No one can save me."

"Mag! No no no no no!" Emily went to her knees, tears cascading down her fawn cheeks as she clutched her best friend's hand as if she could physically tether her to the world of the living.

"Shh, it's going to be okay," Mercy soothed. "We'll always be friends, remember?"

"B–but you won't be here!" Emily sobbed.

"But we get to take love with us," Mercy said. "Em, I'll never forget you. I promise. I don't have much time left, and Khenti needs to return to his home. Help me see him off, okay?"

"O–okay." Emily wiped her eyes with the back of her hand, though her tears continued to fall.

"Help me stand. I want to walk with Khenti to the tree," said Mercy.

They all lifted Mercy to her feet. Then Khenti put his arm around her shoulder and Hunter put her arm around her waist. Xena took one of her hands and Jax took the other. Together, joined by love, then went to the doum.

"I can stand by myself now. Thanks, guys," Mercy said.

"Do we have to do some special magic to open the gate?" Jax asked Hunter.

Khenti answered before she could. "No, my friend. I may open the gate to my home easily, and then I must deal with the jackal-headed guards who await me." He stared grimly at the center of the cluster of doum palms.

"Khenti kitten, I have researched your patron goddess, Hathor," said Xena. "I believe if she is invoked the jackals will have to stand down until your goddess appears, even should your father try to bully you, but he is only a demi-god, so he must wait upon your goddess before he acts." Xena sighed dramatically. "But goddesses can be quite busy, so . . ."

Khenti nodded. "Yes, magnificent Xena Warrior, I had already concluded that I must invoke Hathor's presence or my father's guards will simply hold me hostage until he arrives—to send me back to Duat."

"Does Hathor usually come when you invoke her?" Hunter asked. She stood beside Mercy—remaining close—watching Mercy with worried turquoise eyes.

"The divine Hathor and I have spoken frequently, but usually when she was visiting the Underworld and was near the gate I guarded." Khenti cracked his knuckles nervously. "Truthfully, I have never before invoked her presence."

"She will listen and come at your call. I feel it deep in my bones," said Xena.

"Then I shall go forth and invoke Hathor with confidence, as I have the word of a such a magnificent familiar." Khenti smiled at Xena.

The cat person's round cheeks flushed pink. "Oh, kitten! Thank you for the lovely compliment." Xena went to Khenti and threw her arms around him, hugging him tightly. "I have loved getting to know you, Khenti kitten. You have made my life brighter. I shall never forget you."

Khenti held Xena close. "You are the most incredible feline I have ever known. But if you ever speak to Bast, please do not share that with her."

Xena stepped out of his embrace, laughing softly as she wiped tears from her eyes and licked them from her fingers. "It shall be our secret." Then she rose up onto tiptoes and licked him on his cheek.

Jax came to him next. At first he offered his hand to shake, and then Jax said, "Ah, hell. A handshake won't do it." He and Khenti embraced. "If you ever need help back there in your Underworld, just give me a call—or however you'd do it. I'd be happy to fight beside you. Anytime."

"Thank you, Jax. You are a good friend. I trust you shall look after Hunter and Xena and Emily?" Khenti asked.

"Always," said Jax.

Crying softly, Emily pushed past Jax and hugged Khenti. "I really don't want you to go."

"Emily, you are also a good friend. Perhaps I shall see you, and the family of your heart, again."

Emily wiped her eyes as she stepped out of Khenti's hug. "I hope so."

Khenti turned to Hunter. "I find it very difficult to say good-bye to you, Cosmic Witch. Thank you for using your power to bring me here. Thank you for welcoming me into your home. Thank you for making my time away from my world incredibly pleasant—and *thank you* for introducing me to Buffy Summers. I wish I could have binged all of the seasons with you."

Hunter grinned through her tears. "Well, come back! We'll have a *Buffy*-a-thon!"

Khenti pulled her into his embrace. "If I can, I will. On that I give you my word."

Finally, Khenti looked down at Mercy, who stood unsteadily beside him. "Have you changed your mind?" he asked her.

Mercy nodded. "No. It is okay with you?"

Khenti kissed her gently and smiled. "Yes. Of course."

"Then go ahead. I'll follow you in a sec," said Mercy. She could feel Hunter's shocked gaze on her, but she walked, relying heavily on Khenti's strength, to the cluster of trees with him. Mercy stopped there and leaned against the coarse bark of the centermost doum palm.

Khenti turned to face Hunter, Jax, Emily, and Xena. "You have made my visit to your world a joyful experience. Please know that there is a demi-god in the Egyptian Underworld who will eternally care for you." He paused and met Mercy's gaze. "And please know that I shall always, *always* be Mercy's faithful friend."

Then Khenti lifted his hands so that his palms faced the Egyptian trees. "I am Khenti Amenti, son of Upuant, servant of Hathor, and I command this gate to open for me!"

The center of the doum palms began to glow and a large opalescent oval materialized. "Khopesh! To me!" Khenti commanded, and the sickle-shaped blade appeared in his hand instantly. He straightened his shoulders and strode through the glistening disc.

The disc didn't disappear. Beyond its surface Khenti was still visible. He halted just a few yards from the gate and took a defensive stance, weapon raised. Within moments huge warriors materialized, their jackal heads fierce with glowing scarlet eyes. Each was armed with a wicked-looking spear, and held a shield with Upuant's symbol—the outline of a jackal—etched in ebony.

"In the name of my mother, Meryt, beloved of our goddess, I invoke blessed Hathor!" Khenti's voice echoed from his world through the gate. "In my name, Khenti Amenti, I invoke faithful Hathor! And I shall not move from this place until the goddess to whom I have sworn service appears and hears my petition!"

Hunter and Xena moved to Mercy, each on either side of her. Jax and Emily followed. Everyone except Hunter stared breathlessly through the portal to Khenti's world—waiting for his goddess to appear.

Hunter touched Mercy's shoulder so that she turned and faced her sister. "What did you mean—that you would follow him in a sec?"

It was getting more and more difficult for Mercy to catch her breath. She wasn't in pain, but the numbness in her body was pulling her under. It would have been so easy to just slide down the side of the tree and let it claim her. She could close her eyes and give in to it. She could finally rest.

But Mercy couldn't rest. Not yet. Maybe not forever. Or at least for however long it took for her to clean up the mess she'd made in the Egyptian Underworld.

How was she going to explain it all to Hunter? She couldn't tell her about the hex and about the choice Freya had given her. Hunter would never let her go. She'd take the curse on herself—of that Mercy had no doubt at all.

I can't let her. Oh, Freya, give me the strength I need to last for just a little longer.

Of course, daughter. Freya's musical voice lifted from her soul, her heart, her veins to echo through her body. *You have made the honorable decision, and I shall bless you for your bravery.*

Suddenly, warmth washed through Mercy. She was able to draw a full, deep breath and she stood straight as Freya's blessing gifted her with borrowed strength.

"Mag? You have to talk to me!" Hunter said.

"I know. I'm sorry. I—I couldn't tell you before, but now I have to die in Khenti's world. I made a mess there and I have to fix it," said Mercy.

Beside her Xena sobbed softly. "But kitten, there is no Summerland in Khenti's Underworld, and that means there is no Freya, no Abigail—and eventually no me to be with my kitten in eternity."

Mercy wiped the tears from Xena's cheeks. "I know and I'm sorry. I wish I had time to explain. You'll just have to trust me. I wouldn't do this if I didn't have to."

"No!" Emily sobbed.

Mercy stepped out of Xena's arms. "Em, it's going to be okay. Remember, we'll always be best friends, no matter where we are. Stay close to Hunter, 'kay? Do that for me?"

Weeping, Emily could only nod.

Jax put his arm around Em. Tears leaked down his umber cheeks, but his voice was steady. "I'll be here, too. I give you my word."

"Thank you. I love both of you," Mercy told her friends—the family of her heart. Then she turned back to her favorite person in any world. "H, I gotta go. I gotta die in Khenti's world. I—I don't have time to explain now why. Please trust me. Please believe that I'm doing the right thing, *with* Freya's blessing."

Hunter shook her head back and forth, back and forth. "No. No, Mag. Stay here. Let me try one more time to figure out something to save you! Tyr is with me again! My magic is super strong! I can do this."

The sense of preternatural clarity was back, and everything finally fell into place for Mercy. "I have no magic." She studied her sister. "You were right. You are the Chosen One."

"I don't want it to be true!" Hunter angrily wiped away her tears.

"But it is. You gotta Buffy for me. You can heal the trees. You can close the gates. You can make everything right again. All it takes is for me to leave this world so that our magic isn't fragmented between the two of us anymore—and, H, I'm leaving our world anyway."

"No! I was supposed to leave, *not you!*"

"You'll see," Mercy said. "When I'm gone you'll feel it. Hunter, your blood and body—everything about you is tied to this land—to this *calling*. You are a Gate Guardian—the magnificent Cosmic Witch Hunter Goode, daughter of the powerful Kitchen Witch Abigail Goode, sister to the faithful Green Witch Mercy Goode—who will love you always, no matter where she is."

Hunter snorted a sobby laugh. "Are you really talking about your-self in the third person?"

Mercy grinned. "Why not? That's what Xena did when she gave me her spark of immortality."

"Well, when we feel our immortality we tend to feel it in the third person," said Xena as she licked her hand and smoothed back her hair. "Kitten, are you truly joining Khenti?"

Mercy touched Xena's tear-dampened cheek. "I am. I have to."

"But I don't understand!" cried Hunter. "Just stay!"

Mercy put her arms around her sister and held on to her tightly. "I wish I could."

"Explain it to me!" Hunter insisted.

Mercy continued to hold on to her sister. "I can't now, but someday—Hunter Jayne Goode—someday I'll explain it to you in the Summerlands with Abigail beside us and all the other Goode witches surrounding us with their love. I give you my oath—so mote it be."

Hunter stepped out of her arms and tried to smile. "So mote it be." Then she added, "I always knew you'd leave me for some guy."

"That I would *never* do!" But Mercy returned her twin's smile. "And I can never really leave you. All you have to do is look in the mirror to see me."

"You really have to go?" Hunter said.

"I really have to go," Mercy repeated. Then she turned to Xena. "I'm sorry. I don't know how long it'll take, but I'll see you again someday in the Summerlands. I promise. I love you, Xena. And I'll miss you every single day."

Instead of replying, Xena walked around Mercy to face Hunter. "My kitten, please forgive me."

"For?" Hunter asked.

Xena looked at Mercy. Her smile was a mother's—tender and un-conditionally loving. Then she returned her gaze to Hunter. "Freya bound me to your sister. I must go with her. Forgive me?"

Fresh tears flowed down Hunter's face. Behind her, Emily was weeping in Jax's arms. Hunter nodded, and drew in a long, shaky breath before she could speak. "I forgive you. I'm glad you'll be with Mag. She'll need you. It can't be easy to die alone in a strange world."

Xena put her hands on Hunter's shoulders. "You will not die alone, not in this world or in any other, precious kitten." As Xena continued to speak her voice was amplified with the power of her prophecy. *"You will live a long life. You will keep your city and your people safe. You will find love and happiness—and you will also be gifted with a daughter, as well as a partner who will be by your side when you draw your last breath. And then you will join our precious Abigail, our loving Mercy, and me in the Summerlands where we will frolic together for an eternity. You will never be alone."*

"So mote it be," whispered Mercy.

"So mote it be," said Xena firmly. Then she turned to Mercy. "Shall we begin our next adventure, my kitten?"

"I'm ready," said Mercy. "Help me?"

"For eternity," said her faithful familiar. She faced Hunter again. "I shall leave this with you, kitten. I know Abigail would approve." With a practiced flourish, Xena took off the well-worn bathrobe and handed it to Hunter, who clutched it like a lifeline.

Then, naked except for a pair of pink, fluffy slippers, Xena took Mercy's arm and together they walked through the portal.

On the other side of the opal disc, Mercy paused and turned. Hunter was there—just on the other side of the portal. Through the glowing gate, she spoke to her twin—her other half. "We'll never really be apart. We can't be. I promise I'll find my way to you in the Summerlands, just take your time getting there. Goode guarantee!" Mercy lifted her already graying hand and held it up to the portal.

Through tears, Hunter smiled and lifted her hand. She pressed it through the portal so that she could hook her sister's pinky finger with her own. Pinkies still entwined, the twins tapped their knuckles together before their hands separated, fingers fluttering like birds as they spoke together one last time. "Sisters of Salem!"

Then Mercy, with a magnificent Maine coon padding beside her, strode to Khenti to face the jackals—and the goddess who had just materialized, white horns glistening, dark eyes compassionate and wise.

"Speak, Khenti Amenti! Your goddess shall hear your petition!"

The opal disc faded and was once more simply the bark of a cluster of ailing doum palms.

THIRTY-EIGHT

Hunter was empty. She'd lost the most important part of herself. Her heart had walked out of this realm and into another. She would never be whole.

I'm still here. I'm alive.

"And Mercy's gone."

Hunter didn't know who had spoken, didn't know who was crying. She only heard sobs as soft and hushed as footfalls on snow and felt the pain of loss, the ache of loneliness, and—

She smoothed her fingers over her talisman, sucking in a breath as it scorched her fingertips.

Ouch! Hunter's lips moved, but no sound emerged. Time had stopped. The world had stopped. A tear glistened on Emily's cheek, frozen halfway between her eye and her chin.

"Do you want to leave this place and live a new life?" A voice like silk drifted between her ears.

Her pendant glowed bright against her skin, casting light against the doum palm that was the same silvery white as the full moon. "Tyr?"

"Hunter?"

Her breath caught in her chest. Tyr had never spoken to her before. Not directly. Not with words. She'd only known he was there through the heat of her talisman and the pinpricks of energy that hummed against her fingers whenever she cast spells. She'd felt his absence, too. A hollow pit had formed in her stomach when she'd forsaken him. Over time, it had filled with lead, pulling her toward despair, pulling her closer to Amphitrite. But Hunter had made the decision to seek love over power, and her god had returned to her.

She was the first Goode witch to choose a god over a goddess. She was the first Goode witch to do a lot of things. She could leave, even now. She could start over and be free . . .

Hunter's ponytail brushed her shoulder blades as she shook her head. "I have to stay."

"But what do you desire?"

"I want to make my mom proud, and my sister, and my friends. They would want me to stay," she said, her gaze sweeping over Emily and Jax. "I survived. I won. I'm still here and that means something. Goodeville may not be one hundred percent great one hundred percent of the time, but it's my home. A Goode witch belongs here. *I* belong here. I'm not leaving."

"You always follow your heart."

"My heart left." Hunter swallowed.

"Like Mother Moon, your heart has always been in Goodeville. You only need your true magic to find it."

Energy sizzled and crackled against Hunter's skin as sparks exploded in the air around her like a thousand shooting stars. Heat washed over her, a hot shower on a cold day, a steaming mug of tea in snowy winter, comforting and soothing. Power shot from her fingertips, the fiery blue of a burning star, lifting her off the ground. She was a supernova, changing, evolving, bursting with new life.

This is what it meant to be a Guardian of the Gates, one of the Sisters of Salem. *This* was magic.

Scenes played behind her closed lids—the school, Main Street, bonfires in wooded fields, swimmers in the lake. She felt *everything.* Puffs of happiness and joy fluffy as cotton candy against her fingertips and pain that poked and stung like cockleburs. She felt the air that blew through the cornstalks and slipped past whispering lips. Rudders that churned lake waters. Pebbles that shifted under footsteps. She was a part of this town, and this town a part of her.

And then came the ancient trees and the gates they represented— the Norse apple tree, its buds swollen, ready to burst into bloom, its gate sealed by Abigail Goode's sacrifice; the Hindu banyan tree, its waterfall of aerial roots and thick trunks supporting weak, decaying branches; the Japanese cherry blossom tree, its hanging branches cracked and splintered, unable to flower; the Egyptian doum palm, its green, fanlike leaves shriveled and falling from its four surviving trunks; the Greek olive tree—its once beautiful trunk, now twisted and weathered like a dying behemoth. Each withering tree had a crumbling gate, an easy exit for the evil that lurked in the Underworld on the other side.

Hunter cried out as she felt each tree's pain like a wooden spike through her heart.

"Heal them!" Her voice came from deep within, from the earth below and the heavens high above. *"Heal these trees, mend these gates, protect this town. So I command, so mote it be!"*

A scream tore from her lips as a final burst of sizzling heat shot through her and a pulse of azure light blazed through Goodeville.

Hunter's feet met the earth, and her eyelids fluttered open as the ground beneath her trembled. A doum palm trunk shot out from the dirt, replacing the one that had burst into ash only days before. She had healed it. She had healed the gates. And Hunter Goode was well on her way to healing herself.

She exhaled as the fuzzy warmth of happiness and peace radiating from the ancient doum palm wrapped around her like a well-worn sweater.

She walked backward, staring through the restored doum and its verdant palm fronds to the shimmering gate beyond until she felt Jax and Emily by her side.

Jax looked down at her, his dark eyes wide. "You did it." He breathed.

"And your hair!" Emily thrust her phone in front of Hunter.

A streak of white colored her brown hair, the reflection of the moon upon dark waters. A reminder of her duties. A reminder of her home.

Emily tucked her phone back into her pocket and glanced up at the doum's verdant palm fronds. "Does this mean it's over? All the bad stuff. All the death."

Hunter ran her hand over the band of white hair, brushing stray strands behind her ear. "Those things were always here, and they always will be. But we'll fight them," she said, reaching out to take each of their hands in hers. "And we'll do it together."

EPILOGUE

TWO WEEKS LATER

Hunter plucked a freshly baked pie from the front porch steps and leaned against the open screen door as Jax, Emily, and Kylie hopped into Em's car.

The back window rolled down, and Jax hung out the opening. "Thanks again for breaking your Marvel movie ban!"

Hunter shook her head. "For the last time, it's not a ban! I just don't care about them."

Jax's brow pinched. "Not possible!"

His shout was followed by the mechanical whir of the passenger window as it sank into the door. "I agree with you, H. The whole movie was confusing," Kylie added with a flip of her hair. "At least we got theater popcorn."

"You were confused because they're all connected!" Jax said with a groan. "You can't watch the most recent movie and expect to know what's going on."

"Guess this means we're bingeing all one hundred Marvel movies at this weekend's sleepover!" Emily hollered before she put the car in reverse and backed out of the driveway.

Jax tossed his hand into the air. "There aren't one hundred!"

"You're obsessed, Jax Ashley!" Hunter shouted as Em and Kylie burst into laughter.

The trio had picked Hunter up and dropped her off at school every day since joining her on a two-day hiatus from school, practices, and their own lives to help Hunter sort out hers and the end of her sister's. It hadn't been as difficult to explain away Mercy's absence as they'd all thought it would. Turns out, when at 100 percent Gate Guardian power, there was a spell for pretty much anything.

Jax, Emily, and Kylie also opened their homes to her. Well, Jax more figuratively than literally. After the Jana Ashley fiasco, Hunter would most likely never be allowed in his family home again. But her friends had made sure that she wouldn't be alone if she didn't want to be.

The gold bangles Kylie had insisted she borrow tinkled and sparkled in the porchlight as Hunter waved to her friends.

She wasn't sure if two wrongs made a right or if Kylie, confronted with evil and death, had decided that life was too short to hold on to anger no matter the cause. Either way, Hunter was grateful for the opportunity to mend their friendship.

She lingered at the threshold of the open front door until Emily's car was nothing more than a gleaming spot in the distance.

"Home sweet home," she said to no one, since no one waited inside. She set her keys in the oyster shell bowl on the whatnot table and tossed her bag onto the couch on her way to the kitchen.

She opened the note taped to the plastic wrap covering the top of the lattice crust and read aloud, "'From the Medfords. Another thank-you for saving us.'" Hunter took a deep breath, filling her heart with the power of community.

Goodeville had also changed over the past couple weeks. No longer did she feel ostracized or afraid of being found out as a real witch. True, some still gave her space or whispered under their breath as they passed, but most were happy, grateful even, that she was there to help if ever another otherworldly being was loosed in their small town.

Hunter set the pie on the counter next to the others and turned the knob of the gas stovetop and lit the burner under the half-full teakettle before shuffling toward the pantry.

Today was the day. Tonight was the night. Now was the moment.

Her hand lingered on the doorknob. There had to be another way to procrastinate, another movie to see, another extra-credit assignment to complete.

She chewed her lower lip.

No, if she didn't try to contact her mom and sister now, she never would. Plus, they had to want to talk to her. Or maybe they didn't. Maybe they were glad to be away from her. Maybe Mercy and Xena couldn't even come to her. They might still be in the Egyptian Underworld, fixing whatever it was she'd had to fix there. Or maybe they had fixed the problem, but didn't want to see her. Maybe—

She shook her head, clearing the swarm of negative thoughts. "You're being ridiculous. You know time passes way differently in the Underworlds. What seems like weeks to me could be months, years, or even decades to Mercy and Xena."

But what if she wasn't being ridiculous? What if Mercy and Abigail were actually mad at her? What if Mag had realized that Hunter should have been the one to die and not her? What if her mother was resentful that she hadn't taken action that night at the apple tree? Both times, Hunter had frozen. Both times, someone else had paid the ultimate price.

She exhaled a shaky breath and pulled a tall mason jar of salt, a box of long matches, and a wicker bin of Mercy's prepared tea sachets off the shelf.

"Pull yourself together," she scolded, setting the items on the kitchen counter.

The teakettle whistled, spitting a cone of hot steam into the air.

Hunter took a sachet from the bin, turned off the burner, and grabbed a mug from the rack, the phrase *Witch, please!* in bold letters across the cup. The sweet, fruity, and comforting scents of chamomile and lavender drifted up from the mug on curling tendrils of steam as Hunter poured hot water over the dried packet of herbs. She held the warm mug in both hands, closed her eyes, and inhaled deeply.

In times like this, when the only noise was of the old home shifting in summer winds and the night sky chased away the sun, Hunter heard them—footsteps on the staircase, laughter in the halls, her mother and Mercy discussing plants and food and love. They were echoes, and like every sound, the memories would eventually fade.

Hunter swallowed, and her eyelids fluttered open before they could swell with tears.

She would see her family tonight.

She took the fuzzy bathrobe, the one Xena had worn nearly every time she'd morphed from a majestic Maine coon to an even more regal human, from the apron hook outside the pantry door and slipped it on over her T-shirt and jeans.

Wrapped in her mother's bathrobe, matchbox in the pocket, mug of tea in one hand, and jar of salt tucked under her arm, she pushed open the back door of the Victorian home she had chosen to live in forever and stepped into the night.

The crescent moon hung high in the sky casting a faint glow over the backyard, Mercy's greenhouse, the rows of white pillar candles Hunter and her friends had laid out for their private celebration of Mercy, and the path to the family cemetery. Hunter could walk the property in a blizzard, in a rainstorm, in black as pitch, but she could hear her sister's voice in her head.

There's supposed *to be some ceremony involved, H.*

Hunter smiled, adjusted the jar of salt under her arm, and snapped her fingers. *"Let there be light."*

The pillar candles flamed, illuminating the worn path that led to each Goode's final resting place.

Hunter walked slowly, following the memories of her former self, her former family, whole and real and completely alive, until she reached the cemetery's wrought iron gate.

It unlatched and opened before she had the chance to reach out. Its hinges creaked a word of welcome, a sign of her power, of her connection to this plot of land and the bones resting beneath.

"Merry meet," she whispered as the gate creaked closed behind her.

Merry meet. The wind twirled through her hair, carrying with it the voices of her ancestresses.

The bathrobe swept over the grass as Hunter wound through the grave markers to the iron firepit at the center of cemetery. Pentagram and crescent moon cutouts danced around the pit, revealing the rough bark of dried pine logs and smooth brown coils of cinnamon sticks.

She bent down and nestled the mug in a thick patch of grass before unscrewing the lid to the mason jar.

"*You are the stars in my night,*" she began as she circled the firepit, salt pouring in a big white O around the iron. "*So I say it thrice—I will always remember thee, always remember thee, always remember thee.*"

Color drained from each salt crystal and was replaced with the same blue as the night sky above and the magic coursing through Hunter's veins.

She lifted her bathrobe and stepped into the circle, letting it flutter back around her ankles as she pulled the box of long matches from her pocket. She didn't need them to light the fire. It was another gesture that honored her sister, her mother, and the centuries of magic that came before.

She struck the long match against the side of the box and focused her energy and love on the flickering flame.

"*Mercy and Abigail Goode, hear me. My sister, my mother, my best friends . . . I miss you.*" She dropped the match onto the kindling. "*Come back.*"

Hunter shielded her eyes as blue flames burst from the firepit.

"I miss you, too, my beautiful girl."

Hunter lowered her arm. "Mom?"

Abigail's long hair brushed her back as she danced around a fire of her own, hand in hand with the spitting image of Hunter, and a fluffy Maine coon at their feet.

"Mag!" Hunter cheered, tears spilling down her cheeks. "You came!"

"We're always here for you, H." The words drifted up from the iridescent blue flames as Mercy twirled, her long dress rippling around her.

"We love you." The women spoke in unison. *"And are so proud of you."*

Hunter's heart swelled as she watched her mother and sister and Xena, joy and happiness rolling off them in waves of heat that warmed her cheeks.

"The ancestresses have a gift for you." Mercy's voice floated up to her as the gate creaked open.

Hunter turned as a black-and-tan-striped kitten rounded a gravestone, puffy tufts of coal-black fur sprouting from the tips of each pointed ear.

"Hello, there." Hunter beamed. "Are you my gift?"

A light *mew* was his response as he padded to her, his thin gold chain and tag glinting in the firelight.

Hunter bent down and extended her hand in silent offering.

The kitten sniffed it, tickling her fingers with his long whiskers, before nestling his head in her palm.

She stroked his long fur and ran her hand along his delicate collar, reaching the gold oval medallion that hung in front of his chest.

"Odysseus," she read, smoothing her thumb along the etched letters. "Is that your name?"

He purred as she rubbed the soft striped fur between his ears.

"Are you a cat person, too?"

Odysseus looked up at her, green eyes twinkling, and winked.

ACKNOWLEDGMENTS

Thank you to Team Cast: our amazing agents, Rebecca Scherer and Steven Salpeter; our insightful editor, Monique Patterson; and the hardworking Wednesday Books/Macmillan group, including Jennifer Enderlin, Anne Marie Tallberg, our production team, and a special shout-out to the talented art department who created the gorgeous covers for this trilogy! We heart you!